SHE WAS POETRY IN MOTION. . . .

Alexis Winston was destined to be a champion
—a beautiful young figure skater on her way
to the Olympics. Everything was going her
way. Then, in one split second, her life was
changed forever. . . .

Set against the dazzling world of competitive
ice skating, this astounding novel tells a tender
and sensitive love story—filled with romance
and spirit, joy and triumph.

COLUMBIA PICTURES PRESENTS
A JOHN KEMENY PRODUCTION
A DONALD WRYE FILM

ICE CASTLES

starring
ROBBY BENSON
COLLEEN DEWHURST
TOM SKERRITT
JENNIFER WARREN
DAVID HUFFMAN
and introducing
LYNN-HOLLY JOHNSON as "Lexie"
DIRECTED BY DONALD WRYE
PRODUCED BY JOHN KEMENY
CO-PRODUCED BY S. RODGER OLENICOFF
SCREENPLAY BY DONALD WRYE
AND GARY L. BAIM
STORY BY GARY L. BAIM
MUSIC BY MARVIN HAMLISCH
EXECUTIVE PRODUCER ROSILYN HELLER

ICE CASTLES

A novel by

Leonore Fleischer

Based on a screenplay by

Donald Wrye and Gary L. Baim

FAWCETT GOLD MEDAL • NEW YORK

ICE CASTLES

Published by Fawcett Gold Medal Books, a unit of CBS
Publications, the Consumer Publishing Division of CBS, Inc.

ISBN: 0-449-14154-3

Printed in the United States of America

10   9   8   7   6   5   4   3   2   1

ICE CASTLES

1

As far back as she could remember, Lexie Winston had lived in a world of white. For sixteen years, the springs, the summers and the autumns had come and gone, bringing with them the brilliance of green and yellow and blue and red and browns, but Lexie only drifted through those days, waiting for winter white. When the last leaves abandoned the shivering trees, and the bare branches groped at the frosty sky, when the winds swept over the flat Iowa landscape, carrying the gray, wet chill of the promise of snow, Lexie's heart would grow lighter, like a flower welcoming the sun. She had fun all the year round, but winter was her own, her very special time.

When the first subzero nights struck, leaving behind them mornings of frozen ground and frozen water, Lexie would wake up before dawn, grinning with happiness. By the time the sun had risen, she would be dressed in her down parka, worn over two sweaters, long johns under her jeans, marching in her work boots down to the pond, her precious ice skates over her shoulder. There she would skate on the frozen water, feeling the early morning winds on her temples as she dipped and soared over the rough, uneven surfaces of the ice.

Graceful, free and solitary, Lexie Winston skated as naturally as a salmon leaps through white water, because it was the one thing her body knew best. And even though she skated around cheerfully almost every day of the year on the indoor rink at Beulah's Ice Castle and Five Star Lanes, Lexie knew that her own private world was the frozen pond on her father's farm. For many years it had belonged to her and to her alone, her white world in which she came alive fully.

To say that Lexie Winston loved to skate was like saying that birds loved to fly—and neither needed an audience. Lexie skated for herself alone. Her moves were spontaneous, her jumps and spins performed for no one, but danced out of the sheer joy of the movement. Only when skating out of doors did she attempt the high, bold leaps she enjoyed so much, entrusting her slender body to the air as if air were its rightful element. Her nature responded to the swiftness and the loftiness of the flight; she always counted on landing safely, and she almost always did.

She loved racing, too, swooping along the pond side by side with Nick, trying to match the incredible power of his long, muscular legs. She rarely won against Nick; his legs were so much longer than hers and he was three years older. But winning wasn't what mattered. The race was for the fun of it, and nothing special was gained in the winning. To move, to feel her muscles straining to the limit, to feel the wind against her face as she picked up speed—that was where the triumph came. In the doing.

As she glided and turned now, dipping and soaring like a flake of snow in a windstorm, Lexie's mind sought and shared the perfect harmony, the peaceful purity of her surroundings. She wasn't even aware of the gentle whooshing of her blades as they cut into the snowy ice. Skating like

8

this, alone, she was conscious only of her moves—unrehearsed, a dancer improvising to a strain of music heard only inside her head. She heard a song created out of the whiteness and the peace, a melody of spins and jumps and arabesques and the deeply felt but unspoken emotion she experienced whenever she left the ice in a high, graceful leap like bird-flight, a leap that sometimes Lexie felt could carry her into the sky and away forever.

This morning was especially precious, especially rare and her own. Here, on the pond, she could skate what she felt. Later today, on the rink, she would have to skate the way Beulah wanted her to. A few weeks ago, Beulah had decided that Lexie ought to skate in the Regionals at Cedar Rapids, and she was "preparing" Lexie for it, getting her ready to compete.

Compete. Although the walls of her bedroom in the farmhouse were covered with photographs of skating champions, competition had almost never crossed Lexie's mind. She skated for only one reason—she loved it better than anything in the world. Not more than any *body*—her father Marcus and Nick and even Beulah came first—but there was no *thing* she could imagine that gave her the pleasure that ice skating did. What could the Regionals give her, even in the unlikely event she could win one of the top four places? A medal? She didn't need a medal.

Twenty-five years ago, Beulah herself had won the Regionals. It was hard to picture that heavy, burly, almost clumsy figure as a slim, swift girl in a skating dress, a girl who had stood on the highest dais in the winner's row and bowed her head to receive the ribbon of the first place medal.

Beulah hadn't gone on from there; she hadn't even tried the Sectionals. She'd simply stopped, turned her back on the possibilities and come back to Waverly to grow old. Now she wanted Lexie to take up where she left off, to enter and to win. Beulah was after Lexie night and day to practice, when all Lexie wanted to do was to skate, to dip and glide and turn and leap for her own enjoyment.

Besides, Marcus disapproved of his daughter's competing. He didn't want her to leave home, and she didn't want to hurt him. They had grown very, very close since her mother's death so long ago, and she valued that closeness.

But something in her wanted to give it a try, and she didn't want to disappoint Beulah, either. And so Lexie had promised to take a stab at the Regionals. And every day after school she carried her skates dutifully over to the Ice Castle where Beulah would drill her on the compulsory figures. But that wasn't skating. That was torture, and Lexie gritted her teeth and bore it, consoling herself with the thought that it would all be over in a few weeks. Meanwhile, those very early mornings on the pond, where she could set her own pace and rhythms and movements, were still Lexie's own.

It wasn't that Lexie didn't have talent. Even she, unschooled and untrained as she was, realized that she had a special, natural gift and a certain raw energy that others found a joy to watch. What she lacked was that ferocious competitive spirit that turned little girls of eight into skating robots.

Even if Lexie had been born competitive, where would she get the money? She knew that skaters who were trying to qualify as world class had fathers who could invest upwards of twenty thousand dollars a year in professional training and the finest equipment, as well as hire tutors for their children's school subjects so that they could spend every waking hour on the ice. Competitive skating was an activity for the children of wealthy and ambitious parents. Besides, Lexie was too old. At twelve, Dorothy Hamill had won her first national championship; most figure skaters were competing at the age of eight. At sixteen, Lexie Winston had still to skate in her first Regional competition.

The position of the sun in the sky told Lexie it was time to stop skating and head toward school. Reluctantly, she glided to a stop near the log and sat down to take off her skates. As she leaned over, her hand brushed the rough carving in the bark. Two sets of initials—AW and NP. Alexis Winston and Nick Peterson. Nick had carved them

10

there with his new Swiss Army knife, just before he'd packed his hockey and lacrosse sticks into the Scout and driven away to college. Their last day.

"Write to me," Lexie had begged.

"You bet, Bozo. I'll send you a picture postcard from every whistle-stop between here and Oshkosh, Wisconsin," he'd teased her, his blue eyes glinting with mischief.

"No, Nick, be serious."

"Serious? You want me to be serious? You want a commitment? I'll give you a commitment that will last your time and mine—that'll go down in history. I'll give you a commitment greater than Napoleon gave whatsername!" Brandishing his knife like an Indian taking scalps, Nick had dug deep into the rotting bark of the log, and the chips flew all over the grass. "There!" he cried with a final flourish. "Is that serious or is that serious?"

Yet in six months he'd written her only five letters, and none at all in the last month. He hadn't even called her lately. Was anything wrong? Had he found another girl? A college girl? Lexie shook her head firmly as she dried the blades of her skates and slipped the guards over them. No; no way. She and Nick were born to be together; if she knew anything, she knew that. He was going to be a doctor, and they would get married in a few years. That was the plan. Nothing would change it.

*   *   *

Beulah was waiting for her after school. The middle-aged woman, her hands on her hips—ponderous hips, made larger by overalls and layers of sweaters—stood watching to make sure that Lexie's workout was going according to the rather rough program she'd planned for the girl.

"The long program is the most important part of the Regionals," Beulah said for the hundredth time, but Lexie was not listening as she skated back and forth over her tracings.

"You've got four and a half minutes, and you'll be

under pressure all the time. Now the program we've worked up will give you some fast, strong moves at the very beginning, but you're going to have to work hard in all four corners of the arena. Remember, you get scored for using *all* the ice, not just the center of it, and you want to give them their money's worth. Those five Cedar Rapids judges are no slouches, Lexie. Do the hardest stuff when you're freshest and least tired, and if you think you can't do something perfectly, leave it out of the program. Hear me? Don't take risks." Beulah's voice rasped in Lexie's ears.

"I hear you, Beulah," nodded Lexie. "Don't worry."

"And you got to work on that sit-spin," cautioned the older woman. "It's your weakest move."

"I know, Beulah. I've been trying, but it's still a little wobbly."

"It's compulsory, so you better work harder. We'll do a half hour of that after you finish your tracings. I'm worried about your figures. Your form is for the birds!"

Lexie sighed wearily. She hated tracings, those "compulsory school figures" based on the figure eight. Over and over again, circle after circle after circle. Every curve had to be perfect; all the circles had to be lined up on the same axis. You traced them three times in the ice, and you were supposed to go over your first set of tracings so perfectly that you left only one set of markings on the ice, not three. She'd been at them for two hours now and she was getting dizzy from all those circles. Sometimes, she wished she'd never heard the word *Regionals*.

"All right, Lexie, take a break," called Beulah. "Let's see some figure skating. And make it good."

Grinning, Lexie broke off in the middle of one of her despised circles and skated off to the center of the rink, striking a pose. She started the music in her head and glided forward on her left foot, skating as quickly around the rink as she could to gain momentum for her first jump. It was a split jump, showy, and one of her best moves. Beulah kept harping that she would have only a moment or two to make a strong first impression on the judges.

12

With a surge of power, she left the ice, leaping high into the air with no apparent effort, her arms curving gracefully over her head, her legs wide apart in a perfect split. For a heartbeat, she remained suspended in midair, a small, slender figure in blue jeans, white sweater, white knitted cap and mittens, her long blond ponytail streaming out behind her like the tail of a dragonfly. She had no idea of how lovely a picture she made. Fashioned of grace and freshness, of innocence and charm and the swift motion of a meadowlark, Lexie Winston on skates was beauty itself.

"Not bad," Beulah called grudgingly as Lexie came down from her leap and glided backward in an arabesque.

One leg extended, her body bent to the side like a dancer's, Lexie executed a perfect arabsque and turned gracefully so that she was skating forward for another jump.

"Double axel," ordered Beulah, and Lexie left the ice again, turning twice in midair and coming down on the same foot she had started off with. It was harder to do, but Beulah said it had earned her a couple of extra points with the judges years ago. Someday . . . someday, Lexie decided, she would master the triple axel, if only to prove to herself she could.

"Sit-spin," instructed Beulah, and Lexie's heart sank a little.

Her jumps were good, and her arabesques and spread eagles were things of beauty, but to Lexie the sit-spin was just plain murder. It begins as a standing spin, but the skater must sink immediately and gracefully into a sitting position on the skating knee, the other leg extended parallel to the ice as she spins around, head held high, a bright smile pasted to the face. Then she has to rise again, just as gracefully and—still spinning—come to a perfect stop with arms crossed on the chest. And still smiling.

With a muffled groan, Lexie executed a rather wobbly sit-spin, forgetting, as usual, to smile.

"Again!" ordered Beulah. "Do it again, Lexie. You gotta get it right. Now . . . back straight, head high. Smile! That's better. Keep smiling."

Keep smiling. Keep smiling. Think about something to make you smile, Lexie told herself. Don't think about the Regionals. Think about Marcus. Think about Nick.

Nick was her best friend. She was popular in school and her grades were good. People responded to her; her teachers liked her; the kids thought she was neat; but she found it hard to make *close* friends. Except for Nick, of course. She thought of him skating with her over her pond, daring her to a race, daring her to leap over obstacles at top speed. She always took those dares, cheeks flushed, ponytail flying; she was fearless on blades, as fearless as he.

And her thoughts turned to her father as she usually saw him, sitting at the old kitchen table, drinking his coffee, the first morning chores completed. Marcus would take his break before Lexie was ready to leave for school so that they could spend half an hour together. He'd grin as he'd spin his wild tales for her, stories of his past, of his "barnstorming" days. Lexie knew that barnstorming had gone out when Marcus was still in grammar school; it was his fancy word for "crop dusting." Nevertheless, there had been a time when Marcus had flown through the sky, instead of being tied to the earth, as he was now. And he still dreamed of those days. Lexie never knew whether to believe Marcus' tall tales or not, but it didn't matter. They were etched in his memory as though each event had truly happened.

Lexie's favorite story was about the time Marcus had gotten high on illegal whisky and had turned his plane around and flown right back through the cloud of insecticide he'd just dusted. It had choked him so badly that he'd crashed. But since he had been flying only about fifteen feet off the ground and he came down in a field of mown hay, he'd landed without a scratch.

"And it was that rotgut alcohol that saved me, babe," he'd always tell her at the finish of the yarn. "Stuff was so strong and poisonous it like to kill any DDT ever made. Woke up feeling better than ever."

"Oh, Daddy." Lexie would smile, shaking her head. But she loved the tale; there was a daring about it that tickled

14

her. She felt the same way sometimes, as though nothing could hurt her, no stunt was too dangerous to pull. She was Marcus' daughter, no two ways about that.

Frowning, she practiced the same figures over and over, tracing them into the ice, while Beulah watched her with a critical eye and folded arms. She wished Nick were there. On or off the ice, she loved being with Nick, to watch him smile at her, to see his large blue eyes sparkle with mischief.

Thinking about Nick now, Lexie lost track of her timing and stopped. Abruptly, the music in her head shut itself off. That was her signal, her mind's private signal to her body that she'd done enough for one day. Another few minutes and fatigue would set in. Quit before you're tired, Beulah had always told her. Being tired doesn't do you any good at all. That's when you make your mistakes.

Pulling the knitted cap off her head and shaking her long, tousled hair free, Lexie skated swiftly to the edge of the rink and sat on the barrier as she unlaced her skates. They were good skates, her Phantoms, but they were getting pretty old. Daily use had stretched them out a little, and they didn't fit as tightly around her heels and ankles as they should. They'd soon need regrinding, too, and that was expensive. Lexie sighed. Beulah had been talking about new skates for the Regionals, but Lexie knew better. New skates, really good ones, cost the earth.

"Daddy will never go for it," she had told Beulah again and again.

As Beulah watched Lexie dry her blades with a soft old towel, she announced, "Tomorrow morning I want you here by 6:00 A.M. Every second between now and the Regionals counts double, you know that."

"I know that." The girl nodded, but her face was troubled. She laced up her work boots and stood up, pulling her heavy, nylon parka over her sweater.

Beulah walked her to the door of the rink and patted her warmly on the shoulder. "You were good today, Lexie," she said. "You worked real hard, and you showed

15

me some good stuff. But you need a lot more precision. Tomorrow you've gotta work even harder."

Lexie sighed. "Yes, Beulah."

"Get a good night's sleep, now. Hear?"

"Yes, Beulah. Good night."

Lexie stepped out into the cold evening. It wasn't late, but it was already dark—a moonless night in winter. Crunching her boots into the snow's crust, enjoying the feel and the sound of the crunch, she headed for home. There was still supper to cook and dishes to wash and homework to do and Marcus to spend time with before that good night's sleep. She was tired, and she felt drained. And tomorrow promised to be even harder than today.

Nick Peterson noticed the large ice patches on the road ahead and automatically shifted the Scout into second gear. There would probably be cracks in the asphalt under the ice, but the old car was up to just about anything. Behind him, on the peeling vinyl of the back seat, Nick's baggage shifted, and a hockey stick tumbled forward, narrowly missing his dark head. Pushing it back with one hand while he drove with the other, Nick grinned. But it was a nervous grin, not his usual mischievous smile.

His tackle piled helter-skelter on the seat—his bags, books, sports equipment, dirty laundry—reminded Nick that it wasn't going to be easy to explain. There would be some hard questioning from his old man about what he was doing back home in the middle of the semester. Nick was going to have to come up with some valid answers, and he wasn't sure that there *were* any.

Past the ice, eight miles along the blacktop led him over

some of the few hills in this part of the state. He was getting closer to home now. He was damn tired, his neck and shoulder muscles aching from long hours at the wheel. If he put on a little speed, he could be home in an hour. But he wasn't going home right away. He was going to see Lexie first, and he knew exactly where to find her.

He tried to picture her face, but it kept eluding him. Except for her eyes. They were as blue as his own, large and fringed with long lashes, surprisingly dark for a girl so fair. Her hair was a golden drift, but he couldn't picture it strand by strand. Lexie was three years younger than he, and he had watched her grow up. He still remembered the pigtails that had preceded the ponytail, and the freckles that had gradually disappeared. The face of the child and the face of the young woman kept melding in his imagination—and it was a dear face, one he was eager to see again.

It would be hard explaining to Lexie, too, that he wasn't going to become a doctor.

He spotted the first billboard coming up, signaling civilization. Soon he'd be passing the gas station, then the railroad tracks, then Waverly itself and home. Waverly. Waverly, Iowa. Talk about your small towns. Waverly was just about the smallest town on the planet. A widespread group of farms; a depot for shipping out corn and dairy products; one drive-in movie theater, showing movies a year after they'd opened in Iowa City; a whole forest of silos, a couple of beer joints; one place to dance; a library; four churches; a drug store that made banana splits; a dry goods store that the ladies optimistically called "the department store"; Beulah's Ice Castle and Five Star Lanes and that was just about it. Waverly, Iowa. Home.

Nick drove the Scout down the familiar streets, through the familiar intersections. Nothing had changed in the six months he'd been away, except that the town looked a little seedier, a week or two closer to dying. But maybe that was because he'd become used to more bustle, busier people, the noise and activity of a middle-sized college town instead of this hick village. Nick smiled and shook his

18

head. Waverly wasn't all that different. It was he who'd changed.

As Nick pulled up to Beulah's place and turned off the ignition, he hesitated. He had mixed feelings about being back; something inside him urged him to start up the engine and keep on going. But he knew that he had to face them all—his dad, his girl, and just about everybody else in this damn town, including Beulah. Might as well start now. His shoulders heaved in a sigh, and his blue eyes blinked wearily. He'd been driving for so many hours, over such flat and icy terrain, that fatigue had him confused and depressed. He could feel a headache starting up behind his eyes, tying a band of pain around his skull.

He got out of the Scout, his long legs unfolding stiffly, and rubbed the seat of his worn, faded Levi's. His head wasn't the only thing that hurt.

Beulah's Ice Castle and Five Star Lanes looked just as it always had; it was already so run-down and raunchy that it could hardly get any worse. The building, a long, low concrete bunker covered with beer and cola signs and chicken-wire fencing, was actually a converted truck garage. It was not beautiful. But, then, neither was Beulah.

Nothing inside had changed, either, Nick noted as he pushed open the screen door and the old wooden door behind it. The same weak neon signs for Miller and Bud; the same stained counter top that served as a bar, covered with rings left by wet glasses and burns made by cigarettes; the same customers, just hanging out quietly drinking coffee or beer; the same distant thunder of the balls rolling down the alleys.

A farmer in a plaid lumber jacket called out to him.

"Hiya, Nick."

" 'Lo, Charlie. How areya?" Nick waved.

"Beats the hell out of me," joked the farmer. "What're *you* doing home?"

"Beats the hell out of me," Nick grinned in reply. He passed the bowling alley, where a frustrated bowler was yelling for the pins to be set back up.

"Hey, Beulah! Rack'em up! Come on!" he bawled, getting no answer.

"Hi, Les," Nick offered.

The bowler turned in surprise. "Hey . . . Nick! What the hell you doin' home?"

Nick just shook his head. He knew he'd hear that question a dozen more times before the day was out.

At the door to the rink, Nick stopped, hesitating again. A ball clattered down the old varnished lane and knocked a handful of pins over, and the bowler scowled. He looked up at the tall young man who stood staring past the alleys at the door to the ice rink, his blue eyes troubled. "See Beulah in there?" he called to Nick.

Nick shook his head.

The old Ice Palace was comforting. Its mingled smells of stale beer and old sawdust, of rosin and woolly lumber jackets thawing out, of men's sweat and camaraderie, of dust and Ajax scouring powder and other undefinables made Nick feel that he was home again.

"Say hello to your dad," the bowler called after Nick as he turned his reluctant feet toward the ice rink.

"Sure will," the boy called over his shoulder.

"And if you see Beulah back there . . . tell her to get the hell back on the job," grumbled the bowler.

The rink was on the far side of the ancient concrete structure, built over a natural cold spot so that Beulah could save some dough each year on refrigeration. Aside from Lexie, nobody much used the ice these days, although local pickup hockey matches were played there from time to time. Nick had played center forward for the home team here and he had an aching fondness for the Ice Castle, born out of its creaking comfort and his long familiarity with it as a hangout and a haven.

At the door to the rink, Nick hesitated again. He knew he was letting Lexie down. In fact, he was letting them *all* down, his family and his friends. He'd taken a very special opportunity and he'd blown it.

How? Where had things started to go wrong for him? His grades had been good at first—not great, but good

20

enough to pass without problems. And he was playing center forward on the varsity hockey team, which gave him some status on the campus. It was just . . . he couldn't get *into* it, not like a lot of the guys he saw around him, always fighting for grades. It didn't seem to make any difference to him whether he did well at premed or not. What was one more doctor in the world? Medicine was what other people wanted for him; it wasn't necessarily what he wanted for himself. But how could he explain his restlessness, his dissatisfaction, when he had no words to put to it himself?

Before he pushed open the door to the rink, Nick peered through the windowpane. Although the glass hadn't been wiped clean in years, he could make out two figures inside, on the ice. As he'd expected, Beulah and Lexie were in there, painstakingly going over Lexie's tracings.

Standing silently in the doorway, Nick watched them, the woman and the girl. Beulah hadn't changed one bit—still the same large, weatherbeaten, big-shouldered woman she'd always been. They said she'd been pretty as a girl, but her only beauty now was her long, narrow, cat-green eyes. The ends of her cropped hair straggled out from under a knitted sailor's cap, as usual. On her feet a pair of rubber-soled workman's boots were laced up over her overalls almost to her knees. Even for a woman who did heavy lifting and scrubbing and polishing and pin-setting, Beulah dressed eccentrically. She looked like the town character, and she was.

But Lexie, Lexie had changed. Keeping out of sight behind the barrier of the hockey restraining boards, Nick watched Lexie for a minute or two as she skated slowly around in circles, an unhappy, sober look on her face. He had never seen her so serious when she was on the ice; skating had always been the most spontaneous, joyous part of her life. She was changing, and he was changing. They were growing up. It would alter things between them somehow, he knew, and the thought chilled him.

Beulah looked down at the ice, checking Lexie's blade

marks for double tracings and shaking her head. Nick saw Lexie heave her shoulders in a sigh, and he grinned to himself. There were forty-one compulsory figures recognized internationally by figure skating associations, all of them based on the figure eight. And Lexie hated all forty-one of them, as she hated any routine that interfered with spontaneous skating.

"Straighter!" Beulah called out sternly, and Nick saw Lexie pull her head up higher and straighten out her back a little.

"Hold your head higher and your back will come along," ordered Beulah gruffly. "You on your tracings?"

"Pretty much," said Lexie in a strained voice. She was concentrating hard. It took an effort of will not to look down to see what she was doing, but Beulah had been trying to get her to *feel* her tracings, not only with her feet, but with her entire body.

" 'Pretty much' ain't good enough," Beulah growled.

"Hey, Beulah, come on!" The voice of Les, the bowler, raised in an aggrieved howl, penetrated the rink. "I paid for two lanes. Come *on!*"

Beulah wrinkled her nose impatiently. "Take your money outta the cash drawer," she yelled back, "and go to another alley if you're in such a damn rush."

"Aw, you know there ain't no other alley, Beulah," came Les' reproach. "You got the only bowling alley *in* this ole town."

But Beulah's attention was back on Lexie now. "Figures are thirty percent of your score," she reminded the girl. "Gonna have to do better."

"That's what I say," chimed in Nick.

Startled, both women turned to see the tall young man step out from behind the hockey barrier, grinning. Instantly, Lexie's face lit up like a six-year-old's on Christmas morning, and she skated toward him so fast she appeared to be flying. "Nick!" she shouted happily, running into him full tilt and nearly knocking him down. "Oh, Nick!"

Laughing, Nick spun Lexie around and gave her a big bear-hug.

He's grown, thought Lexie as she looked up at his smiling face. He looks wonderful. I can't believe he's right here; I just can't *believe* it. "Oh, Nick!" And she buried her nose in his parka, laughing with happiness.

"You bum!" hollered Beulah, crossing the ice with a grace surprising in so large a woman. "My turn." And she grabbed him for a hug and a kiss.

Beulah looked up at Nick. He's got a couple inches more on him. Won't be a boy much longer. At nineteen he's damn near a man right now.

"What the hell are you doing home?" Beulah demanded, narrowing her large, clear eyes into slits.

"Couldn't stay away from my girls," smiled Nick evasively, giving each of them a squeeze.

But Beulah wasn't to be evaded easily. "The hell you say," she snorted.

"What'd they do, kick you out?" Lexie joked. She was so happy to see Nick that she couldn't imagine anything being really wrong.

"I quit," Nick said quietly.

Both Lexie and Beulah stared at him wordlessly. Then Lexie gasped, "Nick—"

"What do you mean, you quit?" Beulah demanded. "What the hell did you go and do a dumb thing like that for?"

Nick shrugged, deliberately keeping his voice light. "None of your goddamned business," he told her, but his eyes were serious and a little defiant.

Responding to his expression, Beulah muttered out of one side of her mouth, "Well, at least we all know what *not* to talk about."

An uncomfortable silence fell over them, while Lexie searched Nick's face anxiously for clues.

"You goin' home?" Nick asked the girl.

Lexie nodded eagerly, but Beulah shook her head. "In a while. Her figures are lousy."

"It's okay." Lexie turned large, pleading eyes on Beulah, begging her to let her go with Nick.

But Beulah stood firm. "It's a regional competition," she said with an edge in her voice, directing her words at Nick. "She's a damn good skater, and once in her life she should get out and show what she can do."

Nick nodded his agreement.

Lexie shrugged, her face sullen. "It's no big deal."

"Yeah, it is," said Nick quietly. "I'll see you later," he promised, his face clouding again at the thought of the ordeal ahead of him. "I gotta go home and face the folks. Anything'll be fun after that. Even seeing you."

"Rat!" yelled Lexie, swinging on him and hitting him in the midriff with her small, mittened fists.

Nick pretended to double up, then swung one hand under Lexie's guard and tweaked her upturned nose. "Bozo!"

They scrambled around the ice like a pair of puppies until Beulah stepped between them, pushing them away from each other. "Come on, get going! Get out of here. We got work to do, and not much time to do it in."

As Beulah led Lexie back to the center of the rink, Lexie looked over her shoulder at Nick. "See you later," she shrugged, her face clouded with anxiety over him.

"Yeah," grinned Nick in reply. Don't worry, he begged her silently. Don't look at me like that, Lexie. It isn't the end of the world. But it was the end of something; he knew that as he jammed his hands deep into his parka pockets to find his leather gloves.

Leaving the bowling alley, he stepped into the thin, bitter, winter sunlight. The last thing Nick heard was Les' voice, raised in indignant anguish.

"Beulah! For Christ's sake!"

Nick smiled. Beulah would never pay attention to her lanes while Lexie Winston was on the ice.

3

"Maybe I'm just not smart enough!" yelled Nick, losing his temper at last. It was going to be much more difficult than he'd feared. He had known that his father would get mad at him, but it had never occurred to him that his mother would cry. Her tears were tearing at him, and he was crazy to get out of the house.

"Oh, you got the brains, all right!" Sven Peterson hollered at his son. "You just don't know how to use them. Have you got any idea at all how much money we poured into the last six months, just to keep you comfortable up there in Iowa City? That's a helluva lot of gallons of milk, boy!"

"I know that, Pa, and I'm sorry. I'm really sorry. I wish that I could have taken it seriously, but I didn't. I couldn't. It seemed . . . it just wasn't what I wanted to do. I thought it was, but it wasn't."

"Then would you mind telling your mother and me just

what it is you *do* want to do?" A vein in Sven Peterson's forehead throbbed with rage.

"I'm not sure . . . I thought . . . maybe . . . hockey," Nick said in a low voice.

"Hockey! Are you out of your mind? Do you want to get killed like some ignorant Canuck, maybe lose an eye? Hockey's not a game for anybody with brains. What makes you think you could even earn a living at it?"

"I'm good," Nick replied defensively.

"Good enough for Waverly," his father retorted, his voice heavy with sarcasm. "Maybe even good enough for college. But professional hockey! That takes guts. Have you got guts, son?"

"Now, Sven, that's not fair!" Nick's mother insisted. "You know that Nick is a good boy, a brave boy." She'd stopped crying and was patting her hair into place. A practical woman, Rose Peterson knew when it was time to stop arguing and start salvaging the situation. "Nick, dear, while you're home with us, you might as well work on the farm with Pa. We can use all the help we can get. And you don't have to rush into any decision. As long as you're earning your keep here, you and Pa ought to get along fine. Right, Sven?"

But Nick's father wasn't going to give in that easily. "I never thought I'd live to see the day when a son of mine would be a dropout," he said bitterly. "And you were supposed to have the brains in the family. Some brains! A hockey player."

"Supper," Nick's mother reminded them. "Come to the table, Sven, Nick. Everything is gonna get cold." She wiped her hands on her apron and went into the kitchen to take the roast from the oven.

After breaking the news to his parents and eating his dinner and unpacking and stowing away his gear, it was night, and Nick finally had a chance to think about Lexie. The hour was late, and she probably had gone to bed, but he wanted to see her, to talk to her alone.

He was full of doubt. Now that he was officially out of college, what the hell was he going to do? And why did he have to make his mind up *now*, for the rest of his life? He was only nineteen, he had plenty of time. Why did the decision have to be made this minute? Why wouldn't his folks let him lay back, cool out, take a look around him and see what directions were open to him? The only talent he was sure he had was hockey; he was a damn good center forward, smart and fast and totally without fear. But was hockey a good way of life? It was *one* way, but there must be plenty of others. He needed to talk to Lexie. He hoped she was waiting up for him, and he struggled impatiently with the garage door latch, his thick leather gloves making his fingers clumsy. Being with Lexie was easy and comfortable for Nick and make him forget the self-doubts that gnawed at him. Being with Lexie was as refreshing as drinking from a cool fountain on a hot summer day.

The night sky was clear and unclouded, and in the distance stars shone stilly, not twinkling, content only that their life-light reached the earth. A large, cold moon gave a blue white tint to the crackling snow.

Turning on the overhead bulb in the garage, Nick smiled with satisfaction at the new Rupp snowmobile. Lexie would love this little baby. His dad had traded in the old one only last month, and Nick was seeing this one for the first time. He ran his hand approvingly over the Fiberglass body, examined the front skis and the back treads, patted the heavy plastic windscreen. Lexie really dug snowmobiling, and they would have some fun with this little beauty. He took two helmets down from their pegs on the garage wall, grabbed the ignition key from the rack over the tool bench and turned the motor on. He grinned as he felt the engine roar into life, and they went bounding off over the snow, machine and boy, like a kanga with a baby roo in its pocket.

Lexie *did* love it; her face under the plastic visor of the helmet was all smiles as Nick raced the snow buggy around a tall clump of conifers, over a high bank, and down, down to the foot of the hill. It was like tobogganing, belly-flopping down a steep hill, only at forty-five miles an hour. She adored the feeling of flying, the rush that the speed gave her, sending her blood racing in time to the engine.

Lexie felt the wind cutting around her shoulders, and she snuggled closer to Nick to gain a little warmth. Nick steered the Rupp around the curve of a large boulder and up to the crest of the next hill. As they came to a stop, the front skis hung over the hill, but the back treads held them fast, suspended over an extremely steep drop.

"Wanta try it?" Nick flung the challenge into the wind.

"Why not?" she yelled back, as nonchalantly as she could manage.

Nodding, Nick pulled down his visor and put the buggy into reverse. They backed away from the drop then, and when Nick had built up enough speed and distance, he turned the snow buggy around to head for the edge of the bluff once more. At top speed, they hit the shelf; the snowmobile rose like a bird as they went over. For more heartbeats than Lexie dared to count, they hung in the sky and the incredible silence. Then, with a bounce, they hit the ground and went skidding sideways down the incline, narrowly missing a stand of timber, to brodie to a stop at last. Grinning, Nick took his helmet off and looked at Lexie with a mischievous smile.

"You were scared," he teased.

Lexie could still feel the blood racing through the pulse points in her throat and wrists. "I was not," she lied, her voice cracking a little; she pretended to have difficulty with the helmet's chin strap to give herself an extra moment.

"I wasn't scared," she insisted, shaking her yellow hair free.

"Take off your gloves," Nick ordered, grabbing for her hands.

Laughing, Lexie shook her head and tried to pull her heavily gloved hands out of Nick's, but he was too strong for her, and after a minute's futile struggle, she gave up and let Nick strip off her gloves.

"Aha!" he crowed. "Sweaty palms. You were scared helpless."

"I was not!" yelled Lexie stubbornly. "It's healthy to sweat . . . just before you die."

Both of them broke into laughter at that. Then Lexie tried to tickle Nick through his nylon parka. They poked and prodded at each other, looking for weak spots. Nick's arms went around Lexie's shoulders, and she lifted her face to his, expectancy in her closed eyes. For an instant, he looked at the feathery lashes trembling on her cheek, then he crushed her lips with his own.

The intensity of his kiss took Lexie by surprise. They had often kissed, but the kisses were the sweet, light kisses of childish affection. Lexie was not prepared for this kiss. She broke away, confused, and was immediately sorry, hoping Nick hadn't noticed the implied rejection.

"So what are you doing home?" she asked him lightly, to cover her confusion.

But Nick had noticed it, and her reaction stung him. When he'd taken her in his arms, he'd forgotten how young she was, how totally without experience. The kiss had taken him, too, by surprise.

"Missed you," he said shortly.

"Really?" A broad smile made Lexie's eyes dance and showed her white teeth. Suddenly, she looked about thirteen, and Nick pushed her away, fumbling at the ignition switch of the snowmobile.

Sensing his change of mood, and afraid that she was the cause of his irritation, Lexie jumped off the back of the snow buggy and threw herself onto the ground. Spreading her arms and legs wide, she made an angel in the snow.

"Well, if that's your attitude, you'd just better take me right here," she challenged, her eyes twinkling.

Nick looked at her, amusement tugging at the corners of his lips. Lexie's slenderness was hidden under heavy layers of shirt, long johns, sweater, muffler and ski parka. She might have tempted a polar bear in that shapeless bundle of clothing—but not him.

"Come on, Bozo," he choked. "Get on the machine."

He shook his head and put his hand out to help her up. But Lexie rolled over in the snow, refusing help, and scampered to her feet by herself, then clambered behind Nick on the snowmobile. Slipping her arms around his waist, she gave him a big hug and buried her face in his goose-down parka. Snuggled tightly together, they took off with a roar, the snowmobile's silhouette crossing the empty night sky, skimming the surface of the virgin snow.

*　*　*

The sweet breath of the cows warmed the barn somewhat, but Marcus Winston was still freezing. He could see his own breath as he threw the frigid hay down off the tines of his pitchfork. Hell, he wouldn't be surprised if the goddamn cows gave ice cream! This godforsaken place was swept by every prairie wind from here to the Canadian border. Clomping around the wet barn in his thick Wellington boots, Marcus grumbled as he listened to the weather bulletins on his little SONY portable that sat perched on the manger, its sleek Japanese modernity oddly out of place in the rustic setting.

"Saginaw, two above," droned the weather report. "Meitter, one below, Mantugga, three below, Waverly, zero with a twenty-knot breeze."

"Breeze!" snorted Marcus, glaring angrily at the little radio. "Breeze! Christ, that's some word for a windchill factor of twenty below!" He grabbed up the radio and stomped out of the barn. The "breeze" hit him hard and made him gasp, as its icy fingers searched through the heavy layers of his work clothes and found vulnerable places.

Trudging along the path of packed-down snow that led from the barn up to the house, Marcus continued his grumbling. Somehow it made him feel a little warmer. "A goddamn breeze is seventy goddamn degrees and that's what you get in Memphis, Tennessee on the fourth of September. Who the hell in their right mind would live in an icebox?"

On the back porch, Marcus stamped some of the snow off his boots, but he was too impatient and too cold to get it all. So when he walked into the warm kitchen, he left a wet, muddy trail on the linoleum floor. He never bothered to look down, and even if he had seen his tracks, he wouldn't have cared. It was too damn early to be up and dressed and working; Marcus felt that every morning, when he rose at five. He wasn't cut out to be a farmer.

He set the radio down on the kitchen table and fiddled with the dials, turning past government agricultural reports, farmer's weather stations, rock and roll music, country and western and two gospel stations before he found what he wanted.

As the silken strands of Mozart wove around the kitchen, Marcus began to peel off the heavy layers of his outdoor clothing. He hung up his heavy fleece-lined jacket and a plaid lumberman's shirt, then covered the hook with his cap, a thick, leather affair with a fleece-lined flap that protected his ears and neck.

Marcus Winston was forty and almost looked it. Sun and wind had put the lines in his face, and life had put the gray in his hair and his beard, yet nothing had taken the boyish expression from his blue gray eyes, and his body, freed from the padded clumsiness of his outer garments, was as slender and graceful as a young man's. Once he'd been handsome; he was handsome still, but there was an occasional bitter twist to his mouth and a furrowed vertical line, carved by frustration, between his brows.

Marcus had not been born a farmer; he'd been born a dreamer. He'd been a wild, free spirit when he'd met Betsy so many years ago. He was little more than a boy himself then, a twenty-two-year-old with dreams of breaking records, of flying into space and staying there, a pilot with his head—literally and figuratively—in the clouds.

Betsy was nineteen, but her feet were firmly fixed in the soil. A farmer's daughter, she loved the life on a farm, loved to see the seasons change upon the rich earth, bringing planting and harvest, death and rebirth. And she had taken Marcus' cloud-dreams and brought them down to earth by marrying him and bringing him out to the farm.

Still, it hadn't been bad then because there was Betsy and love and, soon, Lexie. Those had been happy days, and Marcus had worked the seasons around, never minding the endless toil or the bitter weather.

Until Betsy left him. He blamed her for it still, still thinking of her death as her desertion, although she hadn't wanted to die. Even when the pain was slicing her into pieces, Betsy had wanted to live, to stay with Marcus and little Lexie, who was just learning to know her mother. But death had not paid any attention to what Betsy or Marcus wanted, and so he'd been left with nothing more than a farm and a baby daughter and a gravestone and a handful of beautiful, painful memories and unfulfilled dreams. Though many years had passed, Marcus still felt like a stranger on his farm, and now he cursed the weather and the work.

Coffee. What I need is a cup of coffee, Marcus thought as he stumbled around the messy kitchen looking for the can of coffee. Coffee would warm him and wake him up and make him feel almost human again, instead of like a goddamn St. Bernard roaming around the Alps.

Once the kitchen had been a beautiful, comfortable room; the copper polished and the curtains starched. Geraniums had grown on the windowsill in the summertime, and a little pot of holly in the fall and winter. In the spring, Betsy had kept flat dishes of parsley and chives growing. There was always music in the kitchen then, not Mozart, but pop songs for Betsy to sing along with. Good smells came out of the oven, and Marcus looked forward to coming into the kitchen, seeking its warmth and its food and the nourishing presence of his beautiful wife.

Now it was a mess. Dishes were stacked in the sink, and grease-encrusted pots and pans were piled on top of them. The old curtains hung limply at the sides of the windows, like a hound's ears. Bottles and jars and cans stood on the work surfaces, where they'd been opened and abanoned. A crumpled newspaper lay on the table. Lexie did her best to keep ahead of the mess, but lately, with her school work and the extra rink practice with Béulah, things had gone to hell around the house. Especially in the morning, when Marcus needed his coffee.

Now where was that blue can? . . .

Upstairs in her room, Lexie tied a ribbon firmly around her ponytail and checked herself in the mirror. Not too bad, considering she'd had only a few hours' sleep. She grabbed her school books and her blades, picked out a matching scarf-and-mittens set, then raced down the stairs. She dumped her books on the hall table and set her skates in their battered case carefully on top of the books. Then she pulled her parka out of the hall closet and dropped it on the floor near the table. She was almost ready to roll.

The first thing that met Lexie's nose as she opened the kitchen door was the overpoweringly bitter smell of strong coffee. She took a step backward in surprise.

Marcus looked up from where he was sitting at the kitchen table, leafing through an old newspaper. He smiled; he was in a good humor now.

"Hi, babe," he called to her.

Lexie came into the kitchen and kissed Marcus lovingly on the cheek. But she recoiled at what appeared to be a cup of mud he was happily sipping.

"Hi, Daddy. Yecccchhh! What are you doing to your stomach?"

"Campfire coffee. Best in the world," grinned Marcus. "Grab a cup."

Lexie eyed it dubiously. "A plate would be more like it." She took a cup and saucer down from the cupboard above the sink. Boy was the kitchen a mess. She promised herself she would try to get home a little earlier from the rink today and tackle the place with a mop and a scrubbing brush.

"Sorry I overslept."

"That's okay," Marcus assured his daughter expansively. "I got along fine. They say men in their forties can learn to do anything."

"Forty going on fifteen," scoffed Lexie affectionately.

She picked up the battered enamel pot with distaste—where had this old relic come from?—and poured a little of the goo into her cup, wrinkling up her nose at its oozy blackness.

"I can't believe this stuff!" She carried her cup to the refrigerator and filled it two-thirds full with fresh milk. It turned a rather greenish gray color. Tentatively, she took a sip, screwing her face up.

"Out pretty late last night," commented Marcus, a little too casually. "What were you doing all night, boogying?"

"Snowmobiling," said Lexie after one poisonous swallow.

Marcus frowned and set his cup down carefully on the table. "Did I ever tell you about that time a bunch of us were fooling around in a snowmobile and a farmer had set out some traps and one of the guys was decapitated? Had his head taken right off his neck."

"Oh, Daddy," Lexie sighed, casting her eyes wearily up to heaven.

"Fact. I swear. Sure as hell." Marcus nodded vigorously for emphasis. "It was before your mother died." He got to his feet and began to pace around the kitchen animatedly.

Lexie took his place at the table and watched him. The corners of her mouth curled up in fond amusement as she followed her father with her eyes. He's just like a kid, she told herself. Nothing but a big kid. Like Nick.

"You must've been only about five or six when it happened," Marcus continued. "That's why you can't remember. No really strong memory patterns in kids until they're eighteen. Anyway, a bunch of us were down at the VFW drinking and making bets . . ."

"You've never been to the VFW," scoffed Lexie, interrupting.

"Lexie, you wanna hear this moral tale or not?" Marcus stopped his pacing and frowned at his daughter. Jesus, she looked more and more like her mother every day! She was beautiful and growing up a little too fast to suit him.

"Do I have a choice?" Lexie sighed theatrically.

"The deal was that the last one across the lake . . ."

"You gonna tell it the same or a little different?" Lexie wanted to know.

"What's the difference?"

Lexie stood up. "If you're gonna tell it different, I'll make us some good coffee and sit down and listen."

She moved toward the stove, but Marcus reached out one strong arm and grabbed at her. Laughing, he sat down on the kitchen chair and pulled Lexie onto his lap. For an instant, she sat there silently, as she used to do when she was much younger, simply content to be with Marcus, enjoying the warmth and the strength of his lap and his presence. Then she leaned over and kissed his cheek softly.

"Still mad?" she whispered.

"What makes you think I was mad?"

"I'm going to marry him, Daddy." Lexie stood and looked at her father earnestly, watching for his reaction.

"What?" roared Marcus. "That sonofabitch!" A heavy thatch of hair flopped into his eyes as he jerked his head backwards.

Lexie laughed loudly and shook her golden head. "Wait a minute . . . not right away. I'm not going to marry him tomorrow. But I've always been going to marry Nick."

"You have *not* always been going to marry him," said Marcus forcefully. He had little use for Nick, but then he would have little use for any wet-nosed puppy who came to take his Lexie away.

"For the last ten years," said Lexie stubbornly.

When she does that, lifts her chin up like that, she's the image of her mother, thought Marcus with pain. It's not only her eyes and hair, it's the corners of her mouth. "Bull," he snorted out loud. "A six-year-old kid doesn't know who she's going to marry."

"I did," smiled Lexie. "The only problem is I'm not sure he knows that's the plan."

"Damn kid," muttered Marcus, meaning Nick Peterson. "What the hell's he doing home, anyway? Probably got kicked out. Congenital stupidity."

"Get out of here, Daddy!" yelled Lexie, laughing. She

took a swipe at Marcus with her dish towel, but he ducked away from her and ran for the back door.

"I don't want dumb grandchildren!" he hollered as he opened the door, slamming it just before a teaspoon hit it.

As Lexie stood there with her hands on her hips, the door opened again, and Marcus stuck his bearded, unruly head in. "It's not that I don't like him, mind . . ."

"Oh, go on, get out of here!" Lexie laughed, shaking her head. At least he wasn't mad any more. Underneath, he was still a little hurt; Lexie could tell. Marcus was angry earlier in the morning, not only because she'd been out late last night, but because she'd been out with Nick. Her father wanted to keep her a baby forever; Nick wanted her to grow up. She'd never understand men, but she loved and needed both of them. Couldn't Daddy see that she didn't love him less because she loved Nick, too? To her, it was so simple.

* * *

The referee dropped the rubber puck and the center forwards surged over the ice to slam at it with their curved sticks. Six attacked and six defended; leading the attack was Nick Peterson. He skated fast, his stick held out parallel to the ice, his blue eyes wide and alert as the puck passed into the possession of the visitors. Suddenly, he saw his chance, and darting around the defense, he caught up with the puck. Before the other man had a chance to pass it along, Nick cross-checked him enthusiastically, sending him crashing across the ice, skidding into the barrier. The puck now his, Nick turned it rapidly into the other team's attacking zone and over the goal line for a point scored.

The crowd, happy and excited, got to their feet and yelled for Nick and the Waverly Blue Jays. Leading the cheers was Beulah, happy and proud. These were *her* boys, skating to win on *her* rink.

"Come on, you pansies. Get in there!" she yelled hoarsely. "No! Don't check with your goddamn wrist! Let's see the ice run red with blood!"

Lexie giggled, but Marcus, sipping gloomily at a beer, only winced. Beulah made him uncomfortable. She knew it and seemed to enjoy doing it.

"He's fantastic!" Beulah glowed, watching Nick, who played as though every play would put him in the NHL. "The only kid suicidal enough for hockey."

Beulah laughed, and Lexie gasped as a pileup sent Nick sprawling to the ice, only to get up a second later and plunge back into the fight, blades flashing, stick flying.

"It's nice to hear somebody say something nice about him for a change," glowered Marcus.

"Daddy . . ." began Lexie, but Beulah interrupted, looking around herself happily.

"Just look at this crowd," she exulted. "Must be eighty, a hundred people here. That's seventy-five bucks. Just to see your crazy buddy. Maybe if we get another bunch like this next week, we can get you a new pair of skates for the Regionals. Right, Marcus?" Beulah's eyes twinkled maliciously under the brim of her Irish tweed walking hat. She had been baiting Marcus for almost twenty years; it was an old game between them.

But Marcus wouldn't rise to the bait this time. "Yeah, sure, maybe two pairs" was his only comment. He took another pull on the beer can and watched the furious action on the ice. Lexie sighed and turned back to follow Nick.

Attendance at the Waverly Blue Jays' Sunday games had dropped to zilch when Nick was away at college. Now a rowdy, happy crowd was yelling and drinking and enjoying itself, just because one crazy blue-eyed young man was stealing the puck on every other face-off and cheerfully mangling the opposing team in the process.

To Beulah, it meant money in the register. To Lexie, it meant excitement over Nick's victory. To Marcus, it meant a waste of a Sunday afternoon.

With less than a minute to play in the third and final period, Nick was maneuvering across the ice, chasing the puck like a hound dog chases a rabbit. Having caught up with it, having elbowed one opponent and hooked another,

37

Nick was now flashing the puck down the ice in the direction of goal. His big shoulders appeared abnormally large under the protective padding, but he skated with such style and grace that the clumsy hockey protective gear seemed to be tailor-made for him.

Score. He'd pushed the puck through the other team's netting, past the fallen goalie who'd tried to throw himself on it, only to land empty. Goal, and the winning point. As the crowd stood at the barriers cheering, Nick's teammates took turns pounding him and hugging him. Nick raised his arms above his head to wave his stick in a sign of victory. The Waverly Blue Jays had overcome.

After the match, the drinks were on Beulah. The four of them crowded into one of the shabby vinyl booths in the bar, the best booth, in fact. Marcus and Beulah filled their glasses again and again from the bourbon bottle on the table between them. Nick drank a beer or two, very slowly, and Lexie toyed with her can of Tab, not really wanting any.

Lexie felt uncomfortable and apprehensive; she wasn't sure why. These were the only three people in the world she loved and trusted. Aside from skating, these three people *were* Lexie's whole world. Yet, they always all seemed to be tugging her in different directions, so that when all three of them were together, Lexie often felt as though the currents were too deep for her.

Marcus fished around in the Doritos bag and crunched the last remaining chip. "Say, your old man sell off his Holsteins yet?" he asked Nick idly.

"Yeah."

"What's he going to do?"

Nick grinned a little sourly. "Cross-breed with polar bears and spend the rest of the winter in Hawaii." It was only half a joke. Nick's parents had definitely decided to take their long overdue vacation now that he was home from school and able to work on the farm with his brother. So he was feeling very trapped. At least he had gotten rid of some negative energy on the ice today.

Marcus shook his head in disbelief. "*You* going to take

care of the place while your folks are in good old Waikiki?" he challenged.

"Yeah, me and Mike the half-wit," Nick admitted glumly.

"Two . . . "

" . . . of a kind." Nick finished the sentence in chorus with Marcus. He'd heard it a zillion times.

"If you two are through with all this fan-club baloney, I've got a few words to say. There's something I'd like to discuss." Beulah's voice held an edge, and she looked directly at Marcus Winston, who shifted in his seat and evaded her eyes. He knew what was on Beulah's mind.

"What could be more important than finding out why our old buddy here came home in the middle of his first year?" Marcus asked equably, jerking a thumb at Nick.

"Oh, Daddy!" wailed Lexie, distressed.

"Jee-SUS!" Nick raised his large blue eyes to the ceiling and dragged the Cheez Doodles bag over to his side of the table.

"Lexie's competition," said Beulah quietly but firmly. She would not be denied this hearing.

"Subject closed!" shouted Marcus, pounding his fist angrily on the Formica tabletop. All he'd been hearing lately were the damn Regionals, and he was sick of it.

Lexie felt tears sting her eyelids, but Beulah only smiled and said, quietly, "Glad to see you're at least open-minded about it."

Marcus stole a glance at his daughter. Hurt was written all over her lovely face.

"Hell, Lexie's a fine skater," he admitted grudgingly. "But there's a difference between skating in the Seven Counties Kiwanis Competition and . . ." he broke off, seeing the confusion in Lexie's eyes. "Those big things, those big-time contests, well, they're worse than being professional. Little country girl could get eaten alive up there. . . ."

Lexie looked down at the table wordlessly. Her lip trembled and she fought to keep the tears back. How she hated this old quarrel. Marcus' voice grew thick with concern. "Hell, honey," he said, reaching over the table for her hand, "I . . . just . . . don't want you to get hurt."

Shaking her head, Lexie bit her trembling lip. She didn't trust herself to say a word without bursting into tears. Why couldn't Daddy understand how much the Regionals meant to Beulah?

"Marcus Winston, you're so full of bull it boggles the imagination," Beulah exploded, unable to contain herself a minute longer. "Where the hell are you coming from anyway? *You're* what's hurting her! Let her be! She's good. She'd damn good, and you know that I know something about it. She sure as hell has more natural talent than anybody I ever saw, including most of those girls in the Olympics. Let her be, Marcus."

Lexie looked up and across the table at her father. Her eyes were shining, with tears and with something else. With a new vision so clear that Marcus had to close his own eyes to shut it out.

"Let me go, Daddy. It's scary, sure, but I really want to do it." Her pleading eyes searched for her father's, willing him to look at her, to acknowledge her needs.

"We're talking about one competition, for Chrissakes . . ." began Beulah.

"She's too young." Marcus shook his head stubbornly, still not meeting Lexie's eyes.

"I'm too *old!*" Lexie burst out. "That's what I really am." The tears began to spill past her lashes and roll down her cheeks. "It's already too late. If I wait any longer, there won't be any chance at all."

"For what?" asked Marcus warily. He had been taken by surprise at Lexie's outburst.

"For me! Just . . . for me." Lexie stood up and ran out of the cafe. Nick followed her silently, not even looking in Marcus' direction.

"Well, it's for her own good," said Marcus defensively. Then he fell silent, staring into his tumbler of bourbon, aware that Beulah's gaze was on him, half-angry, half-pitying.

"You're going to smother her," Beulah said quietly, her

40

deep voice giving her words a portentous quality that struck a chill in Marcus. "You're going to hold onto her and suffocate her right to death. And she'll hate the hell out of you for it."

Angry and ashamed, Marcus lashed out. "Whatta you know," he snarled. "You run a goddamn broken-down rink and a goddamned broken-down bowling alley in a rummy small town. You wear stupid, men's clothes and you think that makes you a character? What the hell do you know?" The muscles in his jaw jumped and quivered.

Beulah's chin came up, and her green eyes flashed steel. "I won the Regionals," she said coldy, masking her pain.

"Twenty-five years ago," shot back Marcus.

Wounded, Beulah stood up and left the table, moving to the bar. She stood at it with her back to Marcus. He suddenly felt trapped and helpless, frustrated by his own cruelty and anger. He felt a deep rage at himself for the stupid waste of his own life and dreams, and his desire to thwart Lexie's. He knew he was wrong, but he couldn't help himself. Sadly, he got up and pushed through the crowd of drinkers at the bar until he reached Beulah's side. Beulah stood silent, lost in her memories of the past, of her one brief moment of glory, long dimmed.

"B, I'm sorry," he said in a low voice, almost a mumble.

But Beulah heard him, and a thrill of victory coursed through her bloodstream. Lexie was going to skate! Beulah turned to Marcus, her face gentler than he'd ever seen it.

"Everybody isn't afraid, Marcus," she said quietly. "Lexie's scared, but she isn't afraid. I know, I felt that once. Didn't you? Before Betsy died?"

Marcus stood silent, defeat bowing his tousled head. He had no words to meet hers. Beulah had won.

"Don't make her afraid, Marcus. Please . . ." She reached out and touched his arm.

Pulling his arm away from Beulah's touch, Marcus hurried out of the cafe. If there was anything he didn't need right now, it was anybody's pity, particularly Beulah's.

*　*　*

Lexie twisted around to look at her back view in the bedroom mirror. The skating dress hung loosely on her small body, but even so, it was a pretty blue, dark, almost navy, and it brought out the color of her eyes. It was a marvel that Beulah had once fit into it, even twenty-five years ago. In this very dress, a quarter of a century ago, a young and slender Beulah Madison had won the midwestern amateur figure skating championship. Now the dress was to be Lexie's lucky piece; maybe *it* would win the Regionals for her. After all, it knew the ropes.

"We'll take it in here and here," said Beulah around a mouthful of pins, pinching the waist in closer to Lexie's pretty little figure. "It'll be fine. You'll see." She gazed into the mirror, picturing *herself* in the dress.

"Mmmmmmmmmmmmm," agreed Lexie absently.

Beulah looked up sharply at the girl. She appeared to be off in some kind of world of her own, and not a happy one, either.

"You and Nick have a fight?" she asked.

Lexie shrugged. "Nooo . . . I don't know." Then she burst out, "Sometimes lately I don't know whether he really likes me or not. . . ."

"He likes you all right," Beulah remarked dryly. "Maybe too much."

"How can he like me too much?" asked Lexie, really puzzled.

Beulah looked embarrassed. "Well, honey . . . a kid like Nick . . . he's got strong drives . . . and you've been pretty much buddies for years now and . . ."

"You going to tell me about sex?" asked Lexie, laughing. Beulah blushed a deeper red. "Well, I know you kids nowadays know all about that. Not like when I was young. Then, *everybody* got pregnant." She turned her attention back to the skating dress. "Looks a little loose around the middle," she said, deftly tucking in three pins in a row.

Lexie looked at herself critically in the mirror. The

42

dress was so plain, and even a little shabby. She had hoped for a new one of her own, but she hated to let Beulah down. And Beulah had insisted she wear it—for luck.

"It's pretty," she said gently, hiding her disappointment. Beulah drew a deep breath, as though she sensed what Lexie was feeling. "Well . . . I was a lot bigger—don't laugh—even then. Here," she said suddenly, pulling a white collar out of her pocket and draping it over the neck of the dress. It was a round collar of pure linen, a large Peter Pan, and embroidered on one side, exquisitely, was "Lexie," surrounded by tiny roses and daisies. It must have taken her weeks to do it, and Lexie wondered how Beulah's large, rough, chapped hands could create such delicate, lovely work.

"B, I . . . I . . . Thank you." She turned and held the large woman tightly, pressing her fresh young cheek against Beulah's reddened, wind-scarred one.

Beulah returned the embrace briefly, her throat closing with emotion. Then she pushed the girl away. "Get outta here. Go practice your figures or something." Embarrassed, Beulah dabbed at her eyes with a corner of the dress and cleared her throat. "Hell, honey, it's not a crime to be a virgin. Must be a few of you still around. You got plenty of time."

But Lexie was no longer listening. She wasn't even thinking of Nick any more. She was staring at herself in the mirror and wondering if the championship dress would bring her luck in the Regionals.

*   *   *

Lexie zipped the lid closed on her canvas suitcase and straightened up. Had she forgotten anything? Her blades had been reground and tested and sat in their scuffed plastic carrying case. Her skating dress had been packed in layers of tissue so that it wouldn't wrinkle. She had clean underwear and socks and fresh pajamas, her toothbrush and her toothpaste. She even had a bar of complexion soap. She was ready to go.

43

Standing up, she looked around her room, reluctant suddenly to leave its safety and familiarity. On the walls, Scotch-taped to the faded old wallpaper, stuck in the mirror, tacked over her bed, were all the photographs and the posters that had taken the place of the stuffed animals of her baby years. Skaters mostly, photographed in action, in flight, in mid-leap and mid-spin. Tenley Albright. Dorothy Hamill. Dianne de Leeuw. John Curry. Peggy Fleming. Toller Cranston. Champions all.

In one corner of her mirror she'd pasted an old magazine photo of the ice skater, Olympic gold medalist and movie star who had put ice skating on the celebrity map. Skating backward, her long skirt—which had been considered daringly short back in 1932—swirling around her thighs, was Sonja Henie, Norwegian dimples flashing in the smile of an Olympic champion. Pinned to the photograph was a quote by Sonja Henie that Lexie had copied out of a book in her best handwriting, using green ink. The words summed up better than anything she had ever read or heard what Lexie felt about skating:

"It's a feeling of ice miles running under your blades, the wind splitting open to let you through, the earth whirling around at you at the touch of your toe, and speed lifting you off the ice far from all things that can hold you down."

Mixed with the photographs of world class skaters were snapshots of Nick. Nick dressed for the rink, burdened by the hockey player's thick protective padding, but holding his stick triumphantly in his unwieldy leather gloves. Nick in Levi's, at the wheel of the Scout. Nick in swimming trunks, his ribs showing like a little boy's. Nick and Lexie, over and over again—on the ice, on a hayride, at the beach, on the front porch of the Winston farmhouse, dressed up for a dance at the high school. And there were pictures of Marcus, some of them already fading. In a silver-plated frame in a place of honor was the wedding portrait of Marcus and Betsy, two serious-faced kids not a

44

lot older than Lexie herself. Her favorite snapshot showed Marcus in a leather jacket, standing by his crop-dusting plane, one proud hand on the fuselage, the wind ruffling his thick hair on his brow. He looked so young, and so daring. There was a gag photo, too, of Marcus dressed in complete old-fashioned aviator's suit, including silk scarf and goggles, sitting behind the joystick of a De Havilland biplane. Marcus always swore it was the McCoy, but Lexie was almost certain that he'd stuck his face through one of those holes in the photo booth in a Missouri amusement park. Where you could be photographed as a fat lady or Abe Lincoln or Elvis Presley. Never mind. It was Marcus' private image of himself caught in a photograph.

Lexie had lovingly tacked up as many early photographs of her mother and herself as she could find. Betsy was always holding her in those pictures, looking happy and girlish, smiling for the camera held in Marcus' hand. Sometimes Lexie's eyes filled with tears when she stared at those pictures of her mother. There was a funny photograph of Beulah that Nick had snapped at the Ice Castle two years ago. Beulah stood stiffly, proud and pained at the same time. She hated to have her picture taken and had given in only grudgingly.

A few of the photos were of Lexie alone, always on the ice. Lexie as a seven-year-old, her little legs straight in new boots. Lexie in a flying camel at fourteen, rhapsody in motion captured by Nick's long-distance lens. Here on the walls of her room were Lexie's dreams and her hopes, everything that was dear to her and precious, comforting and familiar.

She glanced at them one more time, then picked up her valise and her blades, turned off the light and shut the door of her room behind her.

The wintry sky wore the color of dull lead; more snow was on its way. Lexie crunched through the packed snow in the farmyard toward the tractor where Marcus was kneeling, working on the engine.

"Dad . . . hey, Daddy," called Lexie.

Marcus didn't look up, but his mouth tightened. "On your way, huh, babe?" he asked tersely.

"Yeah." The smile faded from Lexie's face. "They'll be here any minute." Silence fell between them, as daughter waited for father's blessing. But it seemed that Marcus wasn't in a mood to bestow blessings. "I'll be back in a couple of days, three at the most." Again she waited for Marcus to say something, but he bent all his attention to the stubborn tractor.

A car horn honked from the road—once, twice.

"I guess there's your ride," said Marcus grimly, still not looking up at Lexie.

"Yeah." She started to turn away, but her feet wouldn't let her. Desperately, she turned back to Marcus, her face pleading for his love and approval, her large blue eyes darkening.

"Daddy . . . please . . . wish me luck. *Daddy!*"

At last, Marcus looked up slowly at his daughter. She stood silhouetted against the late afternoon sky, a small, slim figure in an absurdly awkward ski parka and small knitted hat. His baby. She was still such a child. And she still needed him so much, more than either of them would acknowledge. He wiped the motor grease off his weathered hands with a filthy old towel. Swallowing his pride and his anger, he nodded to her at last.

"Sure, honey. Hell . . . knock 'em dead."

Her face lit up with joy. She took a step toward her father, to embrace him, but the horn honked again, more insistently this time. And the look on Marcus' face didn't welcome an embrace.

He had given her his "blessing," but it was a grudging one. Lexie felt a stir of anger, too, that he should take no pleasure at all in seeing her grow up, or get no pride from her attempt to accomplish something on her own. At best, they had made only a truce, not peace.

Nick was leaning on the horn now, impatient to get started. It was a long, tiring drive to Cedar Rapids. Obediently, Lexie walked to the porch to pick up her things.

46

Marcus watched her go. A feeling of loss crept over him as he saw her get her valise and begin to run toward the Scout—loss and anger and jealousy. He shook it off with a shrug and turned back to the tractor.

4

"What time is it?" Lexie asked anxiously.

"We got plenty of time," Beulah assured her, covering the face of her watch.

"What *time* is it?" Lexie insisted. She sat scrunched against the passenger door of the Scout's front seat, staring out dismally at the night and the heavy, falling snow. They'd been driving for hours and had reached Cedar Rapids almost an hour before, but Nick had lost his way twice, trying to find the arena. Visibility outside the Scout's windows was zero.

"Eight-fifteen," Beulah admitted with a sigh.

"Oh, no!" wailed Lexie. "It's too late!" Compulsory figures began at eight; they should have been in the arena, safely registered, by seven-thirty. That was another thing —safely registered. How was Beulah going to get Lexie past the registrar without proof of the qualifying tests that Lexie hadn't taken or passed?

"Hold on, honey, these things never get started on time." But Beulah's own voice held an edge of anxiety. She had been elated when they'd set off early today, and the three of them had sung crazy songs and told silly jokes all the way from Waverly. Until they'd gotten lost, and the time crunch had put pressure on them.

Nick, who'd been asking directions, ducked back into the car and turned on the ignition. Snow was powdered on his shoulders and gleamed in his dark hair.

"Well?" Beulah and Lexie turned to him expectantly.

"Man says you can't get there from here," he grinned, teasing. They were only a quarter of a mile away.

*　*　*

"Look for the registration desk," Beulah ordered as they walked quickly through one of the many tunnels leading into the arena. Over the distant loudspeakers they could hear names of girl skaters being called to do their figures, and they quickened their steps.

At the skater's entrance to the fifteen-thousand-seat arena, a registrar sat, tired and harried, dealing with half a dozen skaters and their parents and trainers, all at the same time. Lexie followed nervously while Beulah pushed through to the front.

"Lexie Winston," Beulah called out authoritatively, over the buzzing voices of the others.

"Senior Ladies?" asked the registrar.

"Novice," replied Beulah.

The registrar looked up, surprised. Lexie was at least four years too old for novice class. She shook her head dubiously.

"She have her qualifying tests?"

"Of course," lied Beulah. "St. Claire. Last spring."

With a sigh, the registrar began to check down her long list of names of qualified skaters. Lexie held her breath. She knew her name wasn't on that list, that she had no right even to be there, let alone skate.

"You're late," mumbled the registrar as she continued down the list.

50

"There's a snowstorm," Beulah pointed out.

"For everyone," snapped the woman. "I don't find her here," She frowned.

Nick and Lexie exchanged worried glances, but Beulah stepped forward, bluffing like crazy. "Winston. Alexis Winston." She pulled an official-looking envelope out of her old leather bag. "Here's her acceptance," she lied, starting to remove some papers.

The busy registrar nodded, too harried to care. "All right. There must be some mistake. I don't know who did these lists. They're about half complete," she complained, picking up a form from a stack of them on the corner of her desk. "Here. Fill this in."

Beulah took the form and turned in triumph to Lexie. They exchanged quick, secret smiles. They had made it. Beulah's cool bluffing had worked. Lexie let her breath out at last.

"Aren't you a little old to be a Novice?" asked the registrar suddenly, looking sharply at Lexie.

"Well, I . . ."

"Where are the lockers?" asked Beulah, coming to the girl's rescue.

"Tunnel six and down the stairs. There are little arrows to show you the way."

"Here's her music." Beulah handed over the cassette.

"You the coach?" asked the registrar.

Beulah nodded.

"You're supposed to wear your official entry badges. That's so you can get into the restricted areas," she said, handing over a packet to Beulah. "There's a chaperone?"

"Yes." Beulah nodded at Nick, who took a step forward.

"You're the chaperone?" The registrar's skeptical eyebrow headed way up.

"Sure am," said Nick with his widest smile and most innocent look.

The registrar shook her head, surrendering. She'd been sitting at the desk for six solid hours and she was too tired to hassle with this bunch of obvious losers. "She'll have to wait. There's about sixty girls doing figures tonight. It goes in order, and you have to listen for your name—nobody's going to come looking for you. You miss your turn, you miss the competition. Good luck," she added mechanically.

Arranging to meet Nick and Beulah at section five, Lexie walked down the long tunnel to the locker rooms. There was another official, a woman as tired as the registrar, seated at a desk.

"Hi," said Lexie with a tentative smile. "Is this where I change?"

"Any free locker." The woman waved one free hand. "When you do your figures, you'd better keep your free-style blades with you. Your chaperone can hold them."

"I . . . I only have one set of blades," said Lexie biting her lips.

*   *   *

Lexie stood silently in front of her locker, opening her valise. A heaviness weighed on her that she couldn't identify. She was tired. They'd been driving for hours, a lot of that time in falling snow; and there was the tension of actually getting past the registration desk and into the Regionals. But that wasn't all of it. Carefully, she removed the old blue skating dress and held it up to herself, looking deeply at her reflection in the locker mirror. Why am I really here? she wondered.

The sound of weeping distracted her, and Lexie could see reflected in the mirror, the long corridor of lockers. A young girl, walking on her skates, came around the corner. She was trying not to cry, but she couldn't help herself, and her choked-back sobs had turned into wails. Lexie watched her in the glass, pity for the little girl—for she couldn't have been more than twelve years old—churning her stomach. Then slowly, Lexie turned to her own reflection. Seeing the anxiety written on her face, she asked the mirror again, What am I doing here?

It was very late, close to one in the morning. Nick yawned widely, and the yawn went around the circle to

Beulah next, then Lexie. Tears of exhaustion were forming in the corners of Lexie's eyes. They had been sitting for almost five hours waiting for Lexie's name to be called. When they'd come into the huge arena, about a thousand of the fifteen thousand seats had been filled—with parents, friends, coaches and spectators. Now, there were only a handful; most of the girls had done their compulsory figures and gone to their hotels to sleep until it was time to skate the short program tomorrow.

"You'd better get your skates on," said Beulah quietly.

Lexie nodded and began to tighten her laces. She felt stiff all over and needed the warm-up exercises. On the ice, six sections were marked off by orange traffic cones. In three of the sections, skaters were competing, tracing their circles over and over while the judges, holding clipboards, watched them and graded them. The other three sections were reserved for skaters warming up, and Lexie skated to one of them and worked the stiffness out of her legs and body.

"Melinda Hopper. Alexis Winston. Betsy Meyer," called the loudspeaker.

Lexie skated over to Beulah.

"Head high. You're the skater," the older woman advised. "You can do it."

"Winston, A.?" asked the referee.

"Here," called Lexie, skating quickly and a little nervously over to him.

"Relax. You're not in class," he said, with a friendly but tired smile. The lateness of the hour was getting to everybody. Even the judges were drooping; they'd been there six hours and were beat. They barely acknowledged the three skaters taking their places in the performance sections. But Lexie could see one of them noticing her homemade, twenty-five-year-old skating dress and giving another judge a tiny nudge. There was a smile and a nod in return, as if to say, what do you expect? At this hour it's the bottom of the barrel. Lexie winced and skated to the section assigned to her.

She paused by one of the orange stanchions, reaching

out to touch it as though for reassurance. Then, with a deep breath and head held high, she skated a paragraph bracket, three times on each foot. When she had finished, she skated directly off to the practice area to give the judges a chance to study the closeness and clarity of her tracings on the ice. They paced off the circles to make certain all three were on the same axis and of the same diameter, then they marked their findings on their clipboards.

"Miss Winston, could you do a counter, please?"

Lexie skated briskly into the performance circle and skated the figure calmly and fluidly.

"How's she doing?" Nick asked Beulah as they watched from the sidelines.

"Hard to tell from here. The judges are so tired at this point, it could be an advantage or a disadvantage. I wish she'd wiggle her behind and wake a couple of them up."

"She's doing better than the other two," Nick said loyally.

"She's going against the first sixty, not the other two."

"If I was a judge it'd make a difference," insisted Nick.

Lexie was skating the paragraph loop for the fourth time. Momentarily, she lost her concentration and skated wide, leaving her tracings. Yet, rather than upsetting her, the mistake seemed to have the opposite effect. She recovered quickly and finished the move with an extra snap. Tossing her head defiantly, she smiled at the judges, and one of them actually found himself smiling back, to his surprise.

"I blew it," Lexie said as she skated over to Nick and Beulah. "I almost got through it, then I skated wide." She shook her head angrily, upset with herself.

"Hell, it was so late," Nick put in quickly. "You were fine. What do they expect at one o'clock in the morning?"

Beulah looked a little grim. "Come on, let's get some sleep," she said, touching Lexie lightly on the shoulder. "Tomorrow's the big day. You'll do fine."

But Lexie couldn't sleep. In the other bed of the motel room, she could hear Beulah's heavy, regular breathing, But she felt too wired, too edgy to sleep. Quietly, she slipped out of bed and pulled a bathrobe over her long,

54

flannel nightgown. She opened the door of the room and tiptoed out. She tapped on the door of the next room lightly at first, then more heavily.

"Morning, runt. We late?" A sleepy Nick stood in the doorway, yawning.

"It isn't morning." Slowly, Lexie moved past him into the room, going to the window to stare out at the parking lots and flickering neons that lit this seedy part of town.

"Couldn't sleep?"

Lexie merely nodded.

"Don't worry about your figures. It's only thirty percent anyway," he told her reassuringly, moving behind her.

"Please hold me," said Lexie suddenly, without turning around.

Nick caught hold of her shoulders and turned her around gently. She moved easily into his arms and pressed against him for a minute, her soft hair against his chest. Then he raised her face and bent to kiss her. Lexie returned the kiss almost desperately, pressing closer. Caught off guard, Nick broke the kiss off but continued to hold her.

Lexie couldn't let go. She clung to him, kissing his chest and his neck, wherever she could reach. He caught her close again and kissed her long and hungrily.

"I love you, Nicky," she gasped.

Mouths locked, they edged toward the bed and half fell, half sat on it. Nick slid his hand under her nightgown, stroking her legs while Lexie groaned in excitement.

"Easy, honey . . ." Nick pulled his hand away.

Lexie looked at him, confused, as he rolled away from her onto his back, his eyes not meeting hers but fixed on the ceiling.

"God, you're beautiful," he told her.

Now she was even more confused, and she didn't know what to do or say. Tears squeezed out of her closed eyes and rolled down her cheeks. Finally, she whispered, "Don't you love me?"

"God. Baby, yes," Nick whispered back as he moved to look at her.

"I don't understand."

"Nick uttered a short laugh. "Me neither," he said, shaking his head. "I . . . uh . . . have wanted . . . to make love to you for. . . . I . . . I'm not sure where this is coming from. I mean . . . hell . . . I'm really confused. It's this competition stuff. I guess I'm just wondering whether this is the best time."

"The best time?" Lexie's voice was filled with bewilderment.

Nick leaned over and kissed her. "You think you didn't do well last night?" He waited for her answer, but all he got was a shrug. "You think nobody'll love you if you don't win?" Silence from Lexie.

Nick drew a deep breath and tried to explain better. "I didn't think you really cared whether you won or not. I thought it was just something you wanted to try, for fun."

Lexie sat up slowly. "I did, too," she said at last. She'd been thinking about it a lot. "I don't know. It still is, I guess. When I was getting dressed, there was a girl . . . eleven, twelve . . . she must have done badly. When she came into the locker room, she sat down and just cried and cried. I thought, How could it make that much difference? That sure would never happen to me. But when they called my name, I wanted to win. I really did."

"Nothing wrong with that."

"All I want to do is skate," Lexie went on more quickly. "But they won't let me if I didn't do okay in the compulsory."

"I love you," said Nicky gently. "I'll love you if you win or don't win. I just want it to be good for us . . . you know, *right*."

Lexie nodded. She understood now. Nick didn't want her to come to him just because she thought she'd lost and needed something else to make her feel better.

"Why don't you go back and get some sleep? Early day tomorrow."

"I'd probably get more sleep if we made love," said Lexie slyly.

"Yeah, me, too." Nick grinned back.

At the door, she turned to look at him. "You love me? Really?"

He took her lightly into his arms. "Really do. Good night, baby."

Smiling, Lexie went back to her room. Nick shut the door after her, a troubled frown on his face.

* * *

"Fourteen! Fourteenth!" Nick shouted, pushing through the crowd milling around the arena sidelines to get to Lexie.

Upset, Lexie couldn't stop the tears from welling up. Nick understood at once and grabbed her upper arms. "But that's great! Honey, fourteenth out of sixty-eight! That's fantastic!"

Lexie looked at him dumbly. "It is?" was all she could choke out.

"Sure! You didn't expect to do anything in the figures. It's your weakest thing."

But Lexie was shaking her head miserably. "That far back means I'll never win."

Nick gave her a little shaking, followed by a short kiss.

"Listen, dumbhead, tell you what. I'll race you back through this mob to see who tells Beulah first. Me with the good news or you with the bad."

To Beulah the news was neither good nor bad. It was better than she'd hoped for, but the hard stuff—the freestyle—still lay ahead. First the short program, then the long one. It was make or break there, and she didn't have time for what was already in the past.

"Forget the figures, Lexie," she told her impatiently. "You're skating your short program in the last section before the dinner break. That should be in about an hour. You did better in the compulsory than I thought you would. And better than you had a right to. Now, go and get ready. We'll meet you back here."

"She's really freaked," Nick commented as he watched Lexie run off. "I've never seen her like this."

"Competition does that," Beulah told him. "You think you don't give a damn. Then you get here and it all changes."

"I thought she'd be more . . . like . . . well, like she is at home."

But Beulah was shaking her head, her eyes narrowed, remembering those Regionals twenty-five years ago. "She's young. Pretty sheltered. You don't know what you're made of until you get out there and do it."

"If she can do it on the pond at home, she can do it here."

"Maybe. Maybe not. That's just fun. There are probably twenty skaters here who do it pretty good back home."

"You think she'll blow?"

"Anybody can blow," shrugged Beulah. She turned to Nick, watching his face, and said slowly, deliberately, "Isn't that what happens to you any time you're not in the middle of something simple . . . like a hockey game?"

It took a beat before Nick got it, but when he did, his face flushed in anger.

"That's a lousy thing to say!" he cried hotly, humiliated by her sudden attack.

"Well, you tell me what happened then," demanded Beulah. Her disappointment over Nick's dropping out, combined with the tension she was feeling over Lexie's chances, had released itself in a hostility that surprised her almost as much as it did Nick.

Nick looked at her for a long moment, then turned wordlessly and ran up the ramp leading to the tunnel. Beulah looked after him, furious with herself. "Now why the hell did you go and do a thing like that?" she asked herself out loud.

But she had no answer.

5

Lexie looked around the locker room unhappily. The place filled with girls, being fussed over by their mothers, coaches or trainers, and all of them better-equipped and younger than she. A number of them stared back at Lexie defiantly, taking in the plainness of her blue dress, eyeing suspiciously her long hair, drawn back simply into a golden ponytail. Just look at that dress! Why, it was *old* and not a sequin or a rhinestone on it anywhere. The spectators always enjoyed the glitter of a flashy costume, and every little bit helped with the judges. Lexie suddenly felt very shabby indeed.

When she unpacked her blades, she felt worse. There were girls around her no more than twelve years old, in spiffy little costumes trimmed with glitter, in short and sassy Dorothy Hamill haircuts, and they had two or three pairs of blades, and even two pairs of custom-made boots. The affection Lexie felt for her old Phantoms faded as she looked at the gleaming Gold Test and Gold Star blades being taken from their specially made leather cases to be proudly fitted onto the feet of the young skaters. They were specialist blades—Gold Test for the compulsory figures and Gold Star for the free style. Their carefully honed edges would give any competitor an edge.

As for the girls themselves, Lexie could see how nervous they were. Some who had already finished their short program and had scored poorly were openly weeping with disappointment. Others who had not yet been summoned to judgment were listening with clenched teeth to last-minute advice and warnings and practicing knee bends, kicks and arm stretches as warm-up exercises. In one corner, an eleven-year-old was throwing up into a wastebasket, while her mother hissed her displeasure into the little girl's unhappy ears. Lexie, the only one of the girls to be in the locker room alone, felt very out of place. She had to get out of there. She *had* to.

She laced her boots up as quickly as she could, but carefully, checking to see that the lacings were as tight as possible over her heels and ankles. Then she slipped her skate guards over her blades and started for the door. All eyes were on her. For one thing, small as she was for her age, she was still older, therefore taller, than almost every other girl in the room. For another, she *looked* like an amateur dressed for a Sunday afternoon at the local rink. The others were all dressed like miniature fugitives from the Ice Capades, and most of them wore full stage makeup of rouge, bright blue eyeshadow and heavy mascara. The heavy makeup would look natural under the arena lights, and the dark lipstick around their mouths would provide a frame for their dazzling smiles. Lexie wore no makeup at all, except for some light pink lipstick. As she moved to the door, she could hear the whispers and giggles of scorn.

Somehow Lexie made it through the door with her back straight and a cool, slight smile on her face. But once outside the locker room, her cool dissolved and she slumped against the cinder block wall, feeling tears beginning to well up. Angrily, she looked at her dress; she felt like ripping off the namby-pamby collar with her name embroidered on it. She looked like Cinderella before the fairy godmother arrived—but there would be no fairy godmother for Lexie, she'd have to go to the ball in shabby old rags. For a minute, she gave in to her overwhelming feelings of self-pity. Marcus was right, she told herself, beating her hands in frustration against the wall. This was no place for a little country girl. Humiliated, she sobbed out loud, and the hand striking the wall balled up into a fist.

But the fit didn't last long, and humiliation faded and was replaced by determination. She wasn't there to take part in a locker room fashion show; she was there to skate! All the sequins in the world would not buy her a tenth of a point if her form, style or posture were off, or her edges incorrect. She'd show them! That's what she was here for, wasn't it? To show them—the judges, Beulah, Marcus, Nick and, most of all, herself. To see if she had what it took. Lexie tossed her ponytail over her shoulder and ran down the long corridor to the ice.

At the side of the rink away from the judges' table, Nick and Beulah were waiting for her. Lexie emerged from the corridor pale but calm. Her hands were dry, and she assured the anxious Beulah that her stomach wasn't knotted.

"Are you okay? Are you sure?" Beulah asked again. The whiteness of the girl's face was disturbing. But Lexie began doing knee bends and would say nothing more.

When her turn came, Lexie handed over her short-program music cassette and skated gracefully out onto the center of the ice, assuming a tall, still, waiting position, her hands folded demurely in front of her.

"Alexis Winston, short program" came over the loudspeaker, and her music began to play. Suddenly, Lexie forgot about competing, and coming out of her waiting posture, she moved with the grace and speed of a bird. Dipping and turning, skating on her edges, turning forward and backward in graceful spirals, she built up speed for her first jump, a double axel, rotating in the air as though

61

air were her natural element. As she landed on her toe picks and went into a spin, the audience burst into spontaneous applause. Lexie's form was not perfect, but her movements were performed with a freshness and spontaneity that were infectious.

The arena was far from filled; many of the spectators were taking their dinner break, but at the sound of the applause people began to walk quickly back down the aisles to their seats, to catch at least some of this dazzling girl's unexpectedly dazzling program. As Lexie glided in graceful arabesques, or left the ice in high leaps, the audience cried out its approval of her ebullient style.

Nick and Beulah were shouting themselves hoarse, hugging each other. They could hear the audience's cries of pleasure at a unique performance. These people were seeing something special, a skater of grit and originality, and they appreciated it. As for Beulah and Nick, neither of them had ever seen Lexie skate with so much energy or brilliance.

A final spin, a crossover, and Lexie came to a stop on her toe picks, bowing. The two minutes were up, the short program over. Nothing remained but the judging.

A perfect score is 6.0, but anything in the high 5's—5.7 or 5.8, for example—is considered admirable. Lexie sprinted gracefully off the ice to a huge round of happy applause, directly into Nick's waiting arms.

"JeZUSS, Lexie! My God!" cried Nick, nearly knocking her down in his eagerness to hug her. Beulah came running up as fast as she could, grabbing both of them in a bear hug and squeezing them tightly.

"Hot damn!" she exulted. "Didja see that? Goddamn! Goddamn! Lexie, you were sensational!"

Lexie looked around, dazed and bewildered. She lay limp in Nick's embrace, almost uncomprehending. She had skated on purest instinct and was only now returning to reality.

There was evidently some confusion at the judges' table; the five of them were slow to write down their individual scorings. The crowd held its collective breath, and

Beulah and Nick watched anxiously as the "number girls," in their bright red skating outfits, took the large white pieces of cardboard with Lexie's scores and skated to the center of the ice where everyone could read them.

The judge's whistle blew, and the girls held up the cards, the scores printed on them front and back. In the same instant, the loudspeaker announced the verdicts.

"The scores in the short form: 4.6, 4.8, 4.2, 4.4, 4.5."

Terrible. Lexie's scores were terrible. The crowd made rumbling noises, outraged, then broke into loud booing. Beulah and Nick gasped in disbelief, and the people who had gathered around Lexie to congratulate her pulled away from her, protesting.

"They can't do that!" yelled Nick in anguish. "No! Those rats!"

Dazed, Lexie watched the electronic scoreboard spell out her name and her miserable scores. She felt sick, dizzy. Her head throbbed and her lips and throat were dry. She looked at Beulah, who stared back at her with vacant eyes, unable to credit the judges' decision, unable to utter a word. Finally, she found her voice.

"They didn't believe it," croaked Beulah in a hoarse whisper. "They couldn't believe their eyes." She shook her head uncomprehendingly. They had seen perfection and they were unable to recognize it.

"When you won the Regionals," Lexie asked Beulah slowly, breaking her soda straw with her nervous fingers, "could you tell you were winning?"

Beulah pushed her half-full coffee cup away. "To tell the truth, I don't remember," she said in a tired voice.

But Lexie wasn't satisfied, and she pressed for more information. "There must have been something?"

Surprised, Nick looked at Lexie closely. Two feverish spots glowed brightly in her cheeks and her eyes glinted. Her gaze was fixed on Beulah as though waiting for some great truth to emerge.

Beulah nodded. "I just remember what it was like to win," she said very quietly. Then, her voice dropped to a

63

whisper, "I remember that . . . every . . ." She broke off, unable to continue, and her eyes were filled first with remembered dreams and glories, then with today's tears. "It was like drowning. I couldn't breath. I just . . . started . . . bawling like a baby."

She had failed tonight. Lexie had failed her. Or, rather, she had failed Lexie. For almost twenty years, Beulah had lived on the memory of winning the Regionals. She could have gone on, maybe, become a star, been somebody. But she hadn't. Facing success, she had panicked and dropped out. Gone right back to Waverly and turned herself into the town character so that she'd never have to face what she might have been. In Lexie, she'd seen a second chance for herself. That's why she'd pushed her so hard, forced her to compete. Lexie had a God-given talent, a natural love of skating that was free and pure. And Beulah had tried to tame it, to harness it to tracings and a program so that she could relive her long-ago victory through this spontaneous child who sat beside her now, at the coffee shop counter, looking for answers. Answers she couldn't give, as guilt and the deep sense of failure washed over her.

The intensity of her feelings took Beulah by surprise, but after a long moment she shook them off like a bird dog shakes drops of water off his coat. "Long time ago," she said brisky, dabbing at her eyes with a crumpled paper napkin. "Long time ago."

The long program was the most exciting part of any competitive skating event, and the television cameras had come in early to set up. This event was the one spectators would fill the arena to see, the one the viewers at home would be waiting for—freestyle skating by young hopefuls, tomorrow's Dorothy Hamills. Maybe they'd even spot a champion in the making. Top coaches kept an eye on the Regionals, looking for talent they could develop into championship potential. Energy was at a high level as the arena filled with onlookers, hungry to be entertained.

At rinkside, a booth had been set up with video and

audio equipment and a pair of handsome swivel chairs. Long cables snaked out from inside the booth to form coiled masses of video feed on the edge of the rink. The spectators were kept out of the booth's line of vision, and two stationary cameras were trained on the ice, their high-powered lights tilting upward so that the heat wouldn't mar the perfect surface of the rink.

Inside the booth sat Mitchell Rogers, Cedar Rapids' best known sportscaster, and his guest, a woman in her middle thirties. She was beautiful, with long chestnut hair and eyes that were wide and grey. The woman sat quietly in the swivel chair, (at rest like a hunting animal between forays,) while the technicians fussed with eliminating the feedback from the mikes. Her self-possession was total, but there was a fine-honed nervous edge to her personality; it enhanced her expression and lent interest to an otherwise too-symmetrical face.

"Good evening, ladies and gentlemen, and welcome to the final of the Ladies Regional Competition. With us tonight is the nationally known coach, Deborah Mackland. Well, Debbie, what brings *you* out to the sticks?"

Deborah smiled so radiantly that it was impossible to tell that she despised the nickname "Debbie." "Hardly the sticks," she said in a modulated voice directly into the microphone pinned to her cashmere blazer's lapel. "This is one of the major competitions in the country. And of course there are always a great many fine skaters in this area."

"But isn't it true that most of the top talent is coming out of California, or being trained at places such as your bailiwick, the Broadmoor, in Colorado?"

Deborah leaned back in her chair and crossed one sleek leg over the other. "Talent isn't restricted to certain places. That's what makes skating such a vital and exciting sport."

"I can see I'm going to have a hard time getting you to say anything nasty about our local skaters," purred Mitchell Rogers.

Deborah deliberately fluttered her eyelashes into the

camera. "Why, Mitchell," she purred back, "you just don't seem to bring out that side of my character, I guess."

Rogers was loving it, eating out of Mackland's manicured hand. "What do you think about the little girl—Alexis Winston—who did so well in the short program yesterday?"

Did so well with the fans, but the judges rated her low, thought Deborah, who had been informed. "I'm terribly sorry to have missed it," she assured the camera. "I was here for the evening skaters and there were several exciting talents."

"Well, we're going to get a look at Alexis Winston. She is now ninth in the twelve finalists who will be skating tonight."

"I'm looking forward to it," smiled Deborah graciously. "Thank you, Debbie."

Deborah to you, fathead. "Thank you, Mitchell."

"One of the top woman coaches in the country," added Rogers.

That's two I owe you, thought Deborah, hating the "woman" part of the phrase. I'm one of the best coaches in the country, period. But she smiled her thanks.

" . . . here to see if our good solid midwest stock can compete with the big names of the east and west," concluded Rogers, as the judges came out onto the ice. There was an electric tension in the air and the crowd could feel it.

Deborah Mackland could feel it, too, and it excited her and charged her with double her usual energy. I want a champion, she thought. And if there is a champion here tonight I'll find her.

*   *   *

Lexie stood on the sidelines with Nick and Beulah, waiting for her turn. The Zamboni, the large, motorized ice cleaning machine had just moved like a silent behemoth across the ice, leaving it pristine and ready. One at a time, hopeful girls in expensive costumes, their music carefully selected to show off their best movements, their short hair bouncing, made their appearances on the ice, performed for between four and five minutes and skated off again. Most of them were not memorable, but a few were very good indeed, and Lexie watched them anxiously. They appeared so well trained, every movement precisely executed. Whatever they lacked in imagination, they made up for in form. In the pit of her stomach, Lexie felt a knot of nervousness beginning to grow.

Adding to her nervousness was the crowd's reactions. They would groan and cheer, applaud lightly or heavily, approve or disapprove with what seemed a single voice. And that voice so powerful! Nick felt her mood and rested his arm supportively over Lexie's shoulders.

Then, onto the ice sprinted a girl who had done very well in the afternoon's short program—a redhead in a bright green sequined costume, her mop of hair bobbing like Little Orphan Annie's. The girl had a piquant look, and she'd capitalized on it cleverly. Her program was jazzy and was performed to a bright, cheerful musical comedy score.

The crowd liked the girl; Lexie could tell. They gave her a big hand when she leaped high in a double axel that was both graceful and arresting, and her loops and arabesques were greeted with more applause. The redhead left the ice confident that she had done well, and when the number girls held up her scores—5.6, 5.7, 5.6, 5.7, 5.5— the crowd cheered the results. The scores put the redhead in first place. Lexie's heart sank. How could she beat her? Her own scores so far had been disastrous.

"Pretty good," remarked Beulah as the scores went up on the board. Then she saw Lexie's face. Despair was written all over her features. "Don't worry," Beulah told her decisively. "Lexie. We've still got a chance. Lexie?"

But Lexie only stared vacantly at her, as though she couldn't understand Beulah's words. Beulah's face registered concern.

"Anything you're not sure of, don't try," Beulah warned

67

Lexie as the girl removed her blade guards and got ready to go on next.

"Why?"

"These guys are sticklers." Beulah threw a cold look at the judges. "Looking for perfection. I've been watching them all evening."

Lexie's expression was now colder even than Beulah's. "Only the first three places go to the Sectionals. Right?"

Beulah nodded grimly.

"I don't stand a chance, do I?" Lexie went on. "Not a chance of making up enough points. Soooo, I might as well . . ." she turned and smiled impishly at Nick. He grinned back and they touched noses, tip to tip.

"Have . . . a . . . ball," finished Nick.

"Have . . . a . . . ball," agreed Lexie, echoing his words. She turned and skated quickly onto the ice before Beulah could say another word. But, instead of skating directly to the center and waiting for her name to be called, she speed-skated past the judges' table, her head held high, a wide smile on her face. Flirtatiously, she bobbed her head at them, so that the ponytail streamed out behind her like a golden banner. Then she pirouetted to the center and stood waiting, arms outstretched.

"Alexis Winston. Long program."

The sound of scratchy whirring filtered through the loudspeakers as the taped music started. As her music filled the arena, and Lexie began to move across the ice, the audience fell quiet.

The program that Lexie had decided on left her head entirely. There was nobody out there but herself and her music. She was alone on the ice, alone in the arena, alone in the world. Slowly, with infinite grace, she began to bend backward in a spread eagle, one of the most difficult moves in figure skating to execute well. But Lexie was not even aware that she was executing it. It seemed a logical extension of her body—the curve of her waist, one arm held high, the other straight out parallel with the ice, legs wide apart. In perfect form she began to bend backward, then turned so naturally into a spin and the spin into a

68

backward glide and a sudden leap off the ice into a double axel that no effort at all seemed to be involved.

Beulah heard the audience draw in its breath, saw the crowd lean forward to get a better look at the graceful youngster. Nick hardly noticed the crowd; his eyes were glued to Lexie.

Lexie didn't hear the crowd at all, was totally unaware of the applause or the cheering. Her eyes were closed, and a small, private smile played over her lips, instead of the wide mouseketeer grin she was supposed to be wearing. Dipping and gliding, she sailed across the ice in a backward spiral, then once more the spread-eagle backbend, her head back . . . slowly . . . slowly . . . her hair nearly touching the ice. Suddenly, in perfect time to the music, she arched forward and took off in a perfect split-jump, hanging horizontal in the air, touching down on her toe rakes, leaping once more, touching down as lightly as a feather, then again—in a perfectly-executed double lutz, taking off from a fast outside spiral, her knee bent so low it nearly touched the ice. Turning in the air, rapidly, twice, coming down in a perfect landing that turned into a spin and that spin into a sit-spin—Lexie almost a blur of rapid motion.

Getting to its feet like a beast with thousands of heads, the crowd roared out its approval, cheering and stomping.

For the first time, Lexie became aware of her audience. The sudden awareness of the incredible shouting, stomping, clapping crowd crashed over her like thunder and mader her falter. Her foot buckled under her in the sit-spin, and she fell to the ice.

A gasp, followed by a groan. So perfect, she was so perfect and now it was all ruined!

Beulah felt her heart stop. She tried to catch her breath but couldn't, and she put her hand to her throat, her eyes never leaving the small figure in the shabby blue dress sprawled in the center of the ice.

"Come on, damn it!" growled Nick through clenched teeth. She had to get up. Please, God, she *had* to! Make her get up!

She did. Lexie Winston rose to her feet as though nothing had gone wrong and listened for the music to catch her up as she skated forward into another double lutz, then down into another sit-spin, just to show them she could do it. Effortlessly, she was back in control.

In the stands, Deborah Mackland watched Lexie with intense interest. What impressed her most was not the girl's skating—she was a natural, and her training was all wrong—but the way that the crowd responded to her. When a crowd saw a champion, it knew it. You couldn't fool a smart audience. Yes, something was definitely there, in its roughest form.

Waltz turns, toe loops, flying sit-spins, axels and lutzes —Lexie was ice poetry in motion as she skated to a finish. The music rose and swelled as she leaped, glided and spun until finally, a last spin brought her to perfect rest, dead center of the rink. The blur became a girl in an old blue skating dress with "Lexie" embroidered on the collar. The music stopped.

There was an explosion of sound as the crowd got to its feet, loudly cheering and calling Lexie's name. The arena rocked with the sound of it, the laughing and the thunderous applause.

On the sidelines, Nick was jumping high into the air, waving his arms and yelling in triumph while Beulah stood rooted to the spot, tears of gladness streaming down her face.

Lexie skated to the four corners of the arena and bowed, then sprinted off the ice and into Nick's open embrace. Laughing and crying at the same time, Lexie opened her arms to Beulah, who came forward just as the number girls skated out with Lexie's scores. They turned to see.

"5.2," announced the loudspeakers. "5.0, 4.8, 5.0, 5.2."

In the standings on the electronic scoreboards, Lexie's name moved up . . . to ninth place . . . to fifth. Two short of qualifying for the Sectionals. It was over. She hadn't made it.

70

But the crowd was clapping and stamping in an insistent rhythm, refusing to be quiet. They wanted something, and they wouldn't stop demonstrating until they got it. In the stands, Deborah Mackland kept her eyes on Lexie. On the sidelines, Beulah gave the girl a little nudge forward, and Lexie looked around, confused.

"They want you, Lexie," said Beulah gently. "They want you to circle the ice. Go on, honey. Go on."

Laughing, Lexie tossed her hair back and waltzed out on the ice. Slowly, her smile broad and her eyes sparkling, she skated around the arena, waving at the cheering crowd, thanking them. A rose landed on the ice ahead of her, then another and another. Fans always brought long-stemmed red roses to shower on the winners and the favorites. Although Lexie wasn't a winner, she was an obvious favorite, and soon the ice around the edges of the rink held dozens of roses. Smiling and bowing, Lexie skated up to the flowers and taking care not to catch her blades on them, bent her knees to scoop them up. When she had an armful of roses, she pressed them to her cheek in thanks and skated back to Nick and Beulah. She had never known such happiness; her face and brow radiated it like electricity.

*   *   *

Marcus watched as the Scout came along the back road, bumping up and down on the icy patches. It was so cold that early in the morning that his breath froze on the air, and he buttoned up his leather jacket and tied the flaps of his cap under his chin to cover his ears. The Scout braked slowly to a stop where he stood, and he pulled the door open. Nick put a finger to his lips in a gesture of silence.

Inside, tucked in an old army blanket, her head against the vinyl of the front seat, Lexie lay curled up asleep. She looked about twelve years old, and Marcus could see that she held a big bunch of withered flowers in the crook of her arm.

Nick mouthed silently, "She was great," and Marcus

71

nodded in acknowledgment. Then he reached into the car and began to lift Lexie out. Her eyelids fluttered open.

"Don't wake up, honey," whispered Marcus.

Half-awake now, Lexie opened one blue eye and smiled at him. "Hi, Daddy."

Beulah was asleep, too, in the back seat, and as Marcus hoisted Lexie out, Beulah awoke with a start.

"What's going on? Where are we? Oh . . . Marcus . . . what're you doing here?"

Marcus grinned. "I live here," he reminded her. He lifted Lexie more securely in his arms, and she wrapped her arms around his neck. "They threw me flowers, Daddy," she informed him sleepily. "They threw me flowers." And she clutched the faded roses tightly as her father carried her into the house.

*　　*　　*

Beulah put the cup and saucer down on the counter with such a thump that the coffee sloshed over the rim of the cup. But the gray-eyed woman didn't bat an eyelash. She glanced around Beulah's Ice Castle and Five Star Lanes with an expression so bland and smooth that Beulah could cheerfully have murdered her. Her with her tailored pants and Valentino boots and red fox coat and Hermès bag and scarf. Her with her slender figure and well-cared-for hair and manicured fingernails. Beulah knew her kind. She was class all right, but there was a touch of barracuda to Deborah Mackland that made all of Beulah's hackles rise.

"You're her coach?" asked Deborah, fitting a cigarette into a long, ebony holder.

"Yes," answered Beulah shortly.

"You do good work," Deborah remarked mildly. The tall, crazy-looking woman in the bib overalls could easily and happily throw her out in the snow, and Deborah knew it. But she hadn't dragged her behind all the way to Waverly "Godforsaken" Iowa to be thrown out in the snow. "How old is she?"

"Miss Mackland, let's start over," said Beulah suddenly, biting her lip. "I know who you are, and we both know Lexie's training has been lousy."

Deborah Mackland avoided the issue gracefully. "She's had work in figures" was all she said.

"She's a natural talent," Beulah admitted painfully. She felt very uncomfortable in the presence of this glamorous and talented woman whose name was so well known in the world of figure skaters.

"Well, she was quite impressive," agreed Deborah, flipping her long, thick hair off her brow. It was her only nervous habit apart from cigarettes.

"You want to train her," said Beulah flatly. It was an accusation.

Somewhat taken aback by the other woman's directness, Deborah used evasive tactics once again. "I'd like to see what her goals are."

"Think she's that good, huh?" demanded Beulah. She was torn between feelings of pride in Lexie and of jealousy and distress at the thought of losing her to a professional.

"She looked good," said Deborah, drawing on her cigarette. "Of course," she temporized, "it was only a Regional."

"You want to train her," said Beulah again, stubbornly.

"I want to train her," admitted Deborah, giving in with a smile. "Now, how old is she?" The question was more emphatic than before.

"Sixteen."

Deborah Mackland swore under her breath and angrily ground the cigarette out in the chipped glass ashtray on the counter. Gathering up her purse and her scarf, and throwing her fox coat over her shoulders, she headed for the door. Sixteen! The best years, the *only* years, already down the drain. What a pain. Served her right for coming all the way down here on a wild-goose chase.

"Sorry to have wasted your time," she snapped at Beulah.

Beulah felt a momentary rush of relief. Lexie was still

hers! But guilt overtook the gladness. This could be Lexie's big chance, her *only* chance. Before Deborah reached the door, Beulah called out to her. "She's very quick."

Deborah turned. "Pardon?"

Beulah searched for the words to explain. "I've seen her . . . watch somebody on the TV . . . you know? Somebody like Dorothy Hamill or somebody . . . and pick up the moves right away."

Deborah hesitated. She couldn't get that girl out of her mind. The light, quick figure, the incredible grace, the way she hovered above the ice in those startling leaps . . . most of all, the way the audience had cheered and clapped and stomped and thrown roses. All for Lexie Winston from Waverly, Iowa. She could *do* something with that.

"What about the figures? She's too old to . . ."

Figures *were* Lexie's weakest point. "Figures are only thirty percent now," Beulah reminded her quickly.

Deborah stood at the door, facing out, her fingers lightly tapping the pitted old wood of the door frame, picking at the peeling paint. All at once she turned, smiling. "Yes, they are, aren't they?"

And Beulah felt her heart sinking inside her breast. She'd won, but she'd lost.

Marcus Winston wasn't to be won over as easily as Beulah had been. The three of them sat in the Winston kitchen, with the pale afternoon light fighting its way through the grime on the windows. Marcus glared at the beautiful woman as though she were a cobra ready to strike. He loathed her and her fancy ways and her beautiful clothes and her mild speaking manner and most of all he loathed her determination to take his daughter away from him. Lexie had lost the Regionals, which was what he'd secretly hoped for, and now she should stay home where she belonged.

"You said she was too old," he told Deborah Mackland gruffly. "Why do you want to put her through a whole cotton-picking business, and then she's gonna be too old to win? . . ."

"I said," Deborah interrupted gently, "that normally the best skaters start being . . . carefully trained . . . much younger." What a strange man, she thought, sizing up Marcus. He seemed at once young and old, and he was acting like a petulant child whose pet rabbit was being taken away. Had he no idea of what she could do for his daughter? Didn't he know what a champion could earn when she turned pro?

"Six or seven," agreed Marcus with a grin. "Well, Miss Mackland, you came a decade late."

"Lexie could do it, Marcus," Beulah put in.

"If I didn't think so, I wouldn't be here," agreed Deborah briskly. "I can't afford to waste my time."

"Glad to hear it," said Marcus with false geniality. "Who can? Thanks for dropping by." He stood up politely, as though to see Deborah to the door.

"Damn you, Marcus," Beulah exploded. "Give Lexie a *chance!* This is her chance to be something."

"She *is* something," snarled Marcus, turning on Beulah.

"Are you afraid she might make it?" demanded Deborah, her tone suddenly cutting. "What would happen if she did become a champion? She'd probably leave here, come back only for Christmas. . . ."

"Thank you for taking an interest," snapped Marcus, his face reddening with anger. He picked up Deborah's fur coat and handed it to her. Damn her, anyway! Who sent for her?

*　　*　　*

"I just went up there and skated for them, and they said I could try out." Nick grinned, very pleased with himself.

"That's great," said Lexie flatly. She hoped her unhappiness didn't show. She didn't want to spoil Nick's high moment.

The Scout bumped along the rutted back road that led up to the Winstons' back door. A Ford Granada with rental plates was parked right outside the kitchen.

"When do you go?" asked Lexie in a small voice. She didn't notice the car.

But Nick did. He noticed anything on wheels. "Two weeks. Who's that?"

Lexie saw the automobile for the first time. "I don't know," she replied absently. "You want to do that?" she asked Nick miserably. "Play hockey?"

"Hell, yes!" Hearing the note of hurt in Lexie's voice, he stole a look at her. Her dejected face told the story. "Look, I'll only be gone a couple of days," he reassured her.

"What if you make it?" Lexie wanted to know.

"I sure as hell hope I will. Hey, Lex, how do I know what I want to do? I mean, last year I wanted to be a doctor. Maybe next year I'll be a fireman. . . ." Nick poked her, teasing, grinning, forcing her to look at him.

Lexie did look up at him and she did smile, but it wasn't a very big or a very convincing smile.

"Will you write?" she asked him.

"Hey, I'm not gone yet!" he protested.

"Every day," insisted Lexie stubbornly.

Nick stole a look at her. She was serious. It blew him away. "Maybe every other day," he teased.

"You love me every other day?" demanded Lexie.

He could see that she was close to tears. "Hey, Bozo, I love you," he whispered, wanting to touch her but knowing the tension between them was too great.

But Lexie burst out at him, anger keeping her at a safe distance, at the far edge of the seat. "Why do you have to always go away, then? I mean, if you love me, why can't we be together?"

"We can be. It's just . . . I . . . I mean it's like I'm about to blow up." He groped to find the words to explain the searching he had to do, the quest for something better that drove him around the next corner and the next. "You know I don't even know why; I just have to do something. Lex, I know that we're supposed to get married and that I'm supposed to be a doctor or something and have some

76

kids and . . . hell . . . then we get older . . . and hell, that's the place my folks are at, and Lex, you know . . ."

Lexie looked up at him, searching his face, trying to understand what he was talking about, what was pushing him so hard.

"I . . . I can't explain it," continued Nick. "Just believe that it doesn't mean I don't love you. Right, Lex? Can you believe that? Can you trust me? I love you. . . ."

"If you loved me any more I couldn't stand it," Lexie retorted as she opened the passenger door and jumped out of the Scout.

Marcus, Beulah and a slim, beautiful woman were coming out the kitchen door as Lexie slammed the car door. She had never seen the woman before, but her clothes were sensational, and Lexie found herself staring.

"Hey!" yelled Beulah. "Where you kids been?"

"Nick's got a tryout with the Northstars!" said Lexie sulkily.

"You're kidding!" whooped Beulah.

"Hey, that's great," said Marcus sourly. "Maybe you can make some money banging into walls."

"Excuse me," said the strange woman, heading for the Granada.

"Lexie," called Beulah swiftly, before Marcus could intervene. "This is Deborah Mackland. She's a coach. She wants to train you."

Deborah turned at once and walked toward Lexie warmly, her hand out in greeting. "I saw you at the Regionals in Cedar Rapids. You were wonderful. You have a great natural gift. It would be a shame not to let it take you as far as you can go."

Lexie stared into the woman's catlike eyes, too stunned to speak. For a moment they all stood frozen in the frigid winter afternoon, a tableau of conflicting emotions and ambitions. Then Nick broke the silence with a yell.

"Fantastic!" He ran toward her. "Hey, Lex, that's fantastic! How do you like that?" Scooping her up, he spun her around, while Marcus glared at him as though he could happily kill him. The grin on Nick's face was wide

77

but empty, as contradictory feelings tore at him. *He* was supposed to be going, not Lexie!

"As far as you can go!" hollered Nick. "Hell, how about the Big O? That's spelled O-L-Y-M-P-I-C-S."

But Lexie still hadn't uttered a syllable. She stood staring at Deborah, who laughed and touched her lightly on the shoulder. "Consider it a trial. In six months we should know, one way or another." She was still holding out her hand.

Slowly, Lexie put her mittened hand out and took Deborah Mackland's hand in hers to seal the bargain. The two young women smiled at each other, unaware of the miserably unhappy glances Beulah and Marcus were exchanging.

*　　*　　*

She wasn't going to go home until he talked to her, *really* talked to her. Lexie had made up her mind. For days, Marcus had been drifting around the house like a sad ghost, disappearing at odd times, hardly saying a word. She understood what was eating at him; why couldn't he understand what was bothering her? Today she'd watched as he left the farmyard, and she'd followed him to the pond, determined to speak.

Marcus was sitting on the fallen log on the pond's bank, where Lexie always perched to lace or unlace her skates. He sat silently, staring out at the empty pond, its surface half-covered with windswept snow. As he heard the crunching of her boots, he looked up to see his daughter approaching, her face shy, her lithe young body awkward under all those heavy winter clothes. God, how much she looked like Betsy!

"Hey, Dad, what are you doing out here?" Lexie called, in what she hoped was a light and cheerful tone.

"Hey, look, babe. I'm a grown man. I do what I want. It doesn't have to be smart, just comes with being old."

"Okay," said Lexie quietly, stung by his reproof. She sat down next to him on the log and folded her gloved hands. For a few minutes they sat together in silence, then Marcus began to speak in a dreamy voice.

"You know, in the whole country around here, this was your mother's favorite place."

"I know," said Lexie softly.

"I used to wonder why," continued Marcus as though he hadn't heard Lexie. "I mean, if you're not from around here, it all looks just like white and cold. You know," he almost whispered, his face softening and looking suddenly very young, *"she* was the one who first took you skating. When you were four, or three, something . . . I forget exactly." His eyes took on a look of confusion.

"I know," whispered Lexie. Dimly, she remembered a beautiful woman and a wobbly little girl in leggings and a hooded muffler, the ice skates buckling under her small feet.

"I guess by the time you could start to remember things, the cancer was getting worse, and you grew up thinking you were born with those damn skates on." He stared out over the pond's surface as though watching for something or someone.

"Daddy?" Lexie called tentatively, trying to get his attention. But Marcus wasn't listening.

"Just struck me maybe you should look at this place. Maybe try to see it the way she did. See that rise over there?" His finger pointed. "Can hardly tell it's there, except there's a sharp little shadow-line, and you see the way one hill has different tones of white. When there's a ground fog, sometimes you can't tell where the snow starts, the fog stops and the sky begins. Damned if she wasn't right. It's a beautiful place."

Lexie wanted to touch him, but he looked too . . . apart . . . to return her embrace. Marcus just sat staring out over the pond, his thoughts far away, locked into the past.

"Daddy," cried Lexie almost desperately. "Daddy, I'm not Mom. Dad . . . I want to do this, I really do. It was . . ." She broke off, searching for the right words to make him see how she felt. "I felt a power . . .

79

in *me* . . . and that noise, the noise the crowd makes . . . first time I heard it, I sat right down in the middle of a spin. Like it knocked me right *down*. But then I . . . I don't know exactly how to explain. But I *wanted* it, and I *did* things . . . I skated because I wanted that applause." She had said it, said it all, said it at last. Had Marcus listened? Had he heard any of it? "Daddy?" she whispered, half eager, half afraid, waiting for his answer.

"I hear ya, babe," said Marcus at last. "Well, ya better get back if you're going to get ready to catch the bus."

It took her a full minute before Lexie realized that her father had just given her his permission to go to Deborah Mackland. With a small cry, she hugged him tightly to her, and this time he hugged her back. Then he let her go and turned his gaze back to the ice again. But his expression was a little more peaceful.

"Go on," he told her. "I'll be along in a minute."

Tears filling her eyes, Lexie stood and started in the direction of the house.

"Hey, make some coffee when you get back," called Marcus.

Unable to speak, she smiled and nodded.

"Hey, and you better label that damned kitchen. Otherwise, I'll starve to death."

Lexie threw her head back and laughed, a rich, merry sound that echoed across the frozen lake. "I think my Daddy's growing up," she teased.

"It's hard . . . but he's working at it," grinned Marcus.

Her heart full and her thoughts racing and tumbling over one another, Lexie headed back to the house. For a long time, Marcus sat there, alone with his thoughts.

6

At the foot of Cheyenne Mountain, which rubs shoulders with Pikes Peak high above the rest of the world, sits the Broadmoor Hotel in Colorado Springs. Because of the spectacular beauty of its natural setting and the clarity of its mountain air, the Broadmoor attracts enchanted, sophisticated, moneyed travelers from all over the world. But its impact had never hit anyone the way it did one little country girl from Waverly, Iowa.

Lexie thought her mouth would never close again as she followed the bellman through the high-ceilinged lobbies of the Italian Renaissance hotel. She had never seen as much luxury in her life as she saw now in only one of the lobbies—the rich carpeting, high-backed chairs, tall palms in Oriental vases, the pampered people sipping coffee or drinks with the negligent air of the monied. Was she going to live here? What a difference between this and Beulah's Ice Castle and Five Star Lanes! How would she ever be able to tear herself away to skate?

"Easily," Deborah Mackland told her, after she'd shown Lexie around her own sumptuous, silk-hung suite. "You won't be living here, but in the dormitory with the rest of the girls. And believe me, Lexie, you'll be skating. That's what you're here for, to learn to skate as you've never skated before. Come, let me show you something." She put her arm around the girl and drew her to the balcony outside the French windows. "Look."

There, behind the hotel, rose the majestic beauty of the Rockies. At their foot sat a lake of molten silver and near it, stretches of golf greens with their emerald grasses and turquoise water holes. Closer to the hotel, on the far side of the lake, Deborah pointed out the famous Broadmoor World Arena, where Lexie would be spending almost every waking hour from now on. Next to the rink was a long, low building that housed the girls who were in training to become world class skaters.

"That's the rink across the lake," Deborah said. "This is probably the last time you'll see it from the outside. Let's go."

Lexie bent to pick up her valise. As she straightened up, she felt a touch . . . a gentle, fleeting touch on her hair. Deborah was smiling at her.

"Im glad you're here," the woman said simply. Lexie smiled back. She was terrified, but glad, too.

The ice rink, the Broadmoor World Arena, was the largest and best-equipped that Lexie had ever seen. It held almost five thousand spectator seats. Broadmoor had hosted the World Figure Skating Championships on five separate occasions; more times than any other ice arena complex. Peggy Fleming, the Olympic champion, had trained at the Broadmoor, as had champions Hayes Alan Jenkins and his brother David. The Broadmoor World Arena was legendary, and a silent Lexie followed Deborah around it, almost smothered by her awe. On the ice, two world-famous coaches were working with two girls who could not have been more than eight years old, and both were gifted skaters.

After Deborah pecked Lexie on the cheek and handed her over to Sandy Walslowski, a girl her own age, Lexie finally began to feel more at ease.

Sandy looked about ten or eleven but was actually thirteen. What fooled you was her size—tiny and no more than sixty pounds, ten pounds of that weight in the braces on her teeth. But as soon as she spoke through those braces, Lexie knew that Sandy was no ten-year-old. She had all the advanced wisdom and the brashness of a woman of thirty, and she was the perfect person to show Lexie the ropes.

Sandy and Lexie were to be roomies in one of the smaller bedrooms at Brady Hall, and Lexie followed at a trot after little Sandy, who walked as fast as she talked and never, never seemed to shut up.

"You're not queer, are you?" she asked Lexie, not waiting for an answer, but plowing right ahead. "I mean it's all right if you are—no law against it. There was a girl here last year—whew! I never knew what a Lesbian was until one night we were up late talking and she kissed me! Right on the mouth!"

Right on the braces? thought Lexie with a giggle, but she said nothing.

"Brother!" said Sandy merrily, turning a corner and leading Lexie down the dorm corridor. "To each his own, but you know, it kind of takes you by surprise." Without knocking, she pushed open a bedroom door. "Whatever you're doing . . . caught'cha!" she announced.

Four girls looked up in disgust from their magazines and nail polish bottles, but their annoyance turned to curiosity as they silently eyed Lexie. Sandy closed the door again without a word of introduction and tugged at Lexie's sleeve.

"C'mon, I'll show you the rest of the jail."

Lexie trailed after the smaller girl, who continued to talk a blue streak as she led her through the dining room with its refectory tables and wooden chairs and into the recreation area with its sophisticated gym and exercise equipment.

"About twenty-five girls live here on and off. Most of them off, if you know what I mean. Nice, huh? Well, it's better than reform school . . . almost. Your parents trying to get rid of you or can you really skate good?"

For the first time since they met, Sandy shut up and looked sharply at Lexie, actually waiting for an answer.

"I really skate good," said Lexie quietly.

A long sigh shook the tiny frame. "I was afraid of that." Sandy's delivery and timing were comical and sharp. "Well, we heard all about you already. This place has no secrets. Actually," she continued as they crossed the magnificent main lobby of the hotel and started up a rich paneled staircase, "the business has no secrets."

"Business?" asked Lexie blankly.

"Yeah. The amateur skating business. You're in it now, so you'd better learn about it. We know you haven't qualified for any major competition, and Deborah Mackland's going to defy the laws of God and the Amateur Skating Association by taking on an older woman. Hah! Over the hill age-wise, as they say, and Deborah's going to transform her into a world's champ. Maybe the Olympics. Right, Cinderella?"

Lexie looked appreciatively at her surroundings, which Sandy appeared to take for granted. They had passed through an opulent ballroom and the sumptuous main salon and were now in one of the brocaded "smaller" sitting rooms. Hugging herself for joy, Lexie said. "I hope they don't send the pumpkin."

The walk around the lake to the World Arena was one of the most beautiful she'd ever taken, thought Lexie, as she looked at the awe-inspiring mountains standing like gods in the distance. Sandy was now on the topic nearest to every skater's heart—the "schedule"—and Lexie listened with fascination to her monologue.

"Just before a competition, some girls'll kill for ice time. They come two o'clock in the morning, four, anytime." Lexie could understand that. "Wait'll you see your schedule," Sandy warned her. "You'll wish you were back on the farm picking cotton, Lexie. Figure patches at five-thirty. That means you're up by four-fifteen. Let's see."

Both girls peered closely at the bulletin board on the arena wall, where Lexie's name had just been added to the list and the schedule of her work and studies posted. "Figure patches from five-thirty to eight. Eight to ten, freestyle. Ten to eleven-thirty, ballet."

"Ballet?" asked Lexie, puzzled.

The braces flashed in the sunlight as Sandy grinned. "Yeah. Just in case you ever have to walk somewhere. You still in school?"

"Junior," nodded Lexie.

"You'll get tutored. Then, of course, there's poise."

"Poise?"

Sandy put one hand on her hip and strutted in a comic burlesque of poise. "It's done maaarvels for me, my deah," she drawled, and Lexie broke up. She couldn't help it. Her new roommate was funnier than Don Rickles.

*　　*　　*

While Lexie was in Colorado Springs beginning her training, Nick was in Minneapolis, getting clobbered by a hockey stick and clobbering back as hard as he knew how. He had been given two weeks to try to convince the Northstars that he was necessary to the Minnesota team's survival, and this was the second week. With every scrimmage he grew bolder and more pugnacious, skating hard for the puck, stealing it whenever he could, gaining as much ice as possible and, whenever he was brought down, taking as many of the enemy with him as he could. For some reason he couldn't fathom, he was in a murderous mood, and he went for the opposing players as often as he went for the puck, only harder.

Blind-sided and knocked to the ice by a particularly mean Canadian who spoke only a French patois, Nick got up swinging. But the coach skated toward him quickly and hustled him off the ice.

"Don't worry about it. Your turn next time," he soothed the growling Nick. "Last week of tryouts. Howda ya feel?"

"How should I feel?" asked Nick belligerently. The scrimmage over, he slipped his blade guards on and clumped down to the locker room with the coach at his side.

"Hell, if I were a dumb, thick-headed kid who could skate pretty good and pass pretty good and sometimes even show some signs of scoring . . . shit . . . I'd probably worry myself sick that somebody was just a little dumber, faster and more suicidal," grinned the coach, lighting a cigarette.

Nick rose to the bait. "There ain't anybody more suicidal than me," he retorted hotly.

The coach shook his head. "I don't know why you wanta beat the hell outta yourself playing hockey," he marveled. "I mean, hell, you even speak English, for Chrissakes!"

"I didn't make the cut?" asked Nick, his stomach churning suddenly.

The coach ignored the question. "What were you studying in college? Premed, somebody told me. Hell, boy, you're getting on the wrong side of the bandages, playing hockey . . ."

"Well, am I cut or not?" Nick demanded, his face tense and angry, his knuckles bunching into fists.

But the coach wasn't to be hurried into his answer. "What the hell does a nice kid—smart, not too ugly— want to quit school for? I wish I had some brains. I sure would have gone to college and—"

"Goddamn it!" shouted Nick, interrupting. "All I want to know is about the cut!"

"You're going to Lincoln," the coach said abruptly, dropping his cigarette butt on the floor of the locker room.

"What's Lincoln?"

"One of our farm clubs. You go down there, hang

around for a while, see how you do with some real killers."

The man's words penetrated the boy's anger and dissolved it. He had made the cut! "Hey, that's great!" he beamed, showing all his teeth. "Lincoln! Great, fantastic!" The smile faded for a second, became dimmer by a few watts, as he said, almost seriously. "Where's Lincoln?"

*　　*　　*

Conscious of her brand-new clothes, Lexie walked at Deborah's side through the splendors of the Broadmoor lobby. On her feet were high boots of Italian leather; against her knees brushed a pleated kilt of the finest Scottish tweed; and on top she was wearing a sweater set of real cashmere. Cashmere! It had always been her dream to own a cashmere sweater. The boxes she was carrying contained more dreams-come-true, including professional double-knit warm-up suits with racing stripes, a new skating dress and even a dress of a pearly chiffon for evening. In her new harness leather shoulder bag, Lexie was carrying the most precious, precious dream-come-true of all. A receipt for made-to-measure blades, two pairs, professional boots and skates for the figures and the freestyle; Deborah and Lexie had just come from the fitting. Soon she would be skating on championship blades! She could hardly believe it!

Deborah led Lexie into the tearoom and they took a table, settling the packages around their feet. The round table, covered in a starched white cloth, held yellow roses in a crystal vase and looked out over the sun patio and the lake. Tea and scones appeared as though by magic, but Deborah, like Sandy, took all of this luxury for granted. Lexie was still in the "pinch me" stage. But what Deborah began telling her so earnestly made some of Lexie's rosy glow fade.

"There are five girls the judges have been looking at since the last Olympics. So, they're the ones everyone expects to win. Even if you're as good as they are they'll win because the judges will think you're a flash in the pan."

Lexie gasped in surprise and set her teacup down with a trembling hand. "I don't understand. If I can't win, why—"

"I didn't say you wouldn't win," interrupted Deborah sharply, her gray eyes turning to ice. "I was just giving you an idea of what we're up against."

Lexie shrugged nervously and shook her head. "I don't know," she said, biting her lip.

"If you're not tough enough, you'll never make it," Deborah snapped impatiently. "The pace, the pressure, even the other girls will kill you." She searched for Lexie's eyes and fixed them with her own. "All of this takes a lot of time and money, and I can't afford to waste my time. There are sponsors who put a lot of their money behind my judgment. If I didn't believe in you we wouldn't be here. The only question is: How much do you want it? How much do you really want to win?" She leaned forward over the table, waiting for Lexie's answer.

Lexie tried to sort out her confused thoughts. She had wondered where all this money was coming from. Other girls paid their coaches and paid them handsomely. Deborah Mackland was one of the most famous skating coaches, and Lexie wasn't paying her a dime. Instead, she was living at this classy hotel, skating in the famous arena, shopping for clothes in the best boutiques in Colorado Springs, putting in an order for two pair of blades that cost the earth . . . and now she was told the money was coming from "sponsors!" Sandy had said that amateur figure skating was "a business." All of this puzzled and perplexed her, but Deborah was waiting for her answer. She had to face that question once and for all—Did she want to win? How much?

"I want to," said Lexie, slowly beginning to understand herself. "I want to win very much."

Deborah sat back, satisfied, and took a sip of her

tea. It was going to work out, even though the road ahead of them would be a rough one.

Deborah Mackland had been in the business too long not to face facts realistically, or to know how to make a bad deal better. Lexie was—too old, not yet a winner, unpolished, and an unknown up against five girls who already held various titles, whose names and the consistency of whose performances were known to the judges. How to make it better? If Lexie Winston's name were on everybody's lips, if she were billed as an upcoming star, if everyone *expected* her to win and rooted for her to win—the strong possibility was that she *would* win and become a world class skater qualified to enter the Olympics. Certainly the girl herself had the natural talent and ability, *plus* the looks. She was as wholesome as Dorothy Hamill, and as pretty, but a good deal blonder. She had what it takes, but how to get the point across to the judges?

Publicity, of course, good old American hype. Mentally, Deborah went through her card file of names and addresses, looking to call in some of her outstanding markers. The name she came up with was Brian Dockett.

Brian Dockett. He was local TV out of Minneapolis, not network, not seen nationally, but give him time. And the right story. He was ambitious, and with the right material he would break through into the network. He was young, good-looking, sincere; a newsman whose passion—one of them, anyway—was sports. They were old . . . friends, she and Brian.

Deborah stood in the control booth, watching Brian wind up the news. When the "On the Air" signal blinked off, he left his desk and she left the control booth and they kissed in a friendly fashion.

"Deborah, you are more beautiful than I've ever seen you," purred Brian sincerely. It was true; she was stunning. Her face and figure were those of a magnificent, tawny jungle cat, and she dressed that body to perfection in understated and outrageously expensive elegance.

"Brian, darling, may I say the same for you?" laughed Deborah. This part of her work could be fun, too.

After a long, nostalgic and wine-drenched dinner, Deborah told Brian about Lexie and about her plans for the girl.

"Is she good enough?" asked Brian, enchanted by the glow in Deborah's eyes. It was less of a wine glow than a money glow; Deborah looked that way when she was on to a good thing.

"I've never seen anyone with such a gift," replied Deborah instantly, punctuating her enthusiasm with a wave of her manicured hand. "There's something in her, something natural. You look at her and you know what it's all about. She's rough and old-fashioned, but she's got it!"

"How rough?" asked Brian, with a newsman's sense.

"I can have her ready for the '80 Olympics," promised Deborah with conviction, but Brian shook his head.

"They'll never let you do it. Skating is one place where they don't like upstarts."

"If we can build enough media interest, they can't stop it."

"We?" Brian raised one handsome eyebrow. So that's why Deborah had insisted on picking up the tab for their expensive dinner.

Deborah smiled at him, touching his hand for emphasis. "It's the kind of thing you like to do, and what's gotten you this far. *And* it's what will get you out of a midwest affiliate and to the network. And because you're a darling."

Brian smiled back. He knew a good story when he heard one. "Does she know what's about to happen to her?" he asked with a touch of pity for the child.

"She wants it," nodded Deborah positively. "She may not know what she wants, but the sound of that little tiny crowd in Cedar Rapids literally knocked her right on her behind, and believe me, she wants it."

"You know," mused Brian, swirling the brandy in his

90

glass, "I see this as kind of an Olga Korbut thing. Everybody's darling. . . . You know, we actually ended up like the Russians. . . ."

Now we're cooking, thought Deborah. She leaned forward to hug him briefly. "It's going to be good for both of us. . . ."

"No more one of the best *woman* coaches in the country?" Brian teased her, amused by her ambitions, which matched his own so perfectly.

"That's right," said Deborah coldly, drawing away.

* * *

Lexie stood at the railing of the rink, waiting for her turn on the ice. Sandy was practicing with her coach, who watched her with a sharp but not too favorable eye. The little girl was talented, but sloppy. Though Sandy had a natural grace, her performance was marred because it lacked the clarity that dedicated practice would have given it.

"Every practice is like a performance," snapped the coach, his hands on his hips, as Sandy braked to a stop in front of him. "You don't work in practice, you don't work in performance. You are a lazy girl, Sandra."

Uncharacteristically silent, the little girl looked down at the ice, humiliated.

"You look out there," continued the exasperated coach, pointing to the center of the rink where a tall, slender brunette was skating beautifully. Lexie's eyes followed his pointing finger. Look there at Annette. That's why she was runner-up at the World. Every day she works as if it were the Olympics." The coach blew his breath out with impatience and strode off, calling over his shoulder, "We work tomorrow. Tomorrow. Work." Clearly he had given up on Sandy, and he held no hope out for today, tomorrow or the day after tomorrow.

Skating over to Lexie, Sandy shrugged, but there was no gleam of braces in a smile. She was obviously hurt and depressed.

"She's good," said Lexie as gently as she could. It was no disgrace to be unfavorably compared with a skater as good as Annette.

"She's a machine," grunted Sandy. "Ever talk to her? Ten minutes on how I found somebody to sharpen my skates. Then she runs out of interesting conversations."

"Is she supposed to win the Nationals?"

Sandy nodded grudgingly. "It's sewed up. She came in fourth in the Olympics, second in last year's World's. Number One retired to make a mint with the Ice Capades. So normally that would have meant Number Two, a French girl. Ceciel. But she got hurt . . . or so they say. *I* heard that she went bonkers, nuts, Asiatic. When a skater disappears you always hear she got hurt, but you never know for sure what really happened."

Suddenly, without a word, Lexie moved out from the railing and pushed off into the center of the rink, gaining speed, skating through the practicing girls until she had reached a clear space. Then she lifted off, turning twice in the air for a double axel, landing cleanly, a good jump if not one of her greatest. But she felt good, free. It wasn't clearly a challenge to Annette, but it did register with the other skaters and coaches, who were looking at her in surprise.

In the center of the ice, Annette continued her program. She was apparently oblivious to the new girl and her flash.

With a short laugh, Lexie began hotdogging as fast as she could around the perimeter of the ice, gaining speed, gaining momentum for another jump. When she left the ice it was to rotate once, twice, *three times* in a triple axel. The turns were good, but her landing was shaky, and she wobbled and very nearly fell. Around the arena, there was a collective intake of breath, as everyone's eyes, even Annette's, were fixed on the slender ponytailed blonde. To even *try* a triple axel—the audacity of it!

Lexie skated back to the railing, satisfied for now. As she passed Annette, she gave her a dazzling smile, and the dark-haired girl returned the smile slowly. It was an acknowledgment Lexie Winston was going to be competition.

* * *

When Deborah returned she was furious, coldly furious. She stalked into the dormitory and pulled a frightened Lexie out of the rec room, shoving her into the passenger seat of her BMW. Without speaking a word to the girl, Deborah drove out of the hotel gounds and down the mountain road toward the airport, her lips pressed tightly together, her eyes the color of steel. When they had driven far enough for Deborah to have let off some of her steam, she pulled the car to the side of the road and spoke to Lexie at last.

"The next time you try a stunt like that, it's over. Do you understand that? You can get hurt very easily. Then where are we?" she demanded angrily. "That stupid show-off thing with the triple—"

"But I *did* it," Lexie interrupted in a small voice. "I've been working on it. I mean I wanted to surprise you that I could do a triple—"

"A *lousy* triple."

"You didn't see it," cried Lexie defensively.

"I heard." Deborah's voice was scornful ice. "A lousy triple." She turned Lexie's shoulders until the girl sat facing her, then she met her eyes, forcing Lexie's gaze to lock into hers. "Let me tell you something. Triples may be good crowd-pleasers, but to world class judges it's just a piece of show-off acrobatics. You can't win in this game by that kind of crap. You know what the judges like and you do it better than anybody else. That's what wins. Annette knows that, and so does every coach here. I'm a goddamned laughing stock. You can make a fool out of yourself, but not me."

Lexie sat silent, her cheeks burning with shame as she listened to Deborah. Her lips began to tremble with humiliation, and she felt the tears welling up in her eyes.

"Which is it going to be?" continued Deborah, relentless. "My way, or should I drive you to the airport right now?"

Tears were streaming down Lexie's cheeks, and she didn't answer. Deborah Mackland sat staring stonily through the windshield.

"Stop crying. Control yourself. You're not a baby."

Lexie gulped for air, desperately trying to stem the flood of her embarrassed tears, but losing.

"I said *stop!*" The chill in Deborah's voice cut like a knife.

Biting her lips, pressing her knuckles into her mouth, Lexie finally succeeded in choking back her tears.

"Which will it be?" asked Deborah again. "My way, or do I send you back to Iowa?"

Again, Lexie struggled unsuccessfully to speak. She knew that Deborah's way meant discipline and hard work, no more stunting and no more freedom. At last, she managed to answer.

"I want . . . to stay . . . I . . . want . . ." she gasped.

"All right," said Deborah briskly, and the subject was closed. She turned to Lexie and held her arms open. Lexie, sobbing softly, threw herself into them.

*   *   *

Nick Peterson held the receiver to his ear and listened as the quarters bonged into the pay phone. He was feeling a little guilty; it had been days since he'd been in touch with Lexie. For some reason he'd been putting it off. As he waited for one of the girls to call Lexie to the dorm phone, Nick thought about her. It wasn't as though he didn't miss her—he *did*—but their lives seemed to be taking such different directions.

Lexie's quiet greeting pulled him away from his sour speculations.

"Yeah, I'm okay, I guess," he told her. "I don't know." Something in her voice made him conscious of her unhappiness. "You down?" he asked her.

"Deborah got mad at me about the triple," confessed

94

Lexie. God, how she missed the pond and skating alone and the games of tag with Nick—especially Nick.

"I guess she knows what she's doing," Nick reasoned feebly.

"Sometimes it's hard," said Lexie. "I feel like I don't know anything. I mean, everybody here is so smart. They all know how to dress and say the right things. They've been working with coaches like Deborah since they were kids."

"You'll be all right," Nick replied evasively.

"Sometimes I feel like . . . everything's happening so fast." Lexie hesitated, then said, "Can you come here maybe?"

The plea in her words took Nick by surprise and he felt an uncomfortable pressure on him. Did he want to see her? He loved her, sure, but things weren't going too well. "Hell, we never play anywhere near Colorado Springs. That's out of our league."

Hearing the rejection in Nick's voice, Lexie's disappointment was so acute, she couldn't express it. "Nicky? You wearing long johns? Nebraska's cold . . ." was all the You wearing long johns? Nebraska's cold . . ." was all she eyes. He'd seen it before, and it always made him feel like such a heel.

"Okay, babe . . . gotta run," he said briskly.

"Nicky . . . " Lexie's voice reached out and held him. "I had a dream about you last night."

"Oh, yeah?" His curiosity was piqued. "Tell me."

"No." She giggled. "I'm too embarrassed." She waited for a reply, but Nick, suddenly embarrassed, too, stood with the receiver pressed hard against his ear, wishing that he and she were together, or that she wouldn't press him so hard, wishing a dozen different, conflicting things.

"Daddy and you ought to get together," said Lexie, more cheerfully now. "Neither of you knows how to write. Oh, I got a funny card from Beulah. It said: *Happy Birthday, Queen of the Ice Castle*. Isn't that funny? It isn't my birthday, though, so don't worry, you didn't forget."

Nick clutched the receiver in silence. Hell, he didn't know what Beulah meant any more than Lexie did. Happy Birthday, Queen of the Ice Castle? But what did Lexie want from him? He could barely keep his own life together without having to solve her problems, too. Why the hell was everything always so damn complicated?

7

The campaign for media attention that Deborah Mackland was mounting started off in full swing without any advance warning to Lexie. Lexie was literally asleep when it began.

Lexie. Was she dreaming? A voice called her name. *Lexie.* With the gentle touch on her arm, Lexie woke up. She looked up to see Deborah, fully dressed and smiling, sitting on her dormitory bed. Sleepily, Lexie pushed herself up on one elbow.

"What? Am I late?"

"No. Everything's fine," whispered Deborah, her smile deepening. "I've got a surprise for you."

"A surprise?"

At that moment, in through the bedroom door came a camera crew dragging cables, lights, sound meters, and a television minicam, already rolling. With them came Brian Dockett, wired for sound.

"Act natural," advised Deborah as the camera stuck its videotronic nose straight up to Lexie's face.

"Act *natural!?*" squeaked Lexie, suddenly conscious of her old flannel pajamas and uncombed hair. Pulling the covers up over her head, she dived back among the pillows, terrified. The camera homed in on the wriggling lump in the bed, Deborah laughed out loud and the media hype began.

They followed her everywhere—not only on the ice, but in the dining room, the dorm, the recreation area, Deborah's suite. The other skaters were at first sarcastic, then jealous, then furious. Only Sandy remained loyal. At the outset, Lexie was self-conscious, with the camera's eye always staring, but after a while she became used to it. Finally, she *did* begin to act somewhat more natural. She became accustomed, too, to Brian following her everywhere, to his commentary on her life, her dreams, her ambitions, her trials and troubles, a commentary she heard in her head even when she brushed her teeth.

"Good evening, ladies and gentlemen. This is Brian Dockett with another sports essay. What does it take to become a world class skater in six months? We are about to find out as we follow the training and preparation of Alexis Winston. . . ."

Lexie skated backward gracefully in an arabesque, while Deborah, wearing rubber shoes, coached her firmly from five feet away. Form, Lexie. Smile, Lexie. Head up, Lexie. Form, Lexie . . .

". . . A skater who appeared from nowhere, electrifying the audience of the Central Midwest Regionals last month."

Had it been only a month? It seemed to Lexie a lifetime away. She had trouble even recalling Marcus and Beulah; they seemed to be at the far end of a tunnel, and she couldn't conjure up their faces. Practice, practice, practice. Over and over again the new routines, the unfamiliar programs, were being drilled into her memory, replacing other memories, memories of the spontaneous joy of skating.

98

"Our cameras will follow the transformation of an exceptional raw talent into a world class skater under the guidance of top American coach Deborah Mackland." Shots of Deborah showing Lexie the steps of an intricately choreographed and very showy new routine.

Lexie *is* exceptional, thought Brian. Deborah was right, as usual. The girl had beauty, strength of purpose, a natural gift for skating and a sweetness of personality that came through on film. It would be a dynamite show, dynamite. He smiled at Lexie as he watched her going through the steps of her new program with Deborah and a professional choreographer. She's tired half to death, but she's hiding it. She's got class, and Deborah will pull it out of her.

"That's the time to break into the hard beat," said Deborah, her eyes narrowed. She signaled to the piano player, who broke into the music again. The choreographer showed Lexie the steps one more time, staying in rhythm with the piano. "*And* one and two *and* three and four . . . see? Now try it."

Concentrating hard, almost unaware of the camera, Lexie tried the routine. It was a difficult sequence of moves, and it felt unnatural, too formal, too stiff. She tried it again. Better this time.

But Deborah wasn't satisfied. "Let's try it again. Not too jazzy, all right? This is still figure skating."

"The sensation from Waverly, Iowa has yet to win a major competition," narrated Brian, "but she has already won the heart of everyone she has met."

And she's winning mine, he thought with surprise. She's only a baby, but she's winning mine. I've never met anybody so fresh, so innocent, who is so obviously destined to be a champion. That was a large part of it, of course, getting in on the ground floor with a champion. Yet, that wasn't all of it, not even for a man as ambitious as Brian. Lexie's beauty and openness were beginning to get to him. He wanted to be with her more and more.

It wasn't easy for Brian to take Lexie out. Deborah

watched over them like a mother hawk. At first, Brian felt flattered, thinking that the beautiful Deborah Mackland was more than a little jealous because they had been lovers once. But he soon discovered that it wasn't jealousy at all. Deborah didn't give a damn about Brian. She was protecting Lexie. Lexie had to get her rest; Lexie had to be on the ice at daybreak; Lexie this and Lexie that.

"Damn it, Deborah!" protested Brian. "I'm not going to keep her out all night. All I want to do is to feed her a little dinner. She has to eat sometime, doesn't she? Or do you feed her yourself with a spoon?"

"Very funny, Brian. Really humorous. Lexie is an investment, and a big one. I can't afford to screw around with that. And," added Deborah pointedly, "neither can you, darling."

Brian nodded, subdued. "Granted. But if I bring her home by midnight, may I please buy the child a lobster? She says she's never had one."

"Where does one get a lobster in Waverly, Iowa?" smiled Deborah. "All right. But no later than ten-thirty. I mean it. I'll be waiting up with a rolling pin."

Lexie's introduction to the lobster delighted Brian. She looked so cute with the bib tied around her neck, struggling with the claws and the cracker, biting her lip in concentration.

"I can't do it." she surrendered at last. She dropped the claw onto her plate in despair. "No way. God never intended man—or woman—to eat a lobster, or he would have put zippers in the claws."

Brian threw back his head in a laugh that made the people at the next table jump. She was priceless.

"Here, let me do it for you. It takes practice." He went around the table and, standing at her side, cracked the claws open neatly. Extracting the succulent meat, he held out a forkful. Lexie turned her face up to him gratefully, and Brian was astonished at just how much he wanted to kiss her, right there in public.

He's terrific, thought Lexie as she looked up into Brian Dockett's handsome face. He knows everything. What to order and how to handle it, and how to bring a girl a flower without making a big deal out of it. I've never met anybody like him before.

I've never met anybody like her before, thought Brian, later, as he drove her up to the dorm on the dot of ten-thirty. She's entirely natural, entirely unspoiled. Maybe she'll even stay that way, although the chances are all against it.

"You can put the rolling pin away now, mother," he called to Deborah, who came out to the car to meet Lexie. "We've behaved ourselves."

"Did you have a good time?" Deborah smiled at Lexie.

"Oh, yes!" breathed Lexie. "Wonderful!"

"Since I've been so good, can I take her out again?" asked Brian meekly. "Tomorrow night? There's a good movie."

Deborah shook her head. "Not tomorrow. Full schedule."

"How about the day after tomorrow?" Brian pleaded in mock humility while his eyes twinkled with malice at Deborah.

"All right," relented Deborah. "But no later than ten-thirty."

Brian saw Lexie as often as he could—her time was grudged to him in small doses by Deborah—because he found enchantment in her company. He felt like a teenage boy, curfew and all. Lexie was delighted by everything, always cheerful, always enthusiastic, and the jaded Brian began to find new pleasure in familiar things as he saw them through her eyes. Deborah, on the other hand, began to see that all of this might be very useful to her plans.

Of course, accompanying the camera, Brian still followed Lexie—to her ballet class, to the gym, riding a bicycle along a back country road.

"It is only fitting that her training is taking place here at the famous Broadmoor World Arena where such skaters as Peggy Fleming, Amanda Smith, and Dorothy Hamill, as well as the current favorite for the 1980 Olympics, An-

101

nette Brashlout, runner-up in last year's World Competitions, have skated before her," his narrative ran.

Brian and the camera followed Lexie—to fittings for her new skating dresses, heavily sequined to sparkle under the lights; to the hotel's beauty salon to have her blonde bangs styled and curled, and her eyelashes darkened so that her eyes would appear even bigger than they were; to the jogging track where Lexie was circling for the third time, still keeping her knees up.

Lexie was not only getting used to the camera, she was learning to like it. She was learning to like Brian, too.

"As we report to you this evening, we don't know the outcome of this story. The prestigious figure skating association Qualifications Committee has not ruled on whether Alexis will be able to compete. But when they do, we'll try to let you know. Because by now we are certain that you are rooting for Alexis Winston, too, and want to see her a "champion of tomorrow." This is Brian Dockett. Good night."

Good night, creep, snarled Nick silently as the television set over the bar blared a closing theme, and Lexie's smiling face vanished. He'd taken a lot of ribbing from the other team players while the show was on, because everybody knew that Lexie was his girl. There were whistles and catcalls when she first appeared, a tiny figure in a short skating dress, and gales of Canadian laughter when the turkey in the double-breasted blazer and hairspray said that she "appeared from nowhere." Waverly, Iowa wasn't nowhere. Hell, yeah it was.

Nick felt a certain amount of conflict about the show. He was happy for Lexie, and it had been great to see her up there, getting famous; but at the same time, wasn't she his girl? He wasn't sure he liked all the attention she was getting. She looked terrific, like a princess. No, not a princess, a star. A goddamned star.

Sitting at the bar of Beulah's Ice Castle and Five Star Lanes, Beulah wiped a tear away as the show came to an end. She was so proud of Lexie, so proud. And yet she was sad, too, because she wasn't a part of it any more.

Lexie belonged to Deborah now, and when she became a world champion, it would be Deborah who got all the credit. Nobody would remember Beulah. But, boy, could that girl skate! More than once, Beulah had drawn in her breath, startled by the differences in Lexie's skating style. It was flashier, more dazzling and far more proficient. Her leaps were higher, her spins faster, her turns more graceful, although less spontaneous. Obviously, Deborah Mackland did good work, real good. Who could blame Beulah for being just the tiniest bit jealous?

At home, Marcus leaned forward and snapped off the set, missing Brian's last few words. Pulling the tab on another can of beer, Marcus scowled. I guess this was what she wanted all along. To be a star. Nothing at home had satisfied her. No, she had to go with that snooty bitch and become a star. Now she's famous, and a fat lot of good it will do any of us. Especially Lexie. He reached for the phone impulsively but drew his hand back. She didn't want to hear from him.

After the broadcast, Lexie hung around the dorm for more than an hour, waiting for them to call and congratulate her. But they didn't call—not Nick, not Beulah, not Marcus. Tears of disappointment stinging her eyes, Lexie put on her best new dress and went out to dinner with Brian again.

This time it was a celebration, and Deborah had lifted the curfew—not all the way, but until 1:00 A.M. Lexie was electric with excitement when Brian led her into the best restaurant in the area, and the headwaiter addressed both of them by name.

As they settled into a sheltered corner banquette, Brian took Lexie's hand and kissed the tips of her fingers, slowly, one at a time. A pulse began to beat hard in Lexie's throat. Nobody had ever done that before—that is, Nick hadn't, because he was the only other man she'd dated. She'd never have believed that the brush of a man's lips against her fingertips could raise such feelings in her.

"Happy?" asked Brian softly.

"Oh, yes! Very happy." Lexie's eyes shone and her

cheeks glowed in the candlegiht. She had never looked prettier, nor more grown up.

"No Coke for you tonight," Brian told her with a grin. "Tonight, chateaubriand and champagne. It we don't get busted. Pretend you're old enough to drink."

"I am! I'm old enough to do *anything*!" chirped Lexie. "I feel I could conquer the world."

"You have," said Brian soberly. "You've conquered a large part of your world already. Don't you know that?"

Nobody had ever talked to Lexie the way Brian did, and she found it a little bewildering. But thrilling. Brian was sensitive, compassionate, caring. Being with him was more romantic than she could have imagined; he could stand in for the hero of any novel she'd ever read. And when he kissed her good night, she could smell his expensive cologne. It occurred to Lexie suddenly that there might be more to life than skating, and more men in the world than Nick.

*　　*　　*

The following day, the news came from the network.

"My God!" cried Deborah, her eyes shining. "I don't believe it. It's set? You're certain?"

Brian's pleased grin widened, and he nodded vigorously. "They went for it, an expanded version of the essay series to be made part of Christmas in America."

Christmas in America! The annual Christmas morning television special that went out coast to coast and into millions of homes!

"And Alexis is in?" asked Deborah carefully.

Brian's grin threatened to split his face horizontally.

It had been Deborah's idea initially, elaborated on and expanded by Brian. They would broadcast a showcase of top contenders for the Olympics, four world-class skaters and Alexis Winston. Technically, of course, Lexie wouldn't qualify to be a member of that group—not yet —but Deborah knew that her inclusion would make the qualifying judges take notice of her. Each of the girls would skate a short routine, not in competition with the others, but as a demonstration of her own talents. Only Deborah knew how hard she and Lexie had worked to perfect Lexie's routine. It was Deborah's intention that Alexis Winston stand out even among champions; it was to be the final cannonade in her master strategy of media bombardment. And it was all coming true!

"The network bought it all and only one turndown from the top five," Brian continued.

"Annette." Deborah's eyes narrowed.

Brian nodded. "She's the only one who thinks she doesn't need the exposure."

"To hell with her," Deborah snarled.

"Bobbi Braker. Sally Richards from Canada . . ." Brian ticked the skaters off on his fingers as he named them. "Wen-An Sun from Taiwan, and the *best*—Ceciel Monchet, number two *in the world!*"

"You're kidding!" gasped Deborah. "I thought she went . . . was ill."

But Brian was looking triumphant. "Talked to Thimitch myself. She's apparently all right. He wouldn't admit what went wrong, but he's anxious to get her back in the minds of the American judges. And I offered him a nice noncompetitive exhibition. No pressure."

"No pressure?" asked Deborah with a sarcastic lift of her eyebrow. She shook her head. It was all too perfect.

"How's Alexis?" asked Brian casually. A little too casually.

"She's coming along fine," Deborah replied with the same amount of cool.

"Will she be ready?"

"I think so."

"She's still such a kid," Brian mused.

"You two are getting along very well," Deborah commented dryly.

"I like her."

Deborah shrugged a "why not?" "She's going to be a star" was all she said.

"Boy, you're a heel!" snapped Brian. Deborah had struck a nerve.

And she knew it. "Oh, come on, Brian," laughed Deborah. "Where's your sense of humor? This is a great situation. Nobody loses. Remember that. Not you, not me and especially not Lexie."

Deborah looked around at the luxurious permanent suite she kept at the Broadmoor and smiled like a cat. Everything was going fine, according to plan, according to schedule. Lexie *was* going to be a star. She was going to rise to the top—world champion, gold medal Olympic winner—and take Deborah Mackland right along with her. It was very satisfying to back a winner. Sometimes she still felt a sense of loss at what she had sacrificed to make it this far—an ex-husband and two children had been left behind in New York. Sometimes she missed them, but she was who she'd always been.

"Deborah Mackland, premier world coach," said Brian rather nastily, echoing exactly what Deborah was thinking. Ordinarily, this would have annoyed her greatly, but she was in so fine a mood that she only smiled.

"You haven't done so bad yourself," she reminded him. "This show will bring you into national TV. Maybe it will even carry you to New York. Not bad at all. . . ."

But Brian didn't stay to hear the rest of it. He walked out of the room and shut the door behind him. Deborah looked after him in surprise, then smiled and dismissed him from her thoughts. She had other, more important plans to make.

*　　*　　*

Lexie's last practice session of the day was at eleven in the evening, when the rink was half-empty. Dressed in her best Polar warm-up outfit, she came into the rink carrying her Gold Star blades.

"Where's the TV crew?" one of the girls asked her sarcastically.

Lexie gave her a dazzling smile, a killer grin, then sat

106

down next to Sandy on the bench and began to lace up her boots.

"Snubbing *everybody* or is there a list?" asked the younger girl.

"Watch out. I've got a disease," snapped Lexie, pulling hard on the lace of her boot.

"Yeah," grinned Sandy with a flash of expensive braces. "Success. It's all right. It isn't contagious. Just irritating."

"Thanks." Lexie lifted her boot and checked for loose screws.

"Look," shrugged Sandy placatingly, "I'm easy. It's hard for some of the girls. They've been doing this for a long time. You come along, take their ice time, there's a big PR push, now this Christmas show thing. It's fantastic! Nobody ever got anything like that before. Sure they're mad."

"Screw them!" Lexie snapped.

Sandy looked at her friend in surprise. "Well, so much for the dumb bozo from the sticks," she said dryly.

Lexie had taken herself by surprise, too. "Well, after a while it gets old," she said defensively. "I mean, I'm working my tail off." And it's not much fun, she thought silently.

"What's worse is they know how good you are," confessed Sandy.

"Well, I don't have *time*. I don't care whether they like it or not." She stood up and skated out on the ice with Sandy by her side.

"Me, too?" asked Sandy sadly.

Lexie looked down at the small figure by her side and smiled affectionately. "No, we're buddies."

"Say, maybe when you're a big Olympic star, you'll fix me up with some hot numbers," teased Sandy. "Or maybe you'll let me carry your skates. You never know how many people will be trying to sabotage them."

Lexie burst into a giggle. Sandy was so funny, she couldn't help laughing. Then she deliberately bumped Sandy with her hip, nearly knocking her off balance. Recovering from her wobble, Sandy bumped Lexie back.

They skated and weaved into each other's paths, like a pair of frolicking drunks, bumping each other and trying to trip each other up. Suddenly Lexie caught herself and stopped. Deborah had come onto the ice and was standing watching them, and she was most definitely not amused.

"Alexis," Deborah called. "Let's go to work."

*   *   *

Nick looked into the mirror on the wall of his motel room. He looked like hell. One side of his face was so swollen that the eye had nearly disappeared, and there were huge bruises on his chest and shoulders. He looked as though he had crashed into a wall going fifty miles an hour. He had.

He was twisting and turning to check the bruises on his back when the telephone rang.

"Hello? Oh, hi, Lex. How's it going?"

"Did you see the cover?" came Lexie's breathless voice, bubbling with excitement.

Nick glanced at the unmade bed, which held a copy of *Sports Illustrated*. On the cover was a photograph of Lexie, caught in the middle of a spin. She looked terrific, sexy, a star! Her smile shone halfway across the dingy motel room. The caption on the cover read *Cinderella Champion?* What a media coup—the cover of *Sports Illustrated*. Damn!

"Yeah, I saw the cover. Great!" He tried to put a little enthusiasm into his voice, but he wasn't really feeling much of anything except resentful and badly bruised.

"Nicky . . . I miss you," said Lexie in much more subdued tones.

"Well, you're a star," evaded Nick, feeling like a heel. There was no answer, but he could hear Lexie's pain over the long-distance wires. "Sorry . . . Lex . . ." he said softly.

"Nick." She spoke so low he could barely make out her words, but he could tell she was crying. "Nick . . . I feel

108

funny. I mean, the new program . . . it still feels strange."

Now he was on securer ground. "Wait'll you get used to it," he advised her heartily. "You'll be fine." Then his voice softened. "Hey, Bozo, bet you can't do a triple."

"Deborah took it off my program. I told you," said Lexie, upset again. Didn't he remember anything?

"Oh, yeah."

Lexie pulled herself together. "Thanks for the clipping you sent me about the game. Two goals—pretty good. I guess Sioux Falls has a tough team this year. Don't get hurt."

Nick hesitated, then blurted out the words. "Lex, I quit today."

"What?" Lexie's voice echoed her bewilderment.

"I'm kidding myself, you know?' replied Nick miserably, looking around the small, shabby motel room, his bed covered with clothes waiting to be packed. "This isn't what I want."

"Oh, baby . . ." exclaimed Lexie softly.

"Hell," Nick blustered, "I don't even think I give a damn."

"What are you going to do?"

"I don't know," he answered her with a sigh. "Go home. Maybe work on the farm a while."

"You could go back to school," whispered Lexie hopefully and held her breath.

"Why?"

"I always wanted to be a doctor's wife. . . ."

"Lexie, I don't know what I want," Nick cried. "I mean . . . I just don't know what I really want to do. You know, what really bugs me is that I don't think I really care. Maybe I don't really care about anything."

Does that go for me, too? Don't you care about me either? Oh, Nick, what's happening to us? Lexie's thoughts were an anguished muddle. "Nicky . . . can you come to Minneapolis?" she asked hesitantly, "for the TV show, Christmas. They're going to broadcast it Christmas morning, but we can have the rest of the day." She waited for his answer, but he didn't utter a word. "Please," she begged, ashamed of herself for her need.

"Hey, maybe I don't think I can right now," said Nick at last, his voice thick. "Okay? I'll . . . look, you're doing great. I don't want to screw things up . . ." he broke off, unable to continue.

"I love you," sighed Lexie at last. It was the only thing left to say. She had asked him twice—begged him—to come to her, and he'd refused.

"Yeah, I love you, too," answered Nick. He felt totally beaten, and deeply depressed. Nothing was going right, nothing. Right now he felt nothing ever would. He hung up the receiver and picked up the copy of *Sports Illustrated*. Lexie's golden beauty shone up at him from the cover, teasing him, provoking him. With a curse, he hurled the magazine against the wall.

"Goddamn it! Goddamn it to hell!" He felt like crying.

Lexie Winston hung up the phone and slumped against the wall of the dormitory corridor. She didn't even realize that she was crying. What was going wrong? Why was everybody deserting her? Marcus never wrote, Beulah never phoned, and now Nick was slipping away, no, *pulling* away, from her! What had she done that was so wrong?

Wherever she turned, Lexie saw only blank hostility—from the girls and the other coaches. Only Deborah was there whenever she needed somebody, but there were things she couldn't talk about with Deborah. Not even with Sandy. She needed a familiar face, a comfortable shoulder to lean on.

Brian. There was always Brian. But he wasn't familiar. In fact, he was so strange he frightened her. The way he looked at her sometimes. Hungry. Funny, whenever Nick looked at her that way she felt warm. Brian had the opposite effect. He made her feel chilled all over; sometimes, Lexie actually shivered. But she was drawn to him, to his intensity, his good looks, his easy charm. He flattered her, treated her like a grown-up, like a star. That was it, he treated her like a *star!* To Nick and Beulah and Marcus, she was still a little girl who wanted to ice-skate. To Brian, Lexie was a star.

She took a tissue from the pocket of her robe, blew her nose and dialed Brian's number. She began to feel a little better.

8

Lexie had never seen so much excitement in so small a space. The Christmas show was being shot in an indoor rink in Minneapolis, much smaller than the World Arena, and backstage was chaotic.

In a dressing room that was not very large to begin with, six young skaters were crammed in with six coaches, a couple of makeup men and various people from Brian's staff, all clutching clipboards and all looking nervously at their watches. The coaches were whispering last-minute advice to girls who couldn't hear it because of their anxieties, and the makeup people were darting around the room with open pancake boxes and combs. Lexie backed herself against a wall, as far out of the way as she could squeeze, and kept her eyes on the others, especially on Ceciel Monchet, the legendary French champion, a curly-haired girl with strange, wide eyes, who sat silent while her coach tied and retied her expensive boots.

Suddenly, Brian popped his head in to check if everyone was present and ready to go. His eyes sought out Lexie against the far wall, and he smiled at her reassuringly and gave her a wink. He looked especially handsome today in a tight, short ski jacket, his hair brushed and fluffed into thickness by the makeup people. Lexie managed to smile back, but her heart wasn't in the feeble wink she essayed.

Brian's second assistant, shhhhing them like a librarian, shooed the skaters out of the dressing room and into a straight line backstage. From where they stood, the skaters could see the rink, with Brian standing in the middle of the ice, on skates. Behind him was a golden curtain crowned by the symbolic Olympic rings.

The lights on the monitors blinked from red to green, and music came up suddenly, startling the girls. To the tune of "The Stars and Stripes Forever," a double line of Ice Cadettes, in spangled red, white and blue skating outfits, whooshed onto the ice and ended up on both sides of Brian, who stood smiling until the music stopped.

"Merry Christmas, ladies and gentlemen, boys and girls. This is Brian Dockett, presenting—as a part of Christmas in America—the Winter Olympic Preview. We're happy to be part of your Christmas morning, and we are proud to present six young international skating competitors heading for the 1980 Olympics."

The orchestra struck up the Olympic theme, and as each skater's name was mentioned, she skated from the wings and took her place at the center of the ice, until Brian was surrounded by the six.

"From France and currently favored to be World's Champion, Ceciel Monchet. From California and second in Senior Ladies Nationals last year, Bobbi Braker. Wen-An Sun, from Taiwan. Canadian champion Sally Richards. Chris Miller, second runner-up in the world. And . . . introducing . . . Alexis Winston!"

Lexie skated out to join the others, conscious of the lights and the spectators. She knew, too, that even though Brian had begun with Ceciel, the top-rated skater of the

114

group, the best position in the introduction was her own, the last. She stood beside Brian in the spotlight, her arms flung high, the navy blue skating dress with its large center chevron of white making her a standout. Deborah had sought Brian's advice as to which color and pattern would show up best on the small home-screen. But Lexie didn't know about that. She only knew that she felt and looked her best. Her heart was beating so loudly she thought the sound engineers would pick it up on their mikes.

"These are the contenders, ladies and gentlemen, girls and boys, for the 1980 Olympic Games." It wasn't quite the truth, but it was almost the truth.

As they had rehearsed, the skaters joined the Ice Cadettes in a series of simple spirals and arabesques designed to get them gracefully off the ice and into a holding pattern for their individual numbers. Backstage, they almost collapsed with relief; it was the first time some of them had skated before a camera on so small a rink, where every false step would be recorded and televised into millions of living rooms.

Nervous laughter broke through and soon all the girls were giggling, including Lexie. All, that is, except Ceciel Monchet, who stood looking blank and nervous while her coach whispered urgently into her ear.

One by one, as Brian announced them, each girl skated back to present her program.

"That was Chris Miller, second runner-up in the World's. And now, from Taiwan, Wen-An Sun!"

Backstage, Lexie crossed her fingers and made a wish. Daddy, please be watching me. Nick, please be watching me. Beulah, please be watching me. And, dear God, please don't let me make a fool of myself.

In Iowa, Marcus sat alone in front of his television set, and Beulah sat at the bar in a deserted Ice Castle, closed for Christmas. Nick was watching in a bar, too, in Nebraska, alone, morose, confused.

Ladies and gentlemen, Alexis Winston!"

As the orchestra struck up her new music, Lexie skated out swiftly and went into her program, the new one she'd been rehearsing with Deborah and the choreographer for weeks. A showy, intricate, jazzy program, innovative and difficult to perform. In short, a performance guaranteed to knock'em dead.

And Lexie performed it brilliantly, never forgetting to hold her head high and smile brightly into the camera. She seemed to explode onto the ice in a sequence of moves—spins and leaps, camels, lutzes, axels—that none of the girls before her had managed with such confidence or speed. Again and again, the crowd in the small arena broke into applause for her form and style and the effortless way she did the most difficult steps.

Watching at the bar in Waverly, Beulah couldn't believe her eyes. Even she would not have thought that Lexie had so much in her. "My God," she breathed, stunned.

The other skaters were stunned, too. They'd had no idea what they were going to be up against. If they had known, it was doubtful any one of them would have agreed to come on the show. Annette Brashlout was no dummy; she stayed home. But then, she'd seen Lexie skate, and she knew how much effort and sweat she'd have had to put into a program that would begin to equal Lexie's, and all for five minutes in front of a TV camera!

Deborah, watching, was impressed despite herself, and ecstatic, too. It had been worth while—it *had* been. All those hours of effort on her part were paying off and were going to pay off even better. She was never wrong, she congratulated herself. She knew how to pick them, and this girl had shown she had talent even as far back as Cedar Rapids. But this! This was beyond expectation. Lexie was displaying not only her new skill, but the personality and charm of a winner, a champion. She looked fantastic, both in person and on the monitor. She was a hit.

Lexie's music was coming to its loud, splashy finish. Completing her program with a series of showy jumps and stops, Lexie took her bows and, grinning, flew offstage and into Deborah's happy, waiting arms. Lexie was radiant as she accepted the congratulations of the other girls. She'd

116

made it, and everybody knew it. She could hear the applause from where she stood; it was the loudest, longest hand of the day so far.

"Ceciel Monchet, the French National Champion!" announced Brian, and Thimitch, Ceciel's coach, pushed the skater gently forward.

Ceciel made her entrance slowly, out of synch with her music, and skated to the center of the ice, where she seemed to hesitate before pushing off. Backstage, Lexie didn't watch the TV monitor, so caught up was she in the triumph she'd experienced. But a gasp from the other girls alerted her and she quickly looked up at the screen. Ceciel had fallen to the ice and lay sprawled there awkwardly.

Transfixed by horror, Lexie moved away from Deborah and approached the monitor. The other girls were buzzing as Ceciel pulled herself to her feet and began to skate again, simple little steps such as a child beginner takes. Then, once again, she slipped and fell.

Lexie tried to close her eyes to shut out the awfulness of the scene. But her eyes remained fixed to the monitor in morbid fascination. Although the other girls had skated to the wing to watch Ceciel for themselves, Lexie couldn't do it. Just as she couldn't stop staring at the monitor, she couldn't bring herself to watch the pain of the French girl in person.

By now, Ceciel had skated in a clumsy circle and had fallen for the third time. Swiftly, the Ice Cadettes were sent skimming out onto the ice to cover the tragedy. They blocked poor Ceciel from the camera's remorseless eye, and Thimitch came out onto the ice to rescue his protégé.

"It's all right, dearest," he murmured to her in French. "Don't worry, everything is all right. Come, my dear, come away." The coach led the dazed and blank-faced girl away behind the cover of the smiling, bouncy Ice Cadettes doing a samba on ice.

Lexie shuddered, horror drowning her like nausea. Suddenly, she turned and ran down the corridor to the ladies' room, ignoring the fact that her blades had no guards on

117

them and they might be damaged. Deborah gasped and followed.

In the old-fashioned tiled bathroom, with rows of closed cubicles and lines of mirrors, Deborah noticed automatically that she was looking tired but dismissed the thought with irritation as she looked for Lexie.

The girl was there, down at the end, in a cubicle with the door locked.

"Alexis, please come out of there." Deborah listened. There was complete silence in the cubicle, not even the sound of sobbing. "Everyone said Ceciel wasn't well," explained Deborah, taking a new tack. "Maybe she shouldn't be skating anymore. Lexie!"

No answer. Not even the smallest noise.

"You were a smash! It was everything we'd hoped for and more. Everything we worked so hard to achieve. What we wanted so much to happen has happened, Lexie. Can't you see that? That's the most important thing. Alexis, open the door!"

Silence.

"Damn it, Alexis!" yelled Deborah, suddenly out of patience. She slammed her palm against the cubicle door angrily, and it opened easily. It had never been locked.

Lexie was standing in one corner of the cubicle, behind the toilet, against the wall. Her face was as white and still as the tiles themselves, but she was not crying. That's what scared Deborah the most. Instead, Lexie was dazed and ashen, completely disoriented, huddled like an infant against the wall.

"Lexie," said Deborah horasely, reaching for the girl. Lexie shrank away, pressing herself harder against the wall.

"It's just one of those things, honey," soothed Deborah. "Forget it. What's important is that yesterday nobody knew who you were. Come on, baby, come here."

Lexie took one hesitant step around the bowl and grasped Deborah's hand. Pulling her into her strong arms, Deborah let Lexie collapse against her. She held the girl tightly, patting her head.

118

"It . . . scared me . . . so much," wailed Lexie, wetting Deborah's fur coat with her tears. "I . . . don't know . . . I . . . I . . ."

For the first time in years, Deborah Mackland felt maternal instincts stirring within her. All she wanted was to make this little girl feel better and stop crying. All she wanted was to see Alexis smile.

"Do you know how many people saw you today?" she asked gently. "Do you have any idea how many people know who Alexis Winston is? I guess maybe fifty million people."

"Christmas morning?" snuffled Lexie skeptically. She was coming out of it.

Deborah laughed. "So it was only twenty-five," she conceded. "That's still a lot more than ever saw Sonja Henie in her entire career."

Keeping her arm tightly around Lexie's shoulders, Deborah drew her out of the bathroom and back into the limelight for the grand finale of the TV program. Skating and smiling, Lexie pretended not to notice that there were only five of them in the finale with Brian, not six.

The success of the Christmas morning special confirmed Deborah's feeling that Lexie was ready to meet the sponsors—those rich men and women who contributed so generously to the upkeep and training of their favorite young amateur athletes. Because Lexie's amateur standing would be violated if she skated for money, she—like many another young competitor—had to accept the generosity of strangers.

Some of the sponsors gave out of patriotic motives—they wanted to groom the best athletes to capture the most gold medals for the United States in the Olympics. It was important to them that the U.S. win, and particularly important that the Iron Curtain countries be beaten.

But there were other sponsors whose motives were less lily white. These were the manufacturers of sporting goods and athletic equipment, the owners of sports complexes, arenas, hotels and so forth. They hoped to profit by Lexie's success. But whatever their motives, all of them had one thing in common: they wanted to back a champion. And Alexis Winston had all the earmarks of a champion. So far, they'd had only Deborah Mackland's word for it. But when the telegrams arrived to invite the sponsors to Minneapolis or to turn on their TV sets and take a look at their investment, they saw for themselves where and how their money had been spent, and one and all were pleased. A champion was in the making.

The time had come for them to meet Lexie, face to face.

When Deborah had sent the invitations to the sponsors, bidding them to Minneapolis for the Christmas special, she had also included a party invitation for Christmas night. "A party," she told Lexie. "Large, lush, expensive, the best food and the best wine and plenty of it."

"Deborah, do we *have* to?"

"Alexis, it's going to take a lot more money to get you ready for competition as a world class skater. And to take you abroad for foreign competition. You have to dress like a champion, for example. And what about the press? They've been very good to you so far, baby, but lunches and junkets and cases of Scotch do not come cheap. No, a party is what we need, and you, my dear, are going to be the star of the party."

"Deborah, I *can't!*" Panic made the sweat stand out suddenly on Lexie's upper lip.

"Of course you can, Alexis. It's not as difficult as learning an axel. All we need is the proper setting to show you off like the jewel you are. Your all-American charm is definitely in your favor, so we don't want you to appear too elegant. Let's leave elegance to the sponsors' wives and girl friends. You're naturally beautiful and naturally sweet, and we don't want to screw around with a winning combination like that. We need to raise quite a large amount of cash to get this show on the road, and the sponsors will certainly want a closer look at their own skating champion .

120

and star. Now . . ." Deborah's eyes narrowed thought-fully. "Where can we hold this wingding? I know, Brian's!"

"Brian's?" Lexie looked blank.

"Oh, yes, our young Brian lives very well," purred Deborah. "Big house, lovely garden. He lives in Lakewest, right outside the city. And you don't find a more luxurious suburb than that. Yes, Brian's house would be absolutely perfect."

Brian's house was everything that Deborah had said it was, and more. Lexie responded to its beauty instinctively; her life had been spent in such drab surroundings, yet she had always known there was a house like Brian's some-where in her future. Outside, in the front garden, Japanese lanterns lit the winter trees; inside, all was firelight and the soft, golden glow shed by porcelain lamps and mounds of caviar and buckets of iced champagne.

A tall Christmas tree, decorated only in giant silver balls, stood in one corner of the living room; brightly wrapped packages were piled underneath its branches in colorful profusion. No expense had been spared to deco-rate the house for the holiday season. Wreaths of pine cones and English holly were bound with red ribbons to every door, and the scent of sandalwood came drifting up from the candles, whose lights were reflected in the many mirrors that made the rooms look even larger.

Lexie caught her breath with excitement and wonder as she came in the front door. Brian, looking as handsome as a movie star in a dinner jacket of midnight blue velvet, kissed both of them—Deborah first, then Lexie—on the lips and wished them a Merry Christmas.

Deborah's eyes gleamed with pleasure and satisfaction as she looked around. Everything was perfect, just as she'd expected.

Lexie and Deborah had come early, so that Deborah could supervise all last-minute arrangements and Lexie could rest and dress. Deborah gave Lexie strict instructions: Don't come downstairs until Brian comes to escort you. You are going to make an entrance. Lexie sighed unhappily, she'd so much rather not. Why couldn't she be there with Deborah to say a simple hello to everybody?

"Because you're a star now, baby, and stars don't say simple hellos. They make entrances."

So, although she soon began to hear party noises downstairs and men's deep voices talking while women's voices laughed politely, Lexie was still banished to an upstairs bedroom. Dressed and ready to go, she sat on a king-size bed deep in the luxury of furs—sable, nutria, fitch, mink, raccoon, opossum, worked in stripes, worked in rounds, banded in leather—that the maid had taken from the backs of the arriving guests. There was an anxiety working in Lexie's stomach, bunching it up, and to relieve that anxiety she wanted nothing more than to hear a voice from home, from Waverly "nowhere" Iowa.

She picked up the phone and called Marcus. He was home. And well. And, presumably, happy. Yes, he'd watched the special. Yes, he was proud of her.

But there was something missing in his voice and, instinctively, Lexie reached out for more.

"I'm glad you saw it, Daddy. I wanted you to come. I . . . it's Christmas and I wanted to spend Christmas with you. . . . I know it's far . . ."

Guilt overtook her suddenly as she realized that it was *she* who was away at Christmas and her father who was at home. And *she* was crying to *him*.

Marcus asked her about Ceciel Monchet, and suddenly Lexie grew defensive. "Yes. No, nobody knows. She just fell," she fibbed. "Everybody says she shouldn't have been skating. They say that maybe she couldn't take the pressure or something."

But Ceciel was only a dim memory now. What was more important was her own brand-new status as a celebrity. "Daddy, Deborah says that twenty-five million people saw me today. Can you believe it?" She looked up from the phone as Brian entered the room to bring her downstairs. "Okay," she said swiftly into the telephone. "I'll call you later. Say hello to everybody for me, okay? I love you, Daddy."

She hung up the telephone and scrambled off the bed, into Brian's open arms. He gave her a warm hug, then held her at arm's length while he scanned her face. "Are you all right?" he asked.

Lexie turned to the mirror. Her lovely chiffon dress, cut low at the neck and snug around the waist, was becoming. Her long blond hair was twisted into a fashionable French knot and piled high. She wore no jewelry except gold hoop-earrings—Deborah's Christmas gift—and very little makeup. But there was a slight frown line cutting between her wide brows, and she smiled at her image to drive it away. Then she turned to Brian again, nodding.

"Because," went on Brian, smiling at her, "the big question outside this room is: Where is the famous Alexis Winston? Some people are beginning to wonder if that lovely lady they saw on television was an illusion or if you're real."

Lexie grinned back mischievously. "Do you think I'm real?" she asked, spreading her skirt with her hands and making a tiny curtsy. She actually didn't *feel* very real, more like a princess trapped in a fairy tale.

Brian took a long look at her. She was beautiful, but in a way new to him. There was a womanly quality about her now that was beginning to replace the former childishness. Her eyes were a little sadder, he noticed, and their expression lent her a dignity and a distance that was terribly exciting to him. She was becoming a star, and therefore unobtainable, and therefore infinitely more desirable.

Brian took a step forward and folded her into his arms. Lexie came willingly and greeted his kiss with eagerness, even though it was the most passionate kiss he—or anybody—had ever given her. Her hands instinctively clutched his head closer to hers, and her mouth opened under his kiss. Without thinking, she pressed her slim young body against him. Barely able to breathe, she lost

123

herself in the kiss, in his closeness, in the excitement she was feeling for him for the first time. For the first time, too, Lexie kissed Brian without thinking of Nick Peterson.

At last, Brian pushed her away. He himself was slightly breathless from the kiss and his own aroused passion.

"You're real," he told her huskily. "God, are you real!" Then he remembered why he had come—to bring her to the party.

"Come on," he said shakily.

Lexie reached for his hand and followed him as he led her from the room. She could hear the buzz of voices rising to meet her as they went downstairs, and hands breaking into spontaneous applause as Lexie entered the room on Brian's arm. For an instant, Lexie pulled back from the sea of avid faces, from the touches of strange hands upon her arms and back, from the eager congratulations. But she could see Deborah standing proudly in the center of the room, Deborah watching her, Deborah nodding encouragement, and Lexie sailed into the crowd with her head high and a smile tacked firmly to her lips.

As Lexie progressed through the crowd of smiling, congratulatory rich people, she became less frightened and more assured. She didn't have to please *them;* they were eager to please *her*. It was Lexie who was the focal point of all their attention, and it was going to be that way from now on. At her side, Brian beamed as he received his share of the compliments and applause. They made a good team, thought Lexie. They looked good together, and it felt right. She watched him and copied his friendly smile and charmingly modest gestures.

By the time they had passed through the throng and arrived at Deborah's side, Lexie was enjoying herself thoroughly. For the first time, she felt as if she belonged somewhere. Here, among all these people who were so willing to accept her, to make her a part of their hopes and dreams. All she had to do was skate . . . and win. And that was all she wanted to do.

Deborah pulled her close and kissed her cheek. "You

look wonderful, darling," she said. "You look like a story-book princess."

How odd, thought Lexie. That's just how I feel. But, suddenly, she wasn't trapped in the fairy tale, she was living it. And almost enjoying it.

"And I have news for you. The Qualifications Committee met and decided, Alexis. They decided in our favor. You're going to skate in the Sectionals, baby. And you're going to win. And become a world class skater. And go on to win again and again, until there's nothing left to win, because you'll have won them all!" Deborah's eyes glittered with the brightness of her dream. "Merry Christmas, Alexis."

"Merry Christmas, Deborah."

When the dancing began, Lexie was whirled from one pair of arms to another. All the men wanted to dance with her, captivated by her grace and beauty. Deborah watched her spin past, locked tightly in the embrace of a seventy-year-old manufacturer of warm-up suits. Lexie was laughing and flirting, and Deborah gave her a warm smile of approval. Deborah, elegantly dressed in understated black that set off her tawny hair and golden skin, kept herself as much in the background as she could; this was Lexie's night.

And Lexie was enjoying it. She had been convinced that she'd be awkward, uncomfortable and gauche. Instead, she discovered graces in herself she'd always dreamed of possessing. And everywhere she went, laughing and chatting and dancing from room to room with a succession of partners, she could feel Brian Dockett's eyes following her, warming her, exciting her. She felt a promise about to be fulfilled, even though she couldn't put a name to the promise.

And then it was time to leave. Everybody was saying good night and how wonderful a party it had been, promising to telephone Deborah within the week. Deborah was glowing, ignited by the pledges of money, lots of money, for her charming, winsome, wholesome champion. The evening had been a success—no, a triumph.

But Deborah's glow began to fade as she looked around to collect Lexie.

"She's upstairs. She's staying," said Brian flatly.

"She's not staying!" Two spots of color rose high in Deborah's cheeks, and her eyes snapped angrily.

"You can't keep her locked up forever, Deborah. You're her coach, not her mother. Or her jailer. She's staying. She wants to stay." This might have been a lie, since Brian had yet to ask Lexie to stay.

"I have a responsibility—" began Deborah, but Brian cut her short.

"I'll look after her. You needn't worry. It's not the fate worse than death, you know. Or don't you remember?" Brian's smile held more than a hint of malice.

"You bastard!" hissed Deborah, her hands curling into claws, and Brian took a backward step, retreating from the anger in her face.

"Look, Deborah," he said placatingly, "I really . . . like . . . Lexie. She's come to mean a great deal to me. I wouldn't hurt her for anything in the world. But you have to give her a chance to live her own life. You're going to turn her into a skating robot if you're not careful, and then she'll lose that vitality, that spark that makes her stand out. You have to handle her very gently now. This is a crucial stage for her, not only in her career, but in her life."

Grudgingly, Deborah had to admit there was something in what Brian said. Lexie had been highly charged tonight, electric with personality, and it came from deep inside her. From the woman part of her, not the skating part. If that side of her was fulfilled, then the skater would benefit as well. Besides, Deborah understood those feelings. There'd been a time, before her career had taken her over, when she'd shared them. And she remembered them now.

She looked at Brian sharply, started to speak, and then changed her mind. "Good night, Brian. And Happy New Year."

126

While Deborah bid good night to the departing guests downstairs, Lexie was standing at the mirror in Brian's bedroom, staring at her reflection in quiet wonderment. She had drunk only one glass of champagne, but it was still glowing inside her. And it wasn't only the wine that was glowing. Her body felt strung as taut as a wire, and a new awareness of herself was taking possession of her. Lexie looked at Lexie in the glass, oblivious to anything or anybody else.

She felt so grown up. What was it? Her body? She let her hands trail down from her cheeks to her neck, then down her chest to rest at her breasts, cupping and stroking them. They were growing, she thought, but that wasn't all of it. Neither was it her sophisticated hairdo, nor her makeup. It was something undefinable, not touchable— the expression in her eyes, perhaps, or her mouth. Her mouth always looked so happy; now it was sad, and the corners turned down just a little. Why am I sad? she wondered. Is it because I'm growing up? Do I want to stay a little girl forever? Daddy's girl? Beulah's girl? No! I want to be a woman.

A knock at the door made her turn away from the looking glass. Brian poked his head in and smiled at her.

"Party's over," he told her cheerfully. He came up behind her and kissed the back of her neck, gently but insistently. She allowed her body to relax against his, and her eyes joined his in the mirror.

"What do all those people want?" she whispered.

Brian shrugged lightly. "Nothing. To see you, to be near something that's exciting . . . a winner . . . and that, my darling, is what you are."

"Why do they touch me like that?" asked Lexie, curious.

Brian sighed a little. He was used to being touched. "I don't know," he said soberly, as if he'd given the matter some thought of his own. "Because . . . they need to have someone do something they can't do. To make them feel that if only . . ." his voice trailed off.

127

"What?" Lexie insisted. She had a burning need to know, to understand, because it was to be so great a part of her future.

"If only they had a chance . . . or the talent . . . or luck . . . or something . . ."

"We're on display, aren't we?" Lexie turned away from the mirror and looked directly into Brian's eyes.

"Yes." Now he broke into a grin. "And damn lucky that somebody wants us to be. Everybody out there tonight— in fact, everybody who saw you today—would change places with you in a minute."

She smiled. That was something she hadn't considered before. It explained a lot. She could understand that, because, if she'd been home still in Waverly and had seen another girl skating so brilliantly for the cameras, she, too, would have longed to change places with her, would have wanted to reach out to touch her.

She touched Brian lightly on the shoulder now. "I want you to know that I understand," said Lexie slowly. "I didn't before, but now I do."

It comes with the territory, Brian thought. It makes you grow up faster than you want to. "Hey, don't worry about it. You're a star," he told her.

A star. That's what Nick said. I'm a star. Deborah said it, too. A star. It made her uncomfortable, and she pulled away from Brian's encircling arm, a frown on her lovely face.

"You want to give it up?" asked Brian quietly.

Lexie shook her head. "No." Shyly, she relaxed back into his embrace.

Brian kissed her lightly on the lips. "Scared?" he whispered, searching for her eyes.

She turned her face up to his. "I don't know what I'm scared of," she confessed.

Brian kissed her again, this time more deeply, and he felt Lexie's lips responding to his. "Nothing. You're not afraid of anything," her murmured into her fragrant hair. Then he took her into his arms and kissed her once more, this time a long, probing and passionate kiss, which the girl returned instinctively. Her hands stroked the back of his neck and his shoulders; she pressed herself into his arms.

9

Nick had been driving for hours without sleep, and his handsome young face looked a little haggard as he turned off the freeway outside Colorado Springs. The winter-chafed roads were rutted in places, and new snow had fallen recently, but the snow-blowers and snowplows were out on the job. The Scout was dirty from the trip and could have used a good washing. So could I, thought Nick with a laugh. So could I.

He'd felt lousy about missing Lexie at Christmas, but he'd been in no shape to see her then. Well, he'd make up for it now. He'd driven all the way up to watch her in the Midwestern Sectionals, then on to the U.S. championship. She would win, too. Nick was sure of that. How they would celebrate!

He wanted to tell Lexie that he'd been wrong, and that she'd been right. The realization that he'd been crippled by his jealousy—her path seemed so clear, while his had been so obscured—had made him determined to see her in person. Lexie was born to skate, born to be a champion, and he would just have to find what he was born to do. One thing was certain. He loved Lexie with all his heart; he knew that now. And he didn't want to be apart from her any more.

Maybe after she won the U.S. championship, they could get married. If she wanted him to go back to school, he'd do it. Study veterinary medicine, maybe. There was good money in that. They'd live in a cold climate where Lexie could skate outdoors most of the year, and he'd grow rich giving cows two aspirin.

Yes, that's what he wanted—whatever Lexie wanted. Most of all, he wanted Lexie. How surprised she'd be to see him! He hadn't called to tell her he was coming. He wanted to see the surprise and the happiness on that beautiful face.

He planned to ask her to marry him. Right away. Sure, why not? Why wait until after the Nationals? They'd need Marcus' permission, but Lexie could get around Marcus. Besides, Nick was certain that Marcus had a sneaking fondness for him anyway, despite his insults and provocations.

By the time he turned into the parking lot of the Broadmoor World Arena, Nick had gotten his second wind just knowing he would be seeing Lexie, watching her skate, watching her win.

The walkways and ramps leading to the arena were almost deserted; the Sectionals had already begun. Nick paid for his ticket and bought himself a program. He heard a muffled announcement and the start of new music as another skater went onto the ice. Nick entered the arena and found himself a seat. Not an easy thing to do because the Broadmoor was packed, filled to the rafters with five thousand spectators. Flags and banners and bunting decorated the hall, and the lively crowd was watching the ice with intense interest.

Nick checked the ice. The girl skating on it wasn't Lexie. He looked over at the electronic scoreboard,

132

searching for Lexie's name. She was in fourth place; somebody named Annette Brashlout was in first. Nick sighed. Those damn compulsory school figures. But she must have picked up a lot of points in the freestyle short program; otherwise she wouldn't be up as high as fourth.

Now they were skating their long programs, which was where all of Lexie's strength as a figure skater lay. Her ability to command the ice with verve and brilliance, and in perfect form, always came through best there. But to move up from fourth place all the way to first would take more than brilliant skating, it would take a miracle! For the first time, Nick felt a twinge of doubt. He began to compute the score that Lexie would need in the long program. Wow! It would have to be damn near perfect for her to win.

For the first time Nick realized that he really *wanted* her to win. Before this, he'd been grudging and selfish. Now he wanted to see his girl a star. Was he growing up? Win, Lexie, win it for both of us. I'll hold the thought, Lex.

A small commotion at the sidelines brought Nick's attention away from the ice. A camera crew was shooting someone coming out of the dressing room and into the arena. Nick thought he recognized that guy—whatsisname—from the TV show. And there, wasn't that Deborah Mackland? Yes. And . . . my God, Lexie!

Lexie walked out swiftly on her skate guards, apparently oblivious of the cameras shooting her every step. She looked ravishing; her hair pulled up in a large chignon; her scarlet skating dress trimmed with sequins that outlined her slender, nubile body. The skirt was the merest wisp of tulle, like a ballerina's tutu, only much briefer, and designed to float around her to emphasize the grace of her moves while she skated. On her face she wore the brightest smile that Nick had ever seen. He almost didn't recognize her, and he sat stunned, watching her greet her well-wishers politely and move on quickly, every contact smooth, superficial, professional.

That wasn't Lexie. That was some glamorous figure

skater complete with camera crew and entourage. Nick didn't know that girl at all.

As Lexie walked to the edge of the ice, her entourage fell behind, keeping out of the star's way. Only Deborah came with her, whispering advice into her ear urgently as Lexie nodded her carefully combed head. Nick leaned forward in his seat to watch Lexie. When she bent to remove her skate guards, she looked over her shoulder at Brian Dockett. Nick caught Brian blowing her a kiss, and he watched, his brows darkening, as Lexie pretended to catch the kiss and press it to her own lips.

But the announcer's voice came over the loudspeakers and Brian was forgotten.

"And now . . . fourth place in the overall standings will do her long program. Alexis Winston."

She skated out swiftly and took her place in the center of the ice, waiting for her music to begin. When it started, it took Nick by surprise. It wasn't Lexie's usual music, but some new, modern jazz with a definite upbeat. Like Lexie herself, it was strange and different.

For an instant, Lexie stood silhouetted against the frozen whiteness of the ice. Then she moved quickly, bursting into her program with that incredible clarity of motion that had marked her at Christmas.

The crowd drew in its breath, and Nick realized that he had, too. He lost himself watching her; he couldn't take his eyes from the brilliant red figure, darting, turning, spinning, gliding, leaping high in the air. For the first time Nick was seeing, without any camera to interpret for him, the new Alexis Winston. And it was almost as though he was falling in love with her all over again, but differently this time. In love with someone distant and inaccessible. With a star. Like the rest of the crowd. They were all in love with her, with Alexis Winston, skating star.

Her first jump lifted her high in the air, and it was followed immediately by a double flip. This variation on the salchow rotated her twice and brought her down on her toe picks to thunderous applause. Nick had never seen a skater jump that high, and his gasp turned to a cheer as

134

Lexie jumped again and again—a double axel, a double flip—and then came down into a sit-spin, her extended leg held perfectly parallel to the ice. As she stood up, still spinning, she moved effortlessly into a backward arabesque, speeding around the ice, using all the corners of the arena as her stage, bursting upon the dazzled spectators like a seagull in flight. She skated forward, lifting high in the air again, arms and legs spread in a split-jump, landing only for the merest space of an instance to glide away, arms wide, a soaring, gliding exotic creature born on and of the ice itself, married to the ice, living on the ice. This was her element—a frozen world to which she belonged, heart and soul.

Nick sat stunned, watching Lexie perform, reacting as one with the crowd. He wasn't aware that he cheered; he didn't know when he broke into applause. All he knew was that his throat was sore and his palms were tingling. And that he had been part of a miracle, witness to a wonder. A spectator at Lexie's incredible show, one of thousands.

Then it was over. Had it been four minutes? It seemed like a lifetime; it seemed like no time at all. But Lexie had come to a silent stop in exactly the spot and exactly the position from which she had begun. Then she flung her arms wide and took a sweeping bow. The audience exploded into applause, not the wrenching, stomping, gut-reaction applause of Cedar Rapids, but a sophisticated, knowledgeable, appreciative applause. Still, it was more than they had given any other skater. Lexie circled the rink gathering up the roses the fans were raining down on her.

Deborah was running forward to fold an ecstatic, triumphant Lexie into her jubilant arms. Still dazed by Lexie and her performance, Nick stood up and began to make his way down to the ice, past the other spectators in their seat. It was hard going, since every seat was taken, and he threaded his way slowly downward.

The judges had finished, and they were now handing out their placards to the number girls. The girls skated out to the center of the ice and held their placards high so that the scores could be read front and back.

Deborah and Lexie turned to watch, holding their breath. Coming down from the stands, Nick paused to read the scores. At the sidelines, Brian's camera crew focused on the cards. And over the loudspeakers, the announcer recited Alexis Winston's scores.

"5.6, 5.8, 5.8, 5.7, 5.9."

The two 5.8's and the 5.9 had done it. The electronic scoreboard went wild, letters rotating as the standings were rearranged. When they stopped, the name Alexis Winston stood in first place, and Annette Brashlout in second.

She'd won! Lexie had won! Nick felt his mouth go dry with excitement as he pushed forward with determination through the yelling, cheering, applauding crowd toward Lexie's group.

He could see them celebrating, rushing forward to grab Lexie, kiss her, hug her. He saw her turn to Brian, saw Brian take two steps forward to gather her into his arms and kiss her, saw Lexie returning Brian's kiss. They were not kissing like friends, Nick felt, but like lovers, even though the TV cameras were on them. Nick stopped dead, staring at Lexie over Brian's shoulder. He wasn't ten feet away from her, but he felt as though light years had suddenly pushed them apart forever.

Breaking the kiss at last, Lexie pulled away from Brian and smiled deeply and triumphantly into his eyes. This was what she'd hoped for, dreamed of. She had won. She was on her way to becoming the champion. Over Brian's shoulder she could see the cheering, faceless crowd, yelling for *her*, Lexie Winston. And in that faceless crowd, one face. One white, shocked face with large, staring blue eyes. One familiar face. One beloved face. One face, now turning away from her astounded gaze. Nick.

"Nick," she mouthed, first joyously, then agonizedly, as she realized what he must have seen. Desperately, she tore herself out of Brian's arms and started toward him.

But the crowd surged forward—the camera crew, the

136

press, dozens of well-wishers—pressing on her, pushing her back, separating her from Nick. Frantically, she pushed through them, although Nick was on his way out of the arena, his back to her.

"Nick," she cried in an anguished voice as she ran after him. "Nick!"

But he didn't turn, and he would have escaped her entirely if a large group of spectators hadn't appeared, cheering Lexie, to block his path. She caught up with him, fighting her way through the crowd, and grabbed at him. He turned, his face dark with fury and pain.

"Nicky! Oh, you came." Lexie threw her arms around him, but he stood still, refusing to return her embrace.

"Come on," Lexie tugged him back toward the ice, but he was stronger than she, and he refused to budge. He gave her a look of such loathing that she flinched.

"In third place," called the loudspeaker, "Suzan Blake."

To polite applause, Suzan skated to the center of the rink where three platforms had been set up at different heights to hold the three winners. She climbed onto the lowest dais.

Lexie, hearing the announcement, turned to Nick. "Please, Nick," she begged. "I have to go." She tugged at him again, but he still stood cold and unmoving.

"Great. Looks like you got everything you need," he said contemptuously.

Deborah was signaling furiously to Lexie through the ocean of spectators.

"Second place," the loudspeaker blared, "Annette Brashlout."

Annette skated forward gamely and climbed the next platform, receiving the loud applause awarded to an almost-winner.

Lexie was frantic. It was her turn to go out there, but she stood frozen. She couldn't leave Nick like this! Without a word of explanation, without a look of forgiveness from him that would tell her that everything was all right between them. He was so angry with her. Finally, he pulled away from her and headed for the nearest exit.

"Nick!" she yelled after him. "What are you doing? Nick—"

"And, we're sure, the next National champion . . ." came over the public address system.

The crowd rose to its feet, cheering and yelling. Lexie ran after Nick and caught up with him again.

"Alexis Winston." The cheers from the spectators were so loud they almost drowned out Lexie's name.

Nick turned away again, and Lexie, suddenly bitter, lashed out at him through her tears, "Maybe you should just go try out for some other hockey team!"

He turned and looked at her. In his face sorrow was so mixed with anger that Lexie took an instinctive step backward. Then a furious Deborah came up through the crowd and grabbed her, pulling her toward the ice where her platform was waiting, empty. Lexie was crying so hard that she could hardly see, but Deborah gave her a push that propelled her forward. Automatically, Lexie skated to the center of the ice and took her place on the center platform, a full step higher than the other two. And just as automatically, she bowed her head to receive the first-place medal on its colorful ribbon, as her music played over the loudspeakers.

But all the time, she was asking herself, over and over, What am I going to do now? Oh, God, what am I going to do now?

*   *   *

Deborah had arranged a victory celebration, sending cases of wine and champagne and mountains of catered food to the house of a sponsor who lived in the poshest part of Colorado Springs. Other would-be sponsors had sent Deborah congratulatory telegrams, and several telephoned offers had already been tendered and were now "under consideration."

Deborah was exultant. Power surged through her, sending up her wattage until she glowed with incandescence. She looked spectacularly beautiful tonight, her thick hair brushed to a glossy smoothness and swirled up on her high forehead. Her catlike slenderness was poured into a form-fitting sheath, and for the first time since she had taken on Lexie, Deborah had allowed herself the luxury of wearing her diamonds. Tonight they glittered at her tawny throat and on her wrists. Next to her, Lexie paled into dimness.

But Lexie would have paled next to anybody that night. All the light seemed to have gone out of her, and she smiled and moved mechanically, waking through her victory party like a small automaton. It was evident to Brian that her mind—and her heart—were elsewhere because he could get no answering glow from his hello kiss. In fact, she pushed him away just as their lips met.

Deborah could have enlightened him because Deborah had witnessed part of the exchange between Nick and Lexie in the arena earlier. But Deborah was in no mood to enlighten Brian. This was *her* party, and she'd earned it. She drifted triumphantly from group to group, receiving their congratulations like the Empress Catherine receiving her courtiers. She'd pulled it off! Deborah Mackland had achieved the impossible—taking a small-town, overage and under-trained skater and turning her into a polished champion in the teeth of everybody's skepticism. It oughtn't to have happened, but it had. Because she, Deborah Mackland, had *made* it happen. This girl was as much her creation as God's.

Now she was one of the top coaches—hell, *the* top coach—not just one of the top *female* coaches in the country. Her future fees would be astronomical, and there would be a waiting list for her services years long. She'd take only the best, the most promising skaters under her tutelage. But first she'd push Alexis Winston to the top—the 1980 Winter Olympics! And she'd see to it that the girl brought home medals of gold, not silver or bronze.

The sponsor's house was lovely, the perfect setting for

so elegant and happy an occasion. The host manufactured custom-styled skating boots and had grown rich and richer on the boom in figure skating that had swept America in the last decade. The house, in a fashionable suburb, even boasted its own skating rink, and some of the most famous skaters in the figure-skating world had given private demonstrations there.

Deborah continued to dazzle her way through the evening, but Lexie had had enough early in the evening. This "celebration" was more than she could bear; Nick's face, angry and reproachful, kept rising up before her eyes to block out any enjoyment. She was totally miserable, and the party was freaking her. Everybody wanted to meet her, to paw at her, to grab her hand or her shoulder, or her dress. Why couldn't they leave her alone? For over an hour Deborah had led her from one group to the next, chanting her litany of praises, making Lexie smile and bow and act like a puppet for the benefit of the "sponsors." She felt like a prize animal being exhibited at a county fair.

All these people acted as if they owned a piece of her. Which, if you looked at it head-on, they probably did. Her father always said that nothing in this goddamned world is free. You're lucky to get what you pay for, but you always wind up paying for what you get. And Lexie discovered suddenly that she was paying, and that the price seemed to be too high. And the skating, her precious skating. All the fun had gone out of it, the natural spontaneity that had made it her most joyous experience. It had become a grim business.

Suddenly, the need to be alone tore at her, filling her with so much pain she thought she'd die. Alone. But where? Lexie looked out of the window, and the little rink below beckoned to her, begging her to come down.

It was small, but perfectly refrigerated so that the surface was steel-hard and not mushy, and it was kept cleared of snow. Around the rink was a low wooden barrier that separated the ice from the patio, where a handful of privileged spectators could sit at cast-iron tables sipping drinks

140

while the skaters entertained them. It must not have been in use lately because the heavy iron chairs and tables were chained down, so that they wouldn't tempt rip-off artists. Yet the rink itself was lit by lanterns glowing in bright colors.

Lexie felt the breath squeezed out of her with anguished longing. Oh, yes. More than anything else in the world, she needed to skate, all by herself, in her own universe. On the ice her thoughts used to come to her clearly, without complication. Alone on the ice, Lexie could solve anything. The ice could bring her Nicky back to her. She was certain of it.

Lexie looked around the room. Brian was backed into a corner by a middle-aged blonde and looked as though he was hating it. Deborah was deep into a business discussion with a pair of tall, serious men, and her attention belonged strictly to them. Nobody was watching Lexie at this moment. This was her chance.

As quickly and unobtrusively as she could, Lexie left the room and ran into the guest bedroom to change. She had dressed there for the party and had left her things. She pulled her blue silk dress off over her head quickly, hearing it rip but paying it no further heed. Then, just as quickly, she slipped into her flannel shirt, tucked it into her jeans and tugged a heavy sweater over her head. Socks. Skates.

Oh, no, she hadn't brought her skates with her! But there had to be skates here; the man who owned this place built the boots! She scrabbled in the guest closet and found some. White boots, beautiful, with freestyle blades attached. Several pairs, all in different sizes. Quickly she found her size and sat down to lace them up. Her socks were too thick, but she jammed the boots over them anyway.

Lexie was past caring. The little rink was calling to her. Offering her peace, and sweet forgetfulness. The skates fit. Not perfectly, but they fit. She slipped them off and ran swiftly down the stairs, holding the boots in her hand.

At the side of the rink she sat down and laced the

boots up again, as tightly as she could. They were good skates, the finest, even if they weren't her own, even if they weren't familiar. Slowly, she made her way out onto the ice.

It was a perfect evening, clear, cold, still. There was no hint of wind, and the cool, high air brought the smell of pine down from the mountains. Lexie skated quietly, alone and almost at peace. She felt the movement of her body as an easy, natural flow. She closed her eyes to feel the spirit of the skating. But it wouldn't come.

Her trained and disciplined body had forgotten how. She'd lost the peace that came with her own place, her own moves. She was accustomed to faster tempos, now, jazzier sound, spectacular leaps and spins, and she had lost her old free self, her old free style. She had to get it back, *had* to. If she didn't, it would never be the same with Nick again.

Squeezing her eyes shut, Lexie tried to conjure up her music. At first, only a note or two, so faint that her inner ear couldn't hear it. Then the melody grew stronger and more familiar, taking over her thoughts, until she could hear it, full, harmonious, haunting. She started to skate to her music.

She began by bending backward, spinning slowly, gathering speed, as she used to do. But it didn't work, and she nearly lost her balance. It made her angry, and she skated quickly across the ice to build up speed for a jump. Oops, not so fast! This rink was much smaller than the ones she had gotten accustomed to, smaller by far than the pond at home. You don't want to go smashing into the barrier like some damn fool hockey player, Lexie.

Some damn fool hockey player. Nick, oh, Nicky! Tears sprang to her eyes, blinding her as she left the ice in a split-jump. Good. Now do better. Remember all the moves you used to make. A backward camel, bending low, arm up over the head. Good. Beulah would like that one. She taught it to me; it had helped Beulah win the Regionals. Dearest Beulah. Now a spin, only a little one, faster, faster. Not so good, Lexie. Try something like a

142

jump instead. Get up a good head of steam for that one. Deborah won't let you do it, but you can, can't you, Lexie? You haven't forgotten how.

Upstairs, at the party, a woman called to Deborah. "Hey, Deb, come see. I think we've found another skater for you."

Smiling indulgently, Deborah moved toward the window and looked out. Down on the ice, a small blonde figure was skating, fast, faster. It looked like . . . no, it couldn't be!

Down on the ice, the small figure, dangerously close to the barrier, lifted off the ice, turned in the air—once, twice, three times, suspended in the air. . . .

"NO! LEXIE!" A silent cry of anguish tore through Deborah. She could see the wooden barrier, so close, so perilously close. She could see Lexie's hesitation in midair, the infinitesimal faltering. . . .

Something was driving Lexie. If she could skate fast enough, far enough, she could avoid that something that was making her crazy. Only a split second away from landing, Lexie suddenly found fear. Her foot buckled under her ever so slightly, and instead of landing on her toe picks, she came down on the flat of her blade. It was an unfamiliar blade, and it skidded underneath her and sent her spinning forward at full speed, crying out in terror.

Upstairs at the window, Deborah Mackland went stiff with horror as she saw the small figure below go crashing into the barrier, saw her catapulted over it to smash into the heavy cast metal of the iron tables and chairs, saw her beloved Alexis Winston tumble headfirst into the jungle of metal, to lie upon the frigid patio, silent and very, very still.

10

All the way to the hospital in the ambulance, Deborah's eyes did not leave Lexie's face. She had never seen anyone so still before, but she had the ambulance attendant's word for it that Lexie was alive. The girl didn't appear to be breathing, though, but lay on the stretcher with her eyes shut, the eyelids not fluttering in the slightest, lashes motionless upon a cheek as white as the pillow that cradled the head. There was no blood, no blood at all.

That's because the bleeding was internal, the chief neurosurgeon explained, after he'd checked over the brain scan. There was definite damage to the inside of the skull, concussion and possibly fracture. But for the moment, surgery did not seem to be indicated. However, it would be a day or two before Lexie could be adequately diagnosed. Deborah assented quietly and went to call Marcus.

The next plane from Iowa City brought Marcus Winston, and he reached Colorado Springs General Hospital early in the morning. Deborah, exhausted, rose from a wooden bench outside Lexie's room; there had been no change, she told him. Lexie had not yet regained consciousness. Still, her coma wasn't total, and that was a hopeful sign.

By the time that Lexie did float up through her ocean of pain to consciousness, two days had passed, and with them had come two more computerized, tomography brain scans. They showed edema—swelling—and blood seepage, but luckily no clots. It was probable that surgery could be avoided altogether.

"Daddy? Is that you? I . . . I can't see you very well," murmured Lexie with agonizing slowness. But the feel of the hand and the smell of rough wool belonged only to Marcus.

"Yes, baby, it's me. It's Daddy. I'm here now, and everything is going to be all right."

Clutching his hand for comfort, Lexie drifted into sleep.

"This kind of thing is difficult to diagnose," Dr. Bramley told Marcus and Deborah as they anxiously awaited the report on Lexie's fourth brain scan. The young specialist glanced at the computer printout in his hand, and once more at the readout—the electronic diagram on the terminal screen. "There's some clotting as a result of hemorrhaging, and of course, the contusion is a bruise on the brain, so there is no damage to the receptors—the eyes. The problem is with the processing center in the occipital lobe. All the muscles and elements of the eyes are normal. That's why it's hard to tell there's anything wrong with her."

But Marcus had a low tolerance for long words and little patience with doctors. "Well, Doc," he demanded, "is she blind or isn't she?"

The neurosurgeon shrugged to show that it was not a question to which he could offer a simple answer. "When she first came out of the coma, she reported that there was blackness. Now she says she can see light and shadow. The clotting may dissolve, or we may be able to do something to alleviate it, maybe drill through the skull and see

146

if we can take any of the pressure off. But let me tell you, the pattern for this kind of thing is that it improves or deteriorates fairly soon after the trauma, then stabilizes, and after that, what you have is what you have."

Deborah sat silent, and Marcus asked abruptly, "When can she go home?"

Home, thought Deborah suddenly. Of course. There's no hope, none at all. A picture of Lexie suddenly rose unbidden into her mind, Lexie sitting in her hospital wheelchair, her head swathed in a high wrap of bandages, her eyes vacant, a look of fear on her young face. Deborah closed her eyes and tried to conjure up an image of Lexie on ice, moving graceful and free, but the image wouldn't come.

"She's going to need a lot of special care," the doctor warned Marcus.

"I understand," Marcus nodded. "I'll take care of her."

Dr. Bramley sighed, "Sorry we couldn't do more," he said, putting down the computer printouts of Lexie's brain. "I understand she was very promising."

"Yes, yes . . . she was very . . . promising," said Deborah tonelessly. She got up suddenly and almost ran from the consulting room.

In the corridor she braced herself against the wall and lit a cigarette with trembling fingers. Drawing the smoke deeply into her lungs, she fought back her rising hysteria. Lexie, blind! And they had been so close . . . so close to the Nationals, so close to the Olympics. Now it was all for nothing. It was over, finished.

But it was more than that, more than the gold medals and the big time. Deborah Mackland had never allowed herself to become personally involved with a skater before. Skating was a business, and she was a business woman. A champion figure skater was a tool of Deborah's trade, and she had always made it a strict policy not to get too friendly with her girls. She couldn't afford it.

But Alexis Winston had been different. So sweet, so real . . . so needful! Maybe it was because Lexie had never had a mother to raise her, or a sister to share things with, but Deborah had found herself being drawn more and more deeply into the girl's life. She hadn't wanted to, but damn it, there it was! She *loved* Lexie and she couldn't —wouldn't—afford the luxury of love. Tears of anger and frustration rose in her eyes, and she threw the cigarette down on the corridor floor and trampled it savagely.

Marcus came down the hall very slowly, shuffling like an old man. He had aged fifteen years in the last couple of days. He stopped a few feet away from Deborah and looked at her with lonely eyes. Once adversaries, they were now uneasily united in misery. Even from a distance, Deborah could see the pain and unhappiness in the man's eyes, and she lowered her lashes so that Marcus wouldn't see the same feelings mirrored in hers.

But he had. "Not so good for anybody, I guess."

Tears trickled out from under Deborah's long lashes. She wiped at her eyes. "No."

"What'll you do? Look for somebody else?"

It struck Deborah for the first time since the accident that she had no idea what she was going to do. "Yes," she said, taking a deep breath. "Sure. That's what I do, isn't it?"

Marcus looked very uncomfortable. He had something on his mind, and he wasn't certain how to say it properly. He wasn't a man who talked a great deal. "Look, Miss Mackland," he began slowly, "I don't think this is anybody's fault. I never wanted a blind daughter, but I can't really blame you for it. Guess I'd like to, but it doesn't make much sense."

"You don't have to make sense," said Deborah bitterly. "I understand."

But Marcus wasn't finished with what he had to say. He came up closer to her and they regarded each other evenly, this beautiful young woman in her expensive clothes and this tall, once-handsome man dressed in farmer's clothes. "Maybe Lexie needs you now more than she did before. . . ." said Marcus.

A stab of fear went through her. She backed away down the corridor from Marcus. "I'm sorry . . ." she stam-

148

mered. "I've got . . . there's nothing I can do." She had to get away, get away from this involvement, from the blind child who needed her friendship now more than ever.

"You could be a friend," said Marcus simply.

Deborah closed her eyes. Part of her yearned to stay, to look after Lexie, to be her friend and even something like a mother. But only part. The rest of her pulled itself together. "I could, but I'm a coach," she said as briskly as she could. "She's blind. There are no blind skaters."

Marcus had recognized the bond between Lexie and Deborah, and he needed all the love he could gather together to help his little girl. "Maybe it's psychosomatic. Maybe it's just temporary."

Deborah looked at Marcus levelly and shook her head. "I can't afford to wait to see," she said in a near-whisper, then brushed past him and down the corridor to the exit.

* * *

Lexie stood at the window, fully dressed. She wore a pair of faded jeans, work boots and an ancient red sweater over a cotton flannel shirt. On her head the white lump of bandage looked incongruous, monstrous and ugly.

Marcus folded the last of her things and clicked the suitcase shut. What could she see from that window? he wondered. It was nearly dark outside—the winter days were so short—but still Lexie pressed her forehead against the glass pane.

Actually, she could see almost nothing, but the glass felt cool against her hot face, and she didn't want Marcus to see the tears forming in her sightless eyes.

"I'll bet you're glad to get outta here," said Marcus with a cheerfulness he was far from feeling. "Bet you can't wait to get home to some of my home cooking—if I don't poison you, that is." He gave a short, mirthless laugh, but Lexie didn't join in the joke.

"What did the doctor say?" she asked quietly.

"Oh, you know. Just a lot of ten-dollar words." Marcus

tried the laugh again. "Means he doesn't know a whole lot more than we do."

The tears were now rolling down Lexie's cheeks, and she kept her face turned from her father. "Daddy?"

The catch in her voice made Marcus stop and look at her. She was so alone there by the window, a little girl lost and afraid.

"Yeah, honey."

"Daddy, I'm not getting better, am I?" Her voice broke.

"Hey, babe, come on," said Marcus, feeling helpless as hell. This was the question he'd been dreading, and even though he knew it would come, he had no answer ready.

"Every day I could see a little better, at first . . ." Lexie said in a choked voice. "Now, it's all the *same*. . . ."

Marcus took a step forward, then stopped. What could he say to her? He wanted to tell her something helpful, something that would ease her mind, but he had never lied to Lexie, and he didn't want to start now. Not now when she needed strength, not weakness. But there was nothing —nothing he could say, nothing he could do. He was afraid to take her in his arms, afraid that if he did, he'd break down totally, and Lexie would know the whole truth. So he stood there, racked by his pain as well as hers, and all he could tell her was "That doesn't mean much. They . . . they say it's the first six months that count. . . ."

"Everybody knows it," insisted Lexie, her voice rising to shrillness. "I can hear it in your voices. Everybody knows but me. I mean I was going on and on to Deborah about how I was going to be back skating in a little while, and she just agreed with me. But she agreed as if she knew it would never happen."

Now she turned from the window, tears pouring down her face. As she turned, she missed Marcus, looking past him. Suddenly she felt as though she were alone in the room, as though she'd lost her father.

"Daddy?" she called on a rising note of panic.

Biting his lips to keep from bursting into tears, Marcus moved close to Lexie. "Right here, honey," he said huskily.

Lexie put out one tentative hand, brushing his sleeve; she clutched at it tightly, as though for protection. "I . . . I can't even see you . . . and I . . . can't see you. . . . I'm blind! I'm blind!" she gasped, sobbing. It was the first time she'd said that.

Marcus drew her tightly into his arms; she was so small and frail. He could feel the tears welling up in his own throat, making it difficult for him to breathe.

"Don't say that, honey. We don't know yet, not for sure. That's what the doctors have been saying. They just don't know yet. Anything is possible."

"What am I going to do?" sobbed Lexie. "I can't see anything!"

Pity ahd helplessness washed over Marcus in a tidal wave of feeling. He hadn't been so wracked since he had watched Betsy die. Lexie was suffering so badly, and he was supposed to be a man, with a man's strength. So why was he so helpless? Why couldn't he take away her agony? All he could do was hold her and pat her shoulder as if she were a baby. "There, there, honey," was all he could say, as if she'd done no more than scratch her knee.

"Help me, Daddy, help me!" cried Lexie, clutching tightly at Marcus' shirt.

How could he help her? He couldn't even help himself. As he rocked her in his arms, his tears mingled with hers.

*　　*　　*

Before she left the hospital, Lexie had two more visitors, Deborah and Brian. They came separately, and each stayed for only a short while. But Lexie hadn't expected them to come at all; she had ceased to expect anything. Still, she went through the motions. When Deborah told her quietly that she was on her way back to the Broadmoor, Lexie nodded. But she didn't ask Deborah if she'd found another skater, and Deborah didn't volunteer the information. Lexie pretended to be certain that she'd be back next year, and Deborah pretended to agree with her. Lexie was glad when Deborah left, but she burst into tears as soon as the door shut behind her.

As for Brian, he played it hearty and encouraging. "Hey, you'll be back with the old 20/20 in no time," he told her in his best sportscasting voice, and Lexie nodded her head. But when he bent to kiss her, she turned her face away.

Beulah called twice a day, every day, making plans for Lexie's homecoming, promising visits and treats and life as it used to be. It was good to hear Beulah's voice, warm and comforting, and to know that somebody back home loved her.

Nick didn't phone, not even once. And Lexie didn't put a call through to him, even though her fingers itched to pick up the telephone and ask the operator for Nick's number. After all, if he didn't want her when she was a star, what made Lexie think he could possibly want her now that she was nothing, a blind rag doll with no future?

When Marcus was allowed to take Lexie home, at last, they flew first class, with Lexie in a wheelchair. Beulah met the plane in Iowa City. She had rented a big station wagon that had enough room for Lexie to lie down in it comfortably. The day was mild, with the first spring scents and feelings in the air, and Lexie longed to see the familiar landmarks that announced home. Marcus remained silent, while Beulah kept up a constant chatter of gossip and small events to bring Lexie up to date on Waverly. Though she talked about everything and everybody, there were three topics Beulah never touched on: ice skating, Nick Peterson and Lexie's blindness.

Lexie's old room didn't feel quite the same. Beulah had gone through it before they'd come home from the hospital and had removed everything she thought could get in Lexie's way or cause her injury. That included the desk —when would Lexie ever write a letter again?—and the rocking chair. The room was now stripped to its barest essentials, and all the furniture was lined up against the walls. Even so, it was several days before Lexie could make her way around it without bruising herself against

152

sharp corners. Even the little rag-rug had to go, once it had tripped Lexie and sent her sprawling.

On her first day home, Lexie refused to leave her room but stayed quietly in her bed, staring up at the shadowed ceiling. Beulah told Marcus not to press her; after all, the child had been through an unbelievable ordeal and was understandably exhausted. She'd come downstairs tomorrow.

But Lexie didn't come downstairs tomorrow, nor the day after tomorrow. She refused to leave the four walls that closed her away from the world, not even when Brian telephoned, not even for meals. Day after day, an unhappy Marcus climbed the stairs with a tray, and day after day, Lexie sent most of the food back uneaten. Even Beulah couldn't get her to eat or to come downstairs, though she visited Lexie daily. The door always closed behind Beulah, and what they said or did in there was a mystery to Marcus.

Nick never came or telephoned, although Lexie knew that he was home, in Waverly, working on his father's dairy farm. She didn't ask about him, and Marcus didn't volunteer any word.

Only Brian called, but Lexie wouldn't talk to him, although he begged Marcus to bring her to the telephone. Lexie wondered whom Deborah was working with now; she was certain that Brian new, but she gritted her teeth so that she wouldn't be tempted to talk to him and ask.

Lexie's vision had stabilized, and she knew it wouldn't change. She could make out the difference between light and shadow and could even distinguish people she knew very well—like Beulah and Marcus—by their perimeters, their outlines. But the inner details, the features of the face, the clothing—these she couldn't make out at all. It was as though there was a big hole in her eyesight, and the inner circle was missing, leaving only the rims. Yet, she didn't look blind, except that she was developing that vacancy of expression so many blind people have, as their thoughts turn inward. Also, she had to walk with her hands outstretched, and she hated that. Perhaps worst of all, she detested the groping she found herself having to do.

The day that Lexie bumped into her bedroom wall, Brian phoned for the last time.

She had thought to try the door, to come out and down the stairs and surprise her father. She'd been cooped up long enough, and through the open window she could smell the first signs of spring. Soon the thaw would come, the ice would melt on the pond, and Lexie would feel warm sunshine on her face. She wanted it suddenly. And so she stepped forward to what she thought was the door, hands held out before her, and walked smack into her wall.

For a moment she stood there, huddled against it, feeling blind and ridiculous. Then her fingers reached up and touched something. Paper. A poster. And next to it, more paper. More posters. Posters of ice skaters—Albright and Fleming and the others, pictures of champions torn out of magazines and pasted to her walls. Pictures she couldn't even see! A great rage washed over her like a huge ocean wave, a rage born out of her helplessness and self-pity. Hatred for those smiling winners, for winners everywhere, shook her small frame, and she ripped the posters off the wall with both hands, then went groping around the bedroom, knocking over her lamp and her radio, tearing down everything her blind fingers could find—the pictures of Nick, of Nick and herself, of Marcus, of herself on the ice, even the one of her mother and herself. With great, sweeping motions, she stripped the walls bare, breathing with difficulty, hearing only the sounds of her rasping, furious sobs.

Downstairs, the telephone rang and rang and rang again. Eventually, Marcus answered it, and Lexie, sitting on the bare floor catching her breath, heard her father's footsteps on the stairs.

"Lex? . . ." Marcus tapped on the closed door. "Lex, can I come in? Brian's on the phone again."

He waited for an answer, but Lexie didn't speak.

"Hell, honey, he wants to know how you're doing."

154

"Tell him," said Lexie softly.

Marcus couldn't hear her through the wooden door. "What?! Goddamn it, I'm not talking through doors in my own house." He turned the knob and the door opened.

"I said, tell him!" cried Lexie harshly. "Tell him how I am. Tell him I can't see!"

"Is that the way you're going to stay?" demanded Marcus. "Shall I just tell him you sit in your room and don't see?"

"Yes! Yes!" Lexie's voice broke in a hoarse sob.

"Oh, hell, honey. I'm sorry. That was stupid." Going into the room, he went to her and wrapped his strong arms around her. Lexie closed her eyes and buried her head in his chest; the rough feel of the winter flannel was somehow comforting.

"He calls twice a week, Daddy," she whispered into the shirt. "Twice a week. It's for his conscience. Don't you see, Daddy? It's not because he wants to. It's because he thinks he *has* to."

Marcus stiffened at the implications of Lexie's words. Then he held her tightly, more tightly than ever. "Yeah, well, okay, I'll tell him," he said, and went downstairs to talk to Brian Dockett.

Brian didn't call again.

Getting Lexie to come downstairs to dinner was Marcus' big triumph, although Lexie appeared to have exorcised some of her demons when she stripped her walls bare. Still, she made conditions—nobody else at the table but Marcus and her, not even Beulah. Lexie was very self-conscious about eating in front of anybody, even her father. She felt gross, trying to find her mouth with a spoon—she hadn't yet graduated to a fork—and needing to have Marcus cut everything up small, like a dog's dinner. Eventually, though, she did agree to come down, and Marcus glowed like a boy on his first big date.

She found it hard to negotiate the stairs, but sooner or later she'd have to learn. The old staircase was so narrow that Marcus had to walk in front of her, which made Lexie very nervous. She held on tightly to both banisters and put one tentative foot on the step below, then the other. Once or twice she stumbled, and Marcus reached a firm hand up to her, steadying her. The single flight of stairs took them five minutes to negotiate, but at last Marcus had his daughter sitting safely at the table in the little dining room, while he went off to bring in the food.

Immediately, Lexie knew that this whole thing was a mistake. Nothing in the room looked familiar to her, not even around the edges. She felt suddenly vulnerable and afraid, and she longed for the safety of her customary surroundings. Her small bedroom with its enfolding walls was her only haven. She had to get out of here.

She stood up shakily, knocking her chair over. Feeling for the table, she groped her way around it, bumping her knees and her shins against the sharp corners of the heavy chairs.

From the kitchen, Marcus yelled happily to Lexie, "You'd be proud of the way this place looks. All neat and everything, almost like your mother would have . . ." He broke off as he came into the dining room and saw Lexie's overturned chair and her empty place.

"Hey!" he yelled. "You haven't touched the fantastic dinner I made." He looked around.

Lexie had made it out of the dining room and was groping her way through the living room on her way to the stairs. Marcus started to go after her but decided that the best thing for her might be to let her work things out for herself. Still, he tried to jolly her, to pretend that nothing was seriously wrong.

"I really outdid myself," he called after her. "Well . . . at least it's edible. Lex . . ."

He saw that Lexie had reached the stairs and was climbing up them like a baby, more on her hands and knees than her feet. All she wanted was the protection of her own room, and it hurt Marcus to the quick. Why did she reject him and push him away when he loved her so much? He'd do anything for her, even give his sight in exchange for hers.

156

"Hey, Lexie . . . I don't expect a lot. Just talk back to me."

But Lexie had made it to her own room and had shut the door.

* * *

"Feels good to get some air, doesn't it?" asked Marcus. It was a bright day, cold, sunny, crisp. The few signs of the false spring had been followed by a cold snap that had frozen the ground, and the pond was hard once more. Spring would be late in coming this year.

Lexie sat in the snowmobile, wrapped in a blanket around her parka. Her bandage was gone at last, and a woolen cap covered her head where the glorious golden hair had been cut away and her scalp shaved. She sat staring ahead of her, unseeing, with no idea of where she was. The snowmobile stopped near the edge of the pond as Marcus cut the engine. Lexie's legs were wrapped in a second blanket, an edge of which was pulled around her waist to keep her warm. Her mitten-clad hands lay unmoving on the blanket, as unmoving as her eyes were unseeing. But little by little, the shapes around the pond—the bare trees and the fallen logs—began to intrude on her sightlessness, and she knew where she was. She turned her face away.

"Still a pretty place, Lex," said Marcus softly. "I bet you can shut your eyes and put together a pretty good picture of it, can't you?"

"I want to go home," Lexie said stonily.

Marcus climbed down off the snowmobile and walked around to Lexie's side. He put out his hand and took her arm gently, helping her down. She came reluctantly, but she had little choice in the matter. Taking two tentative steps forward, she felt the snow under her feet give way to the slickness of ice. She was on the pond. Her eyes widened in fear.

"Remember when you were a little girl and I would pull you around on your skates," Marcus was murmuring to her, as he guided her a few steps further out. But Lexie

157

pulled away from him, spinning around, her boots sliding on the ice. Rushing for the bank, she slipped and fell to her knees, but continued crawling up the embankment, scrabbling with her fingers and toes for a hold.

Brokenhearted, Marcus watched his terrified daughter. Lexie, who had never been afraid of anything! The ice had been so precious to her, so important. He still believed that it could heal her spirit if only she would let it.

"Please, honey," he begged, tears freezing on his cheeks in the wind. "Don't give up, okay? Please don't give up." He ran to her and held her rigid little body in his arms. Lexie kept her face turned away from the ice, not wanting to see even the shadowy, glinting mass of it, wanting desperately to be away from there.

11

Nick Peterson had kept to himself ever since he'd returned home from Lincoln. He never showed up at Beulah's, not to skate or even to have a beer. Beulah had telephoned him once or twice and invited him over; then she'd given up. His old friends never saw him, and he didn't enter the last of the snowmobiling races. The old Scout, which had been visible on all the back roads in days gone by, now remained parked in the Peterson garage.

Marcus had heard that Mr. and Mrs. Peterson had gone to Waikiki for the vacation they'd always wanted and that Nick had stayed behind to look after the dairy farm. So, Marcus went to the farm to look up Nick and ask for his help with Lexie.

Desperate as he was, Marcus would never have faced Nick but for one thing. In the last couple of weeks, ever since he'd managed to get Lexie out of the house for a few minutes at a time, he'd seen Nick. Hanging around the house, hanging around the pond, his large blue eyes fixed on Lexie. Nick evidently had no desire to be seen, since he kept well out of the way. Respecting his wishes, Marcus had made no acknowledgment of his presence, and Lexie, of course, hadn't seen him or sensed him. Nick stayed forty or fifty feet away and hid himself behind the bare trees. But Marcus always felt his presence, and he could see the deep unhappiness in the boy's face even at a distance. It mirrored his own.

The Peterson farm was as different from the Winston farm as the Broadmoor World Arena from Beulah's Ice Castle. It was large and modern, mechanized almost to the point of automation. The Petersons owned four times as many dairy cows as Marcus, and the farm itself always ran in the black. It was an enviable operation, but Marcus didn't really envy it. It took twice as many hours to keep it running as he would be willing to put into it.

He found Nick pushing hay down the feeding chute with a large pitchfork, while half a dozen drowsy, fat cows crowded up to be fed.

"Nice," nodded Marcus genially. "The new feeder outside looks nice. Are you going to put it in?"

"Yeah, it's nice," shrugged Nick grudgingly, "if you're really into the percentage drop of feed pellets per hour."

"What are you into?"

"The percentage drop of feed pellets per hour."

"It's hard to watch somebody you love just . . . give up," Marcus said abruptly. He didn't have the heart to waste words.

"*Loved*. Past tense," Nick replied grimly. One dark curl separated itself and fell over his sweaty brow.

"Then maybe you should do it for yourself," said Marcus softly. "Giving Lexie a hand might be good for you. There's more than one way to give up, Nick."

Nick jabbed his pitchfork savagely into the hay bale and turned away, the muscle in his jaw jumping in anger.

But Marcus wasn't ready to give up. "Don't forget, you've got something here, too," he called after the boy. "You've got something invested in us. In Lexie."

160

But Nick refused to listen, and he stalked off to the other side of the barn, defying Marcus to follow. Anger smoldered inside Nick—why was Marcus coming to *him?* Let that whatsisname—Brian Dockett—that asshole give Lexie a hand. As for me, I want no part of her anymore, he told himself bitterly.

But a secret pang was tearing at him. Why was he watching her, then? Why did he wander over there every day, just to catch a glimpse of her blind, empty face, her groping mittened hands? Why did he keep himself hidden, even though he knew perfectly well that Marcus could see him? Why hadn't he spoken a word to Lexie or telephoned her? They were old friends, even if they weren't lovers any more. Even the most estranged old friend picks up the telephone when tragedy strikes. But no, here he was a damn fool, unable to let go, unable to take a forward step. He was like some goddamned butterfly wriggling on a pin, and all because some ice-skating star kissed a sportscaster. And where was he now, Mr. TV Superstar, now that Lexie wasn't going to be a world champion? More to the point—he told himself suddenly—where are you, Nick Peterson, you who are supposed to be Lexie's oldest friend? He shook his head. No. Friends no longer. Some things hurt too much to heal. Like blindness? What's a little jealousy compared with never being able to see again? But the bitterness rose again, and jealousy claimed him anew. Let Marcus ask Brian. Besides, Lexie didn't want to see him, anyhow. He winced at the word "see," but he shook his head again, stubbornly.

Involved with his conflicts, Nick hadn't even noticed when Marcus turned and left the barn.

* * *

Marcus had been right. Lexie *could* shut her eyes and put together a pretty good picture of the pond. Of all the places in the world, it was the one she knew best. She was familiar with every rough patch of ice, with every wind that blew across its surface in the winter. She could put a name to each tree that grew around the edge of the pond, every fallen log or tree stump she'd ever sat on to catch her breath. She could picture the pond in every season—early spring, when the ice was melting and bare patches began to show around the snowy bases of the trees. And late spring, when green flourished everywhere and paper narcissus dotted the earth in small yellow clumps, while buds unfurled on the tender branches. And summer, when the pond was filled with life and mayflies darted over its surface, food for the frogs. Early fall, when the birch leaves were turning to gold and the grass underneath them was brown and the ducks were making their plans to leave for Miami.

Most of all, Lexie could picture the pond in winter—hard-frozen, a world of ice and quietness, a private universe in which Lexie was the only living creature, skating, happy, peaceful and free.

Didn't Marcus understand? That was why she couldn't go there. Because everything was different now. *Then,* she had possessed strength, grace and power. There was nothing she couldn't accomplish, nothing she wouldn't dare. *Now,* she was a helpless blob, unable to take a step without groping, unable to eat without dribbling, unable to see. She was useless, totally useless, a vegetable, and no place on earth brought that fact home to her more than the pond. Oh, why couldn't Marcus leave her alone? There was no reason for her ever to leave the house again as long as she lived. For what? So that the pond could mock her, laugh at her because nothing was the same anymore? Once she had possessed the freedom of an eagle—but who needed or wanted a bird that couldn't fly?

*   *   *

Beulah ran the warm, wet squeegee over the surface of the ice. That damn refrigeration unit was acting up again, and parts of the rink were turning mushy. The moisture from the sponge laid down a slick coating, and she moved slowly on her knees, like a scrubwoman, repairing the battered sections of the ice.

Why? Beulah asked herself sadly. Why even bother? Who the hell will care anyhow? Nick didn't skate here anymore; the Blue Jays were playing over on the high school rink. Hardly anybody else ever came in to skate. Why was she working her butt off to keep this place in good shape? Why not let it all go to hell? Sooner or later she'd have to. It was too expensive to maintain.

But there was something soothing about the work, about the swish of the squeegee and the rhythmical arm movements. It sometimes helped take her mind off the things that made her sad. Lexie.

She could almost see Lexie now, gliding backward in a graceful arabesque, one arm above her head. Or glumly tracing her school figures, her tongue sticking out just a little as she concentrated on getting them right. She had been so beautiful, Lexie. So free. She was going to be so important . . . before. . . . Beulah sighed deeply from her worn-out boots to her battered old hat. If only . . .

If only what? If only she'd been there to hold out her arm, to keep Lexie from jumping, from crashing into that iron table? If only she could be of some help; if only Lexie would let her come close again! But the girl rejected everything that Beulah had in her power to offer, which was —what? Pity? Of what the hell use was pity, anyhow? It didn't help you to see, when you were blind. She couldn't say as she blamed Lexie, cutting herself off that way from everything and everybody. Nothing could make her see any better, nothing could give her back what she'd lost.

The sound of a bowling ball racketing down an alley cut into her reverie. Beulah stopped sponging the ice and sat up. Who the hell was in there at this hour of the morning? Whoever it was, he hadn't paid for an alley. That was for sure. The lanes were closed. And from the sound of it, whoever it was hadn't hit a single pin. The crash of ball against backboard was unmistakable. It was followed by another ball racketing down the lane, evidently thrown from an illegal height. Who was tearing up the pea patch in there, dammit?

"Dammit!" came like an echo from the lanes, as the heavy ball knocked over only two pins. "Come on, God-damn you!" rasped a man's voice, drunk, by the sound of it.

Irritated, Beulah got to her feet, pulling off her leather work gloves. Some damn fool was in there busting up her alley, and now she had to stop what she was doing and go kick ass. What a pain! She took a deep, angry breath and headed for the pit, coming up inside the third lane and crouching down so that she could see up the alleys.

"What the hell?" growled Beulah. It was Marcus.

"Hey, Marcus! What the hell do you think you're doing?" she hollered.

Without replying, Marcus moved down a lane and picked up another bowling ball. Furiously and without skill or judgment, he barreled the ball down the alley, straight at Beulah's head; she had to jump right smart to avoid getting clobbered. Another pin wobbled and limped around on its axis, finally falling down.

"What the hell is the matter with you, Marcus?" demanded Beulah angrily. "You drunk or something? The alley's not open. Pin boy doesn't come on 'til four."

"You set 'em," suggested Marcus, slurring his words. "Do something useful for a change." He reeled over and hefted another ball, aiming down the lane. Beulah's head looked just like another pin.

"Hey!" protested Beulah in alarm. "I'm still in the lane!" But Marcus was already taking another shot, and the big black ball came charging down at her. With surprising agility, Beulah jumped out of the pit just as the ball came crashing into the pins, sending them flying. Now she was mad, damn mad!

"Damn you, stop it!" she yelled, her face red. "What the hell are you trying to do anyway?"

She ran through the door that led to the bowling lanes and came face to face with Marcus Winston. He was wearing his field boots, not bowling shoes, and they were leaving marks on the varnish. Also, he was standing way over the foul line, almost on the lane itself, and was squinting down over yet another ball. He appeared to be pretty drunk for eleven in the morning.

"I said stop it, Marcus. Now that's *it!* You get the hell out of here, or I'll get Matt down here to throw your ass out! Hear me?" By now, Beulah was almost purple in the face.

Marcus turned to grin at her, but he didn't set the bowling ball down. "Help, poleeeeece!" He mimicked her in a falsetto voice totally unlike Beulah's masculine growl. Then he threw back his head for a sour laugh. "Hell, yes. *Get* the goddamned police. I think I'll play another alley." He turned his wavering steps to the next lane, leaving more footprints on the polished wood.

Beulah glared after him and rubbed her foot angrily against the marks he'd left on the floor. "You got ten seconds to move your ass," she threatened.

But Marcus was looking at her now, seriously, sadly.

"She ever talk to you?" he asked quietly.

The question took Beulah by surprise, and she could only stare at Marcus, who stared back at her helplessly. It was evident now that he wasn't as drunk as he was pretending to be, probably not drunk at all.

"I mean," continued Marcus in the same low, pleading tone, "you go up there and sit in her room all the time. All I ever hear is the damn TV. I mean, what do you two talk about?"

Beulah didn't answer, and Marcus let the ball fly down the alley with a savage motion of his hand. A strike.

"I mean, the two of you both being such skaters and having the same experience . . . winning the Regionals and all . . . you two must have a lot to . . ."

"She won the Sectionals," corrected Beulah quietly. She wasn't angry at Marcus anymore. Even his work boots didn't irritate her. She felt only overwhelming pity for the man and his misery.

"Must have a lot to talk about, you two," repeated Marcus, picking up another bowling ball and letting fly.

This time he didn't even bother to aim; it was a gesture filled with grief and frustration. Beulah just stood there, looking at the ball, which bounced into the gutter.

"We watch TV," she said at last. But she spoke so quietly that Marcus was unable to catch her words.

"What?" he demanded.

"I said we watch TV. We sit in the damn room and watch the damn TV." Beulah's voice carried a burden of hopelessness and despair.

"She can't see it!" Obviously, Marcus had difficulty accepting what Beulah was saying. There had to be more than that! There had to be!

"She listens. She listens and I watch. Okay?"

She snatched up a rag, dropped it on the alley and began cleaning Marcus' footprints off the varnish. It relieved some of her feelings to work.

Marcus stood by, watching her. His face was contorted in pain, and he tried to communicate the heart of his pain to this tall woman who was Lexie's only friend.

"I got all that stuff from school," he explained. "The tapes of her classes, and the stuff the social worker gave me. Notes, and all. Her homework. Her exams. Hell, I don't know what to do. She just sits there and says, what's the use of graduating from high school. Hell, the least she can do is graduate from high school!"

"Why?" asked Beulah bitterly.

Marcus turned on her, anger flooding his handsome face. "Oh, that's great!" he yelled sarcastically. "You're a great goddamn help! I mean, if you hadn't filled her up with all that crap . . ." Now he adopted that falsetto voice again, mimicking Beulah. "You oughtta do it just once," he simpered, then his voice deepened again, husky with anger. "Well, she did—"

Now it was Beulah's turn to be angry, a rage born of guilt. "Don't you start on me, Marcus Winston," she interrupted furiously. "Don't you dare start on me! You sittin' out there holding onto her, like she was some damn doll—" She broke off, unable or unwilling to continue.

The two of them glared at each other, breathing heavily.

166

Each of them felt the other was more to blame; each of them knew that there was no point in placing blame anywhere. Blame wasn't going to help Lexie. If only they didn't feel so damn helpless.

Finally, Marcus broke their locked gazes and turned away. He seemed to have won the fight for control over himself because when he spoke next it was quietly, brokenly and without apparent anger; but with infinite sadness. And sorrow. The sorrow of a man who has lost all hope.

"I want her . . . to be . . . okay. I . . . she's dying out there. Maybe it's my fault," he told Beulah in an agonized whisper. "Maybe it . . . I can't seem to do anything for her. . . . If I could only . . . I just . . . don't want her . . . to be like this. . . . She's all there is . . ." He choked back the tears.

Marcus looked beseechingly at Beulah, who tried to find the words to give him comfort, but failed. She could only stare after him mutely when he turned abruptly and left the rink. If he couldn't help Lexie, who could?

Beulah approached the Winston house for her next visit, with shoulders slumped, and her face set in a grim expression of despair. It had been several days since she'd seen Lexie, several days since Marcus had come to ask her help at the bowling alley. During that time, Beulah had searched her soul in anguish. Had she done all that she could? Was there anything that could relieve Lexie's loss of spirit, something that she, Beulah hadn't thought of? She gave a brief thought to religion but rejected it. It was hardly her business to preach salvation, seeing as she stood in the need of it herself. There was no girl friend of Lexie's own age to be a sister to her now; Lexie's only friend had been Nick.

And where was Nick? Hiding out on his farm, ashamed to show his face around town. He'd let Lexie—all of them —down, and Beulah wondered why, again and again. It wasn't like Nick to do that; in the old days, Beulah would have staked her life against it happening. Just goes to show how little you know about people you think you know real good.

Beulah sighed as she moved up the stairs to Lexie's room. Maybe she could convince the child to shut off the TV today and talk to her a little. It would be a start. But when she pushed open the door to Lexie's room, she gasped in dismay. It was a mess. The photographs and posters that had adorned the walls—Lexie's dreams, Lexie's heroes, Lexie's plan for living—had been ripped down. Bits of Scotch tape were stuck to the wall everywhere, and pieces of the wallpaper had been torn away, exposing the bare plaster underneath.

"Lexie!" Beulah's anxiety increased as she saw that the room was empty. "Lexie?" she asked again, louder, but there was no reply.

"Lexie?" Beulah stepped out into the hallway again and looked around. The door leading to the attic was half-open. No, it was impossible! Lexie couldn't have made it all the way up to the attic. The stairs were treacherous and the attic itself filled with the junk and debris of years. For Lexie it would be like walking through a mine field. And yet . . . Beulah fancied she heard a sound. She went to the door and pushed it open. The half-darkened stairs were empty, but she heard a noise coming from the attic.

Taking tentative steps, one step at a time, Beulah ascended into the attic. Standing in the doorway, almost fearfu, she peered inside. It took her a minute for her eyes to become accustomed to the near-darkness; so it was a minute before she spotted Lexie.

Somehow the girl had negotiated her way through the stacked-up piles of forgotten books and furniture, the dangerous sharp objects that filled the neglected attic. She was sitting on the dusty floor, by the side of an old steamer trunk. The lid of the trunk was open, and Lexie had been pulling things out of it—old, stored clothing—finding them by touch, stroking and feeling the worn-out fabrics.

Beulah stood dumbfounded, then a terrible angry sadness washed over her. There was something so ineffably pathetic about the little girl—and she *was* a little girl, she

168

looked at this moment no more than twelve—sitting on the floor in the dark, blindly clutching an old dress to her cheek. It made Beulah want to break down, right there, and bawl like an infant.

"Lexie," she said softly.

The girl's head came up like a deer's, startled, and she turned her sightless face in Beulah's direction. Instinctively, she held the dress more tightly, as though Beulah had been sent to take it away from her.

"Honey," said Beulah slowly, approaching her as one would a startled deer. "Honey—" She broke off, appalled. "Oh, my God, Lexie," she breathed, unable to take her eyes off the girl.

Lexie's golden hair was a matted mess, tangled, stringy, hanging over her face in colorless, greasy strands. Her face was filthy, not only unwashed, but with dried food caked in the corners of her mouth. Over her torn shirt she had pulled an ancient sweater, which was in holes where the moths had gotten to it. Beulah had some dim memory of that sweater. Altogether, the girl resembled a mangy old cat that had been abandoned in the rain to die.

Beulah's heart turned in her chest, but she fought to control her voice and didn't speak until she was sure the words would sound casual.

"Well, it looks like you're getting around pretty well."

Lexie didn't answer, but her hands had stopped stroking the old dress. She sat very still, but she looked ready to bolt at the slightest start.

"That your mother's stuff, in the trunk?" asked Beulah. She walked over and peered in, then looked around the room, her eye taking inventory. An abandoned sewing machine, a crib, the rocking chair out of Lexie's room— the kind of stuff that belongs in an attic and nowhere else. Dead stuff.

"Come on, Lexie, let's go downstairs."

But Lexie didn't move, not even a muscle in her rigid hands.

"Lex, you've got to get out of here! This is no place for you!" Beulah moved forward and touched the girl on the

169

shoulder, and Lexie shrank back against the trunk, shaking her head.

"Is that your mother's sweater?" demanded Beulah suddenly. "Are you getting stuff out of that trunk? Lexie, is that your mother's sweater? Take it off." Inexplicably, it became terribly important to Beulah to get Lexie out of those old clothes and away from there. The sight of her tiny figure in that moth-eaten sweater enraged Beulah; she was close to hysterical now. She reached for the sweater and tried to tug it from Lexie's shoulders, but the girl clung to it desperately.

"Leave . . . me . . . alone!" Lexie croaked.

"Oh, so you can talk!" Beulah shouted. "If you can talk, you can do something. You can get off your tail and do something!" Once again, she grabbed at the sweater, ripping the sleeve as Lexie twisted frantically in her grasp. "Get it off! Get the damn thing off!"

For some reason, the sweater had come to symbolize for Beulah all the defeat and despair in the household, all the clinging to moth-eaten comforts that were of no use whatever. The sweater of a dead woman had no business on a live woman's back. Its woolen folds seemed to embrace Lexie and bring her that much closer to death—the death of her dreams and hopes. And Beulah's.

Growling low in her throat like an animal, Beulah made another attack on the sweater, this time managing to pull Lexie's determined little body away from the trunk.

"Get out of here!" shrieked Lexie. Hanging on for dear life to her mother's old sweater, she began to fight back in earnest.

But Beulah wouldn't accept defeat, and she brushed away Lexie's fists, snarling with rage. "Poor little Lexie Winston! She was so promising. But then she went blind, and now she just sits in the attic in her dead mother's clothes. Give it to me!" she yelled, as the sweater began to rip under her clutching fingers. "Give it to me! I won't have you wearing that sweater!" She ripped and tore at Lexie, anger and grief mingling in her rasping sobs.

Terrified, Lexie struggled to her feet and tried to escape

the tearing hands, but Beulah pursued her, reaching for the tattered fragments of the sweater.

"You're not . . . going to get . . . away with this," the woman sobbed. "You're not going . . . to do this . . . to me. You're not going to sit up here . . . and I spent time . . . damn you . . . we worked . . ." Beulah's sobs were giving way to gasps.

"Who the hell are you anyway?" demanded Lexie, in tears. "Leave me the hell alone! Go away and leave me alone!"

But Beulah was ripping the last shred of the sweater off Lexie's body with a short, sharp cry. Then she straightened up, trying to catch her breath from the exertion, while Lexie, backing off, stumbled over a chair behind her and nearly fell.

"I'll tell you who the hell I am . . . I'll tell you who the hell I am!" howled Beulah. "I'm a stupid character in stupid clothes, running a goddamned stupid bowling alley and that ice rink. It's goddamned pathetic. And I come up here and I look at you, and I see—" She moved up to Lexie and, seizing the girl by her shoulders, began to shake her. "I see, damn you . . . I spent time . . . I spent *time* so you'd be different!" She shook her again and again, out of control, unable to stop. She had tried to live through Lexie, and both of them had failed.

Lexie's head bobbed wildly, and she couldn't see anything but an angry blur in front of her. The shaking was making her dizzy and ill, and she felt as helpless as a rag doll. With a mighty effort of strength, she pulled herself free of Beulah's violent hands, but the woman's voice pursued her still.

"Now we'll never know what you were made of, will we? What can you expect of a helpless invalid? Hell, nobody blames helpless invalids for giving up." Beulah's voice raised to a pitch that cracked it. "Isn't that what you were doing when you took that goddamned jump? You were looking for a goddamned way out! Well, you sure as hell found one!"

Beulah's words cut into Lexie like a knife and made her

gasp in pain and surprise. A terrible fury gripped her, shaking her as hard as Beulah's hands a minute ago. She searched her mind for the words to fling back at the woman, to make Beulah hurt all over the way she was hurting; but the words were as hidden to her as Beulah's face, and all she could manage was the fury.

"Son . . . of . . . a . . . bitch," she managed to choke out through gritted teeth. "You son of a bitch."

There was so much pain and anguish mingled with the fury, and she was so totally unused to speaking like this that it was doubly shocking and profane.

Beulah stopped, startled. This was the voice of somebody in mortal agony. It brought her back to her senses somewhat.

"I'm sorry, Lex. I just . . . I just can't stand this. I mean, you can't use your mother. Your father's been doing that for ten years. There's no room for you—"

Suddenly, Lexie was screaming and thrashing, coming at her like a wild mountain cat, her claws out. She was following the sound of Beulah's voice, but Beulah, caught by surprise, took a step out of the way, and Lexie ran into an old desk chair, knocking it over.

"Well, if you can see well enough to fight back—" Beulah began.

Growling with rage, Lexie flew forward at her again, her furious hands balled into fists, looking for Beulah to pummel. Again she missed, and this time she tripped over the trunk and went sprawling to the floor. But as Beulah bent to help her, Lexie twisted her wiry body around and caught Beulah amidships with her fist, striking hard.

With a grunt, Beulah caught Lexie and held onto her fists in a grip of steel. Still trying to strike out, Lexie twisted and turned, the lank hair flopping into her blind face, tears of anger cutting clean furrows in her dirty face. For a few minutes the two of them struggled desperately, life and death in this tug-of-war, the older woman holding on for life, the girl screaming incoherent words of pain. Around them, the attic was filled with the shadows of dead

172

things and dead memories, a fitting arena for mortal combat.

At last, exhausted, Lexie stopped struggling. Beulah let go of her wrists; she, too, was worn out. Both of them plopped to the floor, breathing hard, and sat silently in the dust, still face to face. Beulah took a deep breath and spoke, her words heavy with affection.

"All I can say is, you're pretty tough for being blind and only four-ten."

Lexie took a breath. "Five-three."

Beulah smiled and touched the girl's matted hair affectionately. The gesture triggered a release in Lexie, and her shoulders shook suddenly with long, terrible gasps.

"I didn't mean to hurt myself," cried the girl, her face contorted by her howls. "I didn't mean to hurt myself. I didn't mean . . ."

Beulah leaned forward and gathered Lexie in her arms.

"I didn't think you did, honey," she said. It would probably do Lexie good to deny it. She stroked the tangled hair with her work-roughened fingers, soothing the child. "I didn't think you did. It's all right, baby. It doesn't matter now. We just love you and we want you back. Just come back to us."

As she rocked Lexie in her arms on the splintery old attic floor, it occurred to Beulah that they had touched bottom here today, both she and Lexie.

From here, there was nowhere to go but up.

12

Marcus almost tiptoed up the stairs leading to Lexie's room. An hour ago, he'd heard the bathwater flowing into the tub, but from that time on—silence, as usual. Now he knocked gently on Lexie's door and waited, his heart in his mouth, for her to tell him to go away. Instead, the door opened.

Lexie stood in the doorway, fully dressed in clean clothes. She had bathed and washed her hair and had combed out the tangles. It was pulled into a fluffy golden ponytail, though the part wasn't straight.

Marcus' face broke into a wide smile. "Hey," he breathed, beaming at his daughter proudly. "Hey, you look terrific."

But there was no answering smile in Lexie's face. Fresh-scrubbed though it was, the expression was still vacant, the face as blind as the eyes. Marcus' own smile began to die.

"Come on, let's go get some breakfast," he said, and he led the way down the stairs and into the kitchen.

They sat in silence while Lexie sipped at her coffee, making no comment at all on its thickness and bitterness. She crumbled a roll but barely tasted it.

"Wanna go out, Lexie?" Marcus asked tentatively. "Let's go to the pond, huh?"

"All right."

"Uh . . . let's take your skates."

"All right."

Now he stood at the fallen log, looking down at Lexie as she laced up her champion's skates. The blades gleamed under the fine leather boots; the boots themselves hugged Lexie's slender ankles and clung snugly to her heels in a perfect fit.

"Nice boots," said Marcus.

"The best," answered Lexie briefly, with a wry little twist of her lips.

"Ready?" He gave her his hand, and Lexie stood up uncertainly. But she didn't take a step toward the ice. Instead, she held onto her father's gloved hand, her unseeing eyes turned away from the pond.

"That's enough," she said suddenly.

"What's enough?" Marcus was caught off balance, and he looked at her in surprise. But Lexie's face wore no expression at all.

"I don't feel like going out today," she said stubbornly.

Marcus opened his mouth to protest, but it occurred to him that Lexie had already had a pretty full day. Yesterday she wouldn't come down from the attic. Today she was standing at the brink of the pond with her champion ice skates on her feet. Whatever had passed between Lexie and Beulah yesterday—he'd heard the thumps and the screams and the crying but had forced himself to stay downstairs and not interfere—whatever had happened, he was grateful for it. Tomorrow was another day; Lexie could take her first steps tomorrow. He was grateful enough for today.

"Okay," he said mildly, as Lexie sat back down on the log and bent to unlace her skates. "Okay, honey."

It was a couple of days before Lexie had the nerve to go out on the ice. When she did, it was only to take a few tiny, tottering steps forward, clinging to Marcus for dear life. But she took those steps.

Then one day, when they headed for the pond, he noticed that Lexie had brought her old Phantoms instead of her championship skates, and his heart leaped up gladly. It meant that she cared, that she didn't want to spoil her competition blades on the uneven surface of the pond. She had noticed the difference and had made a decision. Marcus felt it was the most positive, hopeful sign of recovery he'd seen since the day she'd washed her hair.

Marcus looked out over the pond as Lexie laced up her boots. They didn't have much time. A few weeks at the most. Winter was just about over, even though the sharp wind carried drifting snow over the surface of the ice. This cold snap couldn't last forever; already the farmer's weather service carried radio bulletins of warm weather coming in from the east and the south. Soon there would be a thaw, and the ice would begin to melt.

But he couldn't think of that today. Instead, his eyes searched the surface of the nearby ice, looking for sticks and small stones the wind might have carried out onto the surface. Anything that could catch in a blade was a hazard, even to a sighted skater. He looked, too, for rough spots in the ice itself, where the rippling of the water had caused it to freeze unevenly. On the large indoor rinks to which Lexie had been accustomed, the big Zamboni machine had kept the ice spotless and perfect, resurfacing it to mirror slickness between uses. All Marcus could do was take his old shovel and clear the pond's surface where Lexie would be skating. He was no Zamboni.

"I guess you know the old pond pretty well," he said quietly.

Lexie nodded her head and looked around. All she could see was a blur of white across which nothing moved.

"Ice is still good and thick," Marcus informed her. "So don't worry about that."

For the first time, something almost like the ghost of a smile flickered across Lexie's face. Flickered and was gone. "I'm worried about standing up, not falling through," she said.

Then, for the first time since her accident had cut her off from everything she'd ever known, Lexie Winston took a solo step onto the ice. For an instant, she felt like a baby; the blades buckled beneath her wobbly ankles and she began to slip a little, but before Marcus could step out onto the ice and give her his hand, Lexie's back straightened, and she bent her knees a little, achieving her balance. Then she pushed her right skate forward, taking a step. Then her left. Again. And once more. She was skating. As a beginner skates, as a little child skates. Nevertheless, Lexie Winston was skating.

Marcus held his breath and kept his feet planted firmly on the pond's bank. He wouldn't go out there, much as he wanted to. She needed to do it alone, even if she fell.

She fell. The wind came up suddenly, catching Lexie in the back and speeding her along faster than she'd intended. Scared, she waved her arms wildly, like a beginner, and she lost her balance and fell. For a minute, she sat sprawled on the ice, bewildered and disoriented. She looked around for Marcus and found him, a dark blur on the pond's bank. A dark, unmoving blur. It was up to her, and she struggled to her feet and found her balance once again.

For another fifteen minutes she skated alone, back and forth on a small area of the ice near the edge of the pond. With each gliding stroke she seemed to gain—infinitesimally—assurance, but it was the assurance of a learning child, not a practiced skater. Still, Marcus' heart lifted as he watched her. She still had so far to go, but look at how far she had come! He was proud of her.

As to what he expected—well, he wasn't sure. Looking at it from a practical point of view, he was convinced that once Lexie gained a small measure of freedom on the ice, she would move with more assurance at home, too, and learn to compensate somewhat for her loss of vision. At the same time Marcus felt an unspoken conviction that somehow, even a little, the ice could restore to Lexie something of what it had taken away. A sense of belonging, of purpose, a sense of her own worth as a human being. These were vague, wordless hopes more than expectations, but they warmed Marcus.

Suddenly the wind shifted and it caught Lexie full in the face unexpectedly. Once more she fell, this time backward, and for a moment it appeared to Marcus that she'd struck her head. Without thinking, he started forward, and out of the corner of his eye, he caught a movement behind him. He turned.

Nick Peterson had also taken an unconscious step forward, coming out from behind a tree. Anger ran through Marcus with sudden heat. What the hell was he doing there? Hadn't he turned Marcus down; hadn't he sworn he no longer gave a damn about Lexie? Marcus opened his mouth to shoo the boy away, to holler at him and cuss him, but the look of pain on Nick's face was so apparent that he closed it again. Marcus realized at that moment that Nick was suffering as much as he was.

Lexie was on her feet again, unhurt. But the wind had risen and was blowing full force in her face, and she struggled against it, vulnerable and suddenly very small.

"Hey, honey," yelled Marcus, cupping his hand to bring his words to her over the wind. "Hey, honey, that's enough for today. Come back home now."

Lexie nodded to show she'd heard and skated slowly back in the direction of the dark blur that was her father. She didn't know about Nick, and Marcus didn't mention him.

*　　*　　*

In the days that followed, Lexie gained new confidence. Every day Marcus brought her to the pond, and every day she skated longer and better. She was learning to recognize the rough parts of the ice, and she ventured further and further away from the bank, until she was moving gracefully around the center of the pond, picking up speed. She had still not tried anything fancy, and Marcus didn't encourage her. It was enough for him to see color back in her cheeks, an occasional smile on her face and the new sureness with which she moved. She talked to him more, too, not about anything important, not about how she felt or what she thought, but about the coming of spring and how bitter his coffee still was and how come Beulah was staying away and wouldn't she be surprised to see Lexie skating.

Marcus, feeling happier than he'd felt in years, spent as much time as he could with Lexie, never telling her that Beulah was demanding daily bulletins on the girl's progress, or that Nick came to the pond every day to watch her from a distance.

Even with all the assurance she had gained, Lexie was still far from secure on the ice. She hadn't been blind long enough to be accustomed to it; she still kept turning her head from side to side to *see*. Every shadow made her veer and swerve; dark objects such as a fallen log were perceived by her only at the last minute and only dimly.

Still, it wasn't long before she tried a jump. Moving over the ice swiftly, she was suddenly overcome by an urge to fly, to lift off and soar high, as she used to. Bending her knee, she jumped. It was a small lift, and a simple one, but as she left the ice, Lexie let go of her instincts and panic seized her. She *couldn't see*—she was going to fall! So, of course, she did fall, landing awkwardly on both skates instead of one. Her feet tangled and she came down in a heap on the hard surface of the pond. Furious with herself and humiliated, she sat dumbly on the ice, unwilling to get up.

"Here. There's a hand in front of you. Grab it!" said a harsh but familiar voice.

Lexie looked, saw the darkness of the leather-mittened hand, then looked up. Nick, it was Nick. His height

180

loomed over her, although she couldn't make out his face, or see the expression on it.

"What are you doing here?" she asked, not taking his hand.

"I came to see you break your ass."

Lexie bit her lip, completely confused. "I can't . . . I can't see you very well, so I don't know if you're kidding."

"Listen to my voice," said Nick. "I'm not kidding." He thrust his hand at her again, and this time Lexie took it and allowed him to pull her to her feet. He was on skates; she could feel it.

Taking Lexie's hand in his, Nick put his other arm around her waist. They skated out over the ice together, with Nick leading strongly. It took Lexie a few minutes to adjust her stride to his longer one, but soon they were moving in unison, and Lexie felt the comfort and safety of it from her toe picks up to her ponytail.

On the bank, Marcus watched the two of them, and he felt torn between satisfaction and jealousy. Still, Nick's being there with Lexie gave Marcus a chance to get back to those goddamned cows. Lately, he'd been neglecting them.

From that afternoon on, Nick and Lexie skated together every day. In fact, Lexie didn't want to go out on the ice without him, didn't want to skate alone any more. The feeling of his arm around her waist, his tall strength supporting hers, filled her with a deep need to be close to him. But off the ice he was cold to her; every day he picked her up and took her skating, then brought her home and left her there. He never stayed to talk to her. He never even came in the door.

Whenever Lexie was on the ice, she felt happy and more secure. At all other times she was confused and plagued by doubts. She knew that she loved Nick, really loved him. But he made it plain that he had changed toward her; he treated her coldly, and whenever she pressed against him, he pushed her away. But, then, why was he skating with her? Why did he come to her every day and guide her around the ice, his strong arms helping to bear her up, if he didn't love her—even just a little? Sadly, she came to the conclusion that she was an object of pity to him. He was sorry for her.

"Don't lean," Nick ordered. "Feel your own balance." He pushed Lexie away from his supporting arm.

"I'm trying," complained Lexie. "It's hard. I keep trying to see where I am."

"Shut your eyes. Do what I tell you."

Lexie hesitated.

"Go on, Lexie. Shut them!" urged Nick.

With an effort of will, Lexie commanded her eyes shut. At once, she felt a different sensation. Suddenly, skating seemed to the girl the only logical way to move. It felt natural to skim along like this, side by side with Nick. Subtly, without even being aware of it, her blades picked up speed to match Nick's, until they were skimming, sailing, gliding along the surface of the pond like twin sailboats. Finally, Lexie was skating smoothly, effortlessly, without hesitation. It made all the difference in the world, not straining to make out what she couldn't see. With her eyes shut, Lexie let her body's instincts take over and do the seeing for her, and the long years of practice came back. Her body wasn't letting her down.

Every day it got better. Every day, when Lexie and Nick stepped out on the ice, she shut her eyes and away they flew. By now, they skated together with the comfort and the familiar grace of a doubles team. Nothing fancy, but always together. The days grew warmer, and a spring breeze brought the smell of the season's growth over the pond. Soon it would be too warm to skate out of doors. Lexie felt a touch of apprehension, because Nick was still not talking to her off the ice. Nothing seemed to be abating his anger; many times Lexie recalled that kiss she'd given Brian, wondering if Nick had seen. And each time she shivered, wishing that moment out of existence.

She never thought about the accident anymore. Resolutely, she had put her plast glories out of her thoughts. Brian and Deborah seemed very far away and very small, like tiny figures on the other end of a long tunnel. Only

182

Nick was real to her now. Right after the accident, she'd spent many miserable hours wondering which promising skater Deborah was coaching now or whom Brian was kissing. But she never thought about them any more. Only her hours on the ice with Nick were real; only then did Lexie come alive.

Those were the only real hours for Nick, too, but he was still determined not to let Lexie know it. He hardly admitted to himself how much he looked forward to picking her up, and how he hated to bring her home and leave her. Their ice time had stretched from a half hour to an hour, then from one hour to two, but there was still a time when he had to let her go. There was something else he was hiding from her, something he was just about to reveal, a little at a time.

Nick had a plan, not completely formed, but still a plan. It involved Lexie, and it involved skating, and most of all it involved Lexie skating by herself. For weeks now, she had been leaning on him, but the time had come for her to learn to stand on her own two blades. He could feel the overwhelming love and dependence pouring out of her toward him, but it troubled him. Lexie, blind, was difficult enough for him to swallow. But Lexie, blind and dependent, was impossible. It would ruin her life and his too if he let it happen.

"Okay, stay loose, easy . . . very smooth . . . all *right!*" said Nick. They had been skating side by side, picking up speed, his arm around her waist. Then, in a single side-stepping move he had eased her away from him and was skating hand-in-hand with her. Finally, he let go, until they were skating side by side, but at a distance. Immediately, Lexie's eyes flew open, and she looked around for Nick.

"Keep your eyes *closed!*" ordered Nick. "Keep skating. I'm right here. I'll talk to you."

Lexie forced herself to relax and keep skating. Again she shut her eyes and listened for Nick's voice. She could feel him still skating alongside her.

"All right. Start to make a gradual turn to the left."

A turn? Lexie's body obeyed the command, and she made a somewhat shaky turn, her first alone since the accident.

"Now ease right," came Nick's command.

A smile crossed Lexie's lips. This was more fun than she'd expected. She eased right and made a one-foot turn, skating toward the bank of the pond.

"Now reverse," ordered Nick. "Slow . . . slowly . . ."

Without thinking about it, Lexie performed a simple three-turn; she was now skating backward over the pond, away from the bank and toward the center. Nick still skated near her, but not as close as before. She kept her eyes shut and listened for his next commands.

"Remember the pond," instructed Nick. "Put the image in your head. Just like you were looking at it. Don't turn your head. I'm right here. Now, pick up a little speed. Do you know where you are?"

Lexie willed her eyes to stay closed. What was the good of opening them? Everything was just one white blur anyway. "North," she said hesitatingly. "I'm heading north."

"That's right."

"The log . . . is to the right. . . ." said Lexie, concentrating.

"About fifty feet," agreed Nick. "Thirty-five. Twenty. Come on pick up some speed on the turn. Now!"

Lexie obeyed, turning more quickly and much more smoothly than before, skating backward away from the treacherous log, back to the center of the pond.

Good girl, said Nick silently. Aloud, he ordered, "Now do an axel."

Instantly, Lexie faltered, lost speed. She shook her head a terrified no. Rotate in midair? How could she?

"Do it!" cried Nick harshly.

Instead, Lexie did another turn, skating away from the sound of his voice.

"Come on, Lexie, do it!" pleaded Nick.

Confused and afraid, Lexie continued to shake her head. She was skating in a wide arc, with no direction to

184

guide her. Her eyes were open wide, and glancing fearfully from side to side, she strained to see what she couldn't see.

"I . . . *can't!*" she wailed.

Nick headed for her, skating hard, his face set in a determined scowl. "Bullshit!" he yelled, reaching her. Grabbing her shoulders, he gave her a little shake. "Come on! We're going round again." He put one hand on her waist and held her other hand, and they skated off together.

As she could feel them gathering speed, Lexie experienced a rush of terror. Nick really wanted her to do an axel! But she still felt like a five-year-old on her first skates. True, she could skate with Nick. But he wanted to let her go to fly alone over the hard coldness of the ice, alone and blind. She wouldn't even be able to see where she was going, where or how she would land. She couldn't.

"No, Nick . . ." she pleaded, but he cut her off.

"We're going to straighten out after this turn and you're going to do it." He gave her a slight push to prevent her from leaning her weight against him.

"What are you doing?" Lexie's voice held a rising note of panic.

"You're gutless," growled Nick in her ear. It was a desperation measure, but it worked. At once, Lexie moved away from him, straightening her body out, picking up speed.

"You bastard!" she snarled over her shoulder. As she came out of the turn, Nick gave her a sharp thrust foward —sharper perhaps than he'd intended—and Lexie shot off ahead of him, skating like fury toward the center of the ice.

"Can't you do it without the TV cameras?" taunted Nick.

Angered by his words, and before she'd stopped to think, Lexie left the ice in a single clean axel. It was instinctive, and it felt right. To be flying again, even in the simplest jump, gave her a sudden rush of pleasure, of

185

simple delight that carried her even higher. Her body was reacting without fear and without hesitation.

"Good . . . great!" Nick was unable to conceal his excitement as he watched Lexie jump forward into the air, her body one perfect line of movement.

But Lexie made a mistake. As she left the ice, she opened her eyes instinctively to check out her landing point. All she could see was a blur, and she turned her head in panic from side to side as she spun in the jump. The overwhelming terror of her accident, that awful fall that cost her her vision as well as her championship, came back to her with vivid suddenness, and fear gripped her heart. In midair, she lost her balance and fell heavily to the ice, still spinning in circles like a human top. As she came slowly to a stop, sprawled out clumsily on the pond, sobs of frustration shook her thin frame.

Nick skated toward Lexie swiftly, concern written all over him, but as he got closer he could see that she wasn't hurt, only scared, bruised and angry. He skated to a stop, just short of her, but didn't hold out his hand or bend to help her up.

"You shouldn't have opened your eyes" was all he said.

Lexie had been crying and holding the surface of the ice with both mittens, as though to hang onto it. At Nick's words, fury and indignation contorted her lovely features, and she reached out blindly for him, hitting out at her unseen enemy. Nick moved easily out of the way of her thrashing fists.

"Come here, you rat!" sobbed Lexie, wanting to kill him. "Come here!"

But Nick stood to one side and watched her. "You're sure a better skater than you are a fighter."

Goaded by his words, Lexie struck out again and again, hitting nothing. All at once, she stopped and rested her hands on the ice, her shoulders slumping in defeat and despair.

"I hate you," she said in a low, husky voice. "I really hate you. You're . . ." She couldn't find the words. "I hate you," she repeated dully. "I really hate you."

"Well, that makes us even," said Nick lightly, to mask his pain.

"You did it on purpose," accused Lexie. "You wanted me to fall."

Nick shrugged. "Maybe. What difference does it make? You just want to give up anyway. Now, are you going to sit there getting your ass wet or you going to get up?" He reached his hand out to help her up, but Lexie pushed it away from her angrily.

"Get your hand away. I don't need you to get up," she said, and struggled to her feet, brushing the loose snow off her jeans and sweater.

For a minute they stood, face to face, and a few feet apart, not speaking. At last, Nick broke the silence between them.

"Well, you wanta quit?" he demanded.

"Why are you doing this?" countered Lexie.

It was the question he'd been asking himself. Why was he doing this when he was still so angry with her, when he had seen her in the arms of another man, seen her face turn up for his kiss? He couldn't get that out of his mind. Why then was he spending hour after hour with Lexie, trying to restore her old independence? Why had he made a plan for her, when he had no plans for himself?

"I don't know," he sighed at last.

Lexie's face crumpled, but she held it together, and after a moment, she shrugged and even gave a small half-smile. Rubbing ruefully at the hip which had born the brunt of her fall, she said, "Well, at least I don't have to be afraid that you feel sorry for me."

At that, Nick gave a great and genuine shout of relieved laughter, and they skated off the ice, side by side, almost like friends. Yet, that night, Nick couldn't sleep, as again and again his restless mind probed into the future, finding it still as hopeless as he'd feared. Whatever lay ahead for him and Lexie, he was scared to death of it.

* * *

Nick and Marcus took their rifles out early the next morning, half-past six, to get the last few buck rabbits of winter. For half an hour they trudged silently through the melting snow, then Nick finally blurted out what was on his mind.

"I still love her."

Marcus looked at him out of the corner of his eye. "I thought so," he said heavily. "All the more reason to stay and help her. What the hell is all this about your leaving town again? Beulah told me you're takin' off."

"When I decided to help," said Nick slowly, his breath making smoke patterns in the frosty air, "I thought . . ." He groped for words. "Actually, I think I wanted to see her get hurt," he confessed.

"Yeah?"

"I can't do it," Nick sighed. All night he'd thought about nothing but getting away. This situation was more than he could handle by himself. Lexie blind, Lexie loving him, him loving Lexie, Lexie blind. It was like a tunnel with only one opening, and he kept beating his head against the tunnel wall.

"Going back to the Northstars?" asked Marcus sarcastically.

"You're too much," grinned Nick. He'd deserved that.

"Well, it sort of seems to me like you just have to get away from anything that looks tough," said Marcus. He was angry, deeply angry at this boy who loved, but was afraid to love enough. Hell, hadn't Marcus held onto Betsy until the day she died and long afterward?

"Ever skate on a pro team?" demanded Nick rather weakly.

"That's easy. You just get beat up. I'm talking about—"

"I know goddamned well what you're talking about," yelled Nick.

"Stop yer hollerin', you'll scare off the rabbits," Marcus told him dryly. "Look," he said with a pretended rush of sympathy for the boy, "I know the moves pretty well. Hell, there's nothin' wrong with playin' hockey, if that's what you really wanta do." He smiled at Nick. "Even if you're good enough, after a couple of years you're through, and you got the same problem. Only you're older and you've lost your room for maneuvering."

Nick listened glumly. Not only did he recognize the unpleasant truth in Marcus' words, but he understood that it wasn't hockey the two of them were talking about. It was life, and Nick's approach to it. And Marcus was right. He was absolutely right. You can't keep running away forever. Sometimes you have to stand still and let life catch up with you. Suddenly, Nick felt very tired. He shivered in the morning cold and took a deep breath.

"You're a real sonofabitch, you know that?" he told Marcus.

"I try" was all Marcus replied, but he felt a pang of elation. Nick had accepted the challenge.

But first, they had to bag some of those goddamned rabbits!

*　　*　　*

Beulah switched on the lights as Nick and Lexie followed her into the Ice Castle. Her frozen fingers fumbled with the keys, trying to get them out of the door.

"God," she muttered. "Five o'clock in the morning. I thought you were kidding." Secretly, she was pleased as hell. She never thought she'd see Lexie on the rink again, but according to Marcus and Nick, Lexie was skating again, and getting better, too. Now that the pond was melting, the Ice Castle was the logical place for them to come.

"Well, how's the old place look?" Nick asked Lexie, and Beulah gave a stifled shocked gasp at his levity.

"Fuzzy," said Lexie sourly, looking around.

Beulah smiled. The kid was all right. "That's the way I always saw it myself," she grinned, giving Lexie's waist a squeeze. "I'll make us some coffee."

Lexie moved forward slowly, finding her way to the rink by a kind of built-in radar she was beginning to develop. Beulah, watching her, could hardly believe she was blind. There was an enormous difference between the despairing child of a few weeks ago and the quietly confident young woman she was seeing now.

Lexie pushed open the door to the ice rink and moved around the hockey barrier to stand at the edge. She felt, rather than saw, Nick come up behind her.

"Soft spot still in the corner?" she asked.

"Yeah, a little bigger."

"Nobody will come in? You're sure?"

"It's five o'clock in the morning, for Godsakes." Amusement mingled with irritation in Nick's voice. "Here are your skates."

In her first hour on the rink, Lexie became familiar all over again with the special idiosyncracies of the rink's erratic surface. But soon Lexie had mastered it; she remembered every bump and ridge, no matter how slight, and she knew the length and breadth of the rink from barrier to barrier.

Beulah sat and drank coffee after coffee, watching incredulously as Nick and Lexie moved around the rink together, as swiftly as a pair of gulls on the surface of the ocean.

"Okay," called Nick suddenly. "Bye-bye, Lexie." He dropped back, leaving Lexie to skate alone. "Make a circle," he ordered, and Lexie obediently leaned outward into a turn. "Faster, let's go!"

Showing an amazing capacity to judge distance, Lexie skated quickly around the rink's perimeter, coming close to the guard rail, but no closer than a sighted skater would.

"Cut to the middle," Nick called, watching her hair flying as her slender body raced around the rink gracefully. "At the corner," he warned. "Now!"

Lexie made a good cut and angled across the ice.

"Halfway!" Nick guided her. "Fifty feet, thirty, ready . . . lay back!"

Moving in a wide arc, Lexie began to arch her upper body backward, in her own version of the spread eagle.

190

Her movements were poetically graceful, and Beulah could hardly believe her eyes.

"Reverse!" called Nick.

Still maintaining the same rate of speed, Lexie pulled herself upright and moved back in the opposite direction.

"Sideways leaning spin!" barked Nick.

"Straight line step sequence . . ."

That was less than perfect, but Lexie still maintained her confidence. She kept her eyes closed, Beulah noticed for the first time, but the girl's body seemed to be in total command of the brain.

Lexie headed toward the end of the rink, listening for Nick's commands.

"Thirty feet, twenty . . . speed turn!" he called sharply.

Lexie made a sharp turn and came back across the length of the ice, gathering speed. It was speed for a jump, Beulah noticed with sense of alarm. Lexie wasn't going to jump! She would break her neck. Beulah stood and opened her mouth to protest, but it was too late.

Lexie left the ice in a single axel, rotated in the air and came down—smoothly. It was not a great axel, but it was a damn good one, and Beulah, with a cry of pleasure, broke into spontaneous applause. Nick smiled, and Lexie grinned, but she wasn't finished yet. Nick was still keeping her on the job.

"Turn!" he called sharply. She was dangerously close to the restraining barrier.

Instinctively, Lexie made the move and skated swiftly away, back to the center and into a standing spin that turned into a sit-spin. Halfway down, the girl lost her control and fell, crashing one shoulder into the ice.

For an instant everybody froze, and Beulah uttered a gasp.

But Lexie was fine, sitting on the ice and laughing at herself.

"Hell," she chuckled as she struggled to her feet, "I did *that* when I could see!"

*   *   *

After that, every dawn saw Nick and Lexie at the rink. Beulah, unwilling to continue crawling out of bed at five, gave Nick a set of keys, and the two kids opened the place, made coffee and skated for two hours before Nick had to go back to the farm and work.

Every dawn saw Lexie stronger, more confident, even bolder. Nick's happiness grew along with Lexie's confidence. She had come this far because of his training. Her courage, maybe, but his training. For the first time in his life, he was beginning to experience a feeling of accomplishment, of personal worth. And he liked it.

"Your old man is so funny," he told her one morning at breakfast—they always ate breakfast at the Ice Castle, behind the bar of Beulah's cafe. "He works his tail off trying to pretend he isn't a farmer."

Lexie smiled fondly as she dropped a pair of Pop Tarts in the toaster. "He says in his head he's still a barn-stormer—"

"He wasn't a barnstormer," interrupted Nick with a touch of something mean in his voice. "He was a god-damned crop-duster. Barnstorming went out in the nine-teen thirties, for Chrissakes."

"He knows it," said Lexie simply. It was a reproach, and Nick felt the sting of it.

"Sorry." But Nick had a point to make. "I mean, if you're going to live your life as a farmer, *be* a goddamned farmer. If you don't want to be something, do something else."

He stopped talking to watch Lexie pour the coffee. She was amazing. Her hands found the cups and she lifted the pot over them, pouring to some beat in her own head that told her how long before the cups were filled. She didn't spill a drop. He was so proud of her.

"You know . . ." he told her slowly, reaching for the exact words that would make her understand. "It's like my being a doctor. I mean, you think you want to be a

192

doctor. Good money, nice life, but is that what you really want to *do?* At school, I used to sneak into classes, and into some of the operating theaters and watch. It was incredible . . . I mean I thought I liked it. I don't know. Parts of it were wonderful, only I kept thinking that maybe I'd run into something that I'd like better. Only then it'd be too late." He broke off, uncertain what to say next.

Lexie had listened to every word intently. She knew that though it was a year later, this was all the explanation, all the apology she was going to get from Nick. She thought that she was beginning to understand—just a little—what drove him so hard and kept him looking around that next corner and the next.

But it was time to finish breakfast and skate. More than anything, Lexie Winston wanted to get out on the ice.

The two of them moved onto the rink and skated together for ten minutes, enjoying the closeness and the privacy. Then Nick fell back and watched as Lexie went through her moves. She hardly needed a command anymore, and she didn't need guidance at all about the length of the rink or the distance between herself and the barriers. She knew the ice by heart now, and she moved over its surface quickly and well, enjoying herself immensely. Beulah had taken to maintaining the ice better, just for Lexie, washing its surface between sessions and trying to keep the rink as cold as the battered old refrigeration unit would allow.

Nick watched Lexie move, glorying in her skill. He could see something of the old Lexie there, something of the girl they once thought would win the gold medal in the Olympics. He stiffened as she left the ice, moving fast, rotating in midair, again and again. She came down perfectly, on her toe picks, with her arms curved in the air, but instead of skating on, she stopped short, breathing hard, the double-axel jump completed.

"A double!" shouted Nick ecstatically. He came racing

from the sidelines to embrace her. "Fantastic! You did a double!"

"Was it perfect?" demanded Lexie from the depths of the plaid shirt that was smothering her. "Was it?" She freed her face from Nick's chest and looked up at him, although she couldn't see him.

Nick held her at arm's length, grinning from ear to ear in delight and pride. "It was damn good." Then he grabbed her tightly again, hugging her without restraint, so proud of her that he didn't see her smile fading as he pulled her closely against him.

"What a girl! Oh, baby!!"

Suddenly, he seemed to realize just what he was doing; she had already realized it and had pulled away from him slightly, reaching out to touch his face with wondering fingers.

"I love you, Nick," said Lexie, against her will. "I . . . I know you don't like me very much anymore, but I . . . love . . . you." She caught her breath fearfully, waiting for his reply. If only she could see his face! Was he laughing at her? Sneering at her? She was trapped in an agony of half expectation, half fear.

For a long moment, Nick stared at Lexie, at the beauty of her face, the light that seemed to pour out of it. He realized that she couldn't see him, but somehow, because she was looking at him so hard with all that light coming straight out of her, words weren't the answer. He was trapped in an agony of his own, struggling to decide between commitment and the possibility of escape.

Commitment won out. Nick took Lexie's hand in his, the hand that was stroking his face. He brought it to his lips and kissed it, then he touched the soft cheek of his beloved, tracing a line with his fingers over her brows and lids, down her nose and along her chin, exploring the smoothness of her skin until he reached her throat, which he stroked. All the while, Lexie arched toward him in passionate longing, waiting for the moment that he would take her into his arms.

It came, and it was worth the wait, for Nick crushed

194

her slim body close in a long, deep kiss that fired them both. Embracing, they kissed again and again, feeding on each other's hungry mouths, touching through the heavy layers of clothing.

"Lex, I want you," murmured Nick, as he kissed her hair.

"Beulah—" protested Lexie.

"It's six." Nick shook his curly head. "She never comes in this early." He kissed her again and again. "My God, you're beautiful," he told her in a passionate whisper.

Lexie felt as though her very spirit was winging out of her body to join Nick's. "Oh, Nicky," she gasped. "My Nicky."

"I've wanted you as long as I can remember," he told her, honestly, for the first time. But Lexie had always known that, somewhere in the depths of her. It was that knowledge that had kept her alive through the worst times, through the days when there had been no Nick to hold in her arms, to kiss. He wants me as much as I want him!

"I don't know where you get these harebrained ideas!" yelled Marcus, pounding the kitchen table with the flat of his hand. He was really mad, and Nick knew he'd have to tread slowly here. He looked at Beulah for her reaction, but she sat quietly with the coffee cup in her hand, her eyes narrowed a little, watching, waiting.

"She can do it!" insisted Nick heatedly. "There's five months until the first competition. That's plenty of time."

"I don't care about any of that," Lexie protested. She looked ready to cry.

"Yes, you do!" Nick turned on her.

They'd been over this ground again and again for a week now, in private. Finally, tonight, at dinner in the Winston kitchen, Nick felt he had to bring it up to Marcus. Nick wanted Lexie to enter the Sectionals in St. Louis. He knew he could get her qualified, even though she hadn't competed in this year's Regionals.

"If you could see, you'd be right back in there at the Broadmoor, with that whole damn business."

"I wouldn't!" insisted Lexie.

"I don't believe you," snapped Nick.

"I can't . . ."

"That's okay, honey," said Marcus swiftly. He smiled at his daughter. "Nobody's going to make you do—"

"If nobody made her do anything she didn't want to," interrupted Nick, "she'd be sitting up there in her room staring at the wall. I don't know whether she can do it or not. I just know she has to try."

"For who?" said Beulah quietly. It was the first time she'd spoken since Nick had brought up the idea of Lexie's skating in competition again. "For Lexie—or for you?" She felt ambivalent herself, even as she asked the question. Was she protecting Lexie, or jealous of Nick?

Nick reached over and took Lexie's hand in his. "For both of us," he said. "If she doesn't try, it'll always be second best, whatever it is." Even me, he told himself silently. "Hell, man, she can *skate!* She can, and goddamn it, she won the Sectionals last year in Colorado Springs. That's all the skaters in the middle of this country. And, by God, that's something!"

"That's pointless and cruel," interrupted Marcus harshly. He was being drawn under the spell of Nick's words, and he didn't want to be. Damn it all, hadn't he let Lexie go once? And look what had happened. How could he send her out there again when she couldn't even see?

"Don't tell me it's pointless and cruel," snapped Nick, waving a spoon for emphasis. "Not trying is what's pointless and cruel. Not trying is wondering for your whole life if you gave up too soon. And who the hell needs that?"

His words sank in, and all four of them sat silent for a minute. Finally, Lexie spoke a little sadly.

"They'll laugh at me. . . ." she said slowly.

"They might," agreed Nick.

But Lexie wasn't finished. "They can't know I can't see," she went on. "Otherwise they'll feel sorry for me."

Once more, they sat stunned, turning Lexie's words over in their heads. Was it possible to pass her off as a sighted person?

"That's gonna be harder," said Beulah wryly.

"They can't know!" insisted Lexie. A fierce light burned in her face, the light of her convictions. Nick had seen it before and it mesmerized him.

"Daddy?" Lexie turned her face toward her father, and he sat contemplating its brightness, while warring needs and desires and responsibilities churned in his mind.

At last, Marcus sighed. "The kid's never seemed too bright," he said, jerking a thumb at Nick, "but he's right. I'm with ya, honey."

With a small cry, Lexie stood up and ran around the table to Marcus, hugging him tightly.

"Goddamn! I sure as hell am!" Marcus whooped, and Nick and Beulah joined in the laughter. Then the laughter faded away, as each of them realized the size of the undertaking that lay before them.

13

The next months were the hardest-working that any of them could remember. Even Deborah at her most ambitious could not have rivaled the amount of training that Beulah gave Lexie. They were on the ice together on the average of fourteen hours a day. Beulah took over Lexie's training from Nick; Nick had taken the girl as far as he could, but he was a speed skater, not a figure skater. Above all, Lexie needed practice in the figures. So, as Beulah trained her, Lexie in her turn trained Beulah, using the best that Deborah had taught her, combining her natural skills with the polish she'd learned at Broadmoor.

As for Marcus, he was relegated not only back to the farm but back to the kitchen, too. He had to cook and clean and tend the cows and mutter, while Lexie spent long hours on the ice.

Nick was working, too, harder than he'd ever worked in his life, even when he was skating with the Northstars.

The farm occupied most of his waking hours because he wanted to get as much as possible done and out of the way before St. Louis and the Sectionals. He was going to go with Lexie, and nothing was going to stand in his way.

At night, Nick and Lexie would meet for a little while, just to kiss, and hold hands and talk a little. Once, they were so exhausted they fell asleep together on the downstairs sofa. Marcus found them there one morning and gave Nick a pretty hard look, but kept his mouth shut.

From early morning until nine at night, Lexie practiced at the rink, while Beulah drilled her on the compulsory school figures, those endless, boring circles. Lexie had never been wonderful at the figures, but at least in the past she could look down and see if she was keeping to her tracings, those first circles skated on a long axis. Now, she had to learn to *feel* her tracings with her body. It was arduous work, but she went at it, for the most part, with astonishing patience, and Beulah checked the circles with as strict an eye as any judge in the world.

Still, the happiest part of the skating day was the moment Beulah called, "All right, Lexie, change skates," and Lexie skated happily to rinkside to exchange her figure skates for her freestyle blades. Then she was like some spirit set free to dance on the ice, to run, spin, glide and, best of all, to fly.

At last the months passed; Lexie received her qualifications to compete at St. Louis. Nick had written a letter explaining that Lexie had been absent from the Regionals because of her accident. But she was completely recovered, he said, not mentioning her blindness. After they sent the letter, they sat for two and a half weeks biting their fingernails. What if the entire skating world already knew that Alexis Winston was blind? But word hadn't gotten out, and the board voted to let Lexie compete.

Finally, the day they were to leave for St. Louis came. Marcus had hired a cousin of Beulah's to make certain the cows were taken care of; Beulah put the "Gone Fishing" sign up on the Ice Castle's chicken-wire fence, and Nick simply split. At least he had some money in his jeans for all his hard work.

It was a strangely silent crew that piled the luggage into the Scout. Each was preoccupied by his or her own thoughts. Each had come a long way in these last few months. For the first time, they had banded together. In the past, they'd pulled Lexie apart—competing with one another. Always and always, each of them had put himself first, while pretending that everything was for Lexie's good. Now, for the first time, they worked as a team, and all of them were working for Lexie's benefit. Not theirs, hers. It was a strange feeling, but a good one. And a sobering one, considering what lay ahead of them. They had entered a blind girl in one of the stiffest skating competitions in the world. And what was more, they had conspired to pass her off as sighted. Were they crazy?

Still, as the journey progressed, the long automobile ride from Waverly, Iowa to St. Louis, Missouri, spirits in the Scout began to rise. Jokes were told, anecdotes swapped, songs sung, until they were laughing almost all the time. The road ran through some of the flattest, dullest stretches in the fifty states, but inside the car, warmth and geniality pervaded.

"The flying wedge," Nick was yelling.

"Fearless," Beulah chimed in.

"Suicidal," added Lexie, giggling happily.

"We have the fastest blade-changing time of any pit crew on the circuit!" yelled Marcus, pretending to spit tobacco out the window.

"Call out distances to walls louder!" snickered Nick, his hands on the wheel.

"You're crazy!" laughed Lexie. "You're all crazy!"

"Damn lucky for you, I'd say," Nick told her, half-seriously.

"Thank God for the loony bin" from Marcus.

Beulah rolled her eyes upward. "God protects fools and little children," she sighed theatrically, "and She sure got her hands full with this group."

Late in the afternoon, Marcus took to spinning yarns.

"A couple of us this one time flew our old beat-up crop dusters into this little town," he began. "Lexie's mom was down visiting family in southern Missouri, and I'll be damned if I didn't do this double back-loop—with a stall. Hell, it's what made your mother fall in love with me, Lexie. That double back-loop. She figured anybody dumb enough to do that in the crates we were flying just *had* to be saved." Marcus let out his best good-ole-boy chuckle and continued.

"When I landed, she came up and said—I remember it as clearly as—well, she said, 'I just want to take a real close look at somebody who wants to kill himself in front of a whole bunch of people.' And . . . well, I guess my head was still buzzing from the spin . . . because I just sort of looked at her with a dumb look, pretty much proving her point for her. And she said, 'I don't wonder flying like that is reserved for the deaf and dumb.' Well, she was so damned pretty I just up and asked her to marry me."

Marcus sat back with a look of smug satisfaction on his handsome, bearded face, until Beulah said, loud and sassy, "That's the clearest piece of nonsense I ever heard."

Nick roared with laughter, nearly choking on his Doublemint, and Lexie, giggling uncontrollably, managed to gasp out, "I believe you, Daddy."

"Thanks, honey," Marcus smiled. "Pay you later."

A strange feeling began to possess Lexie; with surprise, she recognized it as happiness. Sheerest, purest, blissful happiness. Here in this dusty old car, blind as she was, Lexie suddenly felt a surge of the greatest joy she'd ever known, and it all but knocked the breath out of her. Where was it coming from? Even last year, when she'd been on top of the world, on her way to becoming a champion, surrounded by the prospect of wealth and fame, she'd not been happpy. Not like this. Why?

It struck her, all at once. She was surrounded by love. All of these people here with her in the car—her three most precious friends—loved her. And in a new way.

For the first time, they were all getting along together, cooperating to build something good. Nick, Beulah, Marcus—there hadn't been a harsh word among them for a long time, now. The friction had vanished and had left in its place a warm feeling of love and peace and kindness, the kind of feeling that Lexie used to find only on the ice. She used to have to run away into her own world to find love. Now she had it with her always. That's what was making her happy.

Suddenly she felt as if she could actually see their faces, they were so clear in her mind. Beulah—weather-beaten and strong-boned, but somewhere in there was the girl that used to exist, the girl who won the Regionals so long ago. And Marcus—under those straggly whiskers was the face of a country boy; you could see his boyishness in his blue eyes. Lexie could never, never forget Marcus' eyes.

And Nick. He was so handsome, with his jet black hair, a curly lock of it on his forehead, his eyes so large and blue with lashes as long as a girl's. Nick, he was almost too pretty. Yet, Lexie could picture him so clearly in her mind's eye it was as though she was actually seeing him. And he had something more than good looks. It was manliness, just beginning to show, to hint at the person he was going to be.

Lexie hugged herself silently. This was a lot of happiness for one small ice-skater to bear.

Hours later, when the Scout's headlights cut the darkness of the freeway, Marcus took the wheel while Beulah dozed a little. But Lexie was wide awake, staring ahead into darkness as Nick and Marcus talked softly together, man to man.

"You sorry?" Nick was asking. "I mean, did you ever say to yourself that you should have stayed barnstorming? Maybe not have gotten married?"

Marcus thought a minute, giving the question the respect it deserved. "It sounds kind of stupid," he said at last, "but that was a big moment in my life, a big moment. But, no, I wouldn't trade." He shook his head to emphasize the negative. "Nope. That lady and I, we had some good times . . . the best kind of times. Hell, no. I wouldn't trade. It was a good life." He paused, then added softly, "Too good, maybe."

He glanced over at his daughter. Tears were spilling down Lexie's cheeks. Marcus took one hand off the wheel and wrapped his arm around Lexie's shoulders. "I guess the thing I regret the most is that you never knew her very much, honey. I know you remember her, and we talked about her and stuff, but for you, it's all this time not having a mom. . . ."

Embarrassed, Marcus felt a lump rising hard in his throat, threatening tears. But he couldn't stop his flow of words. It was the first time he'd ever spoken of this to Lexie, and he couldn't stop. This time was too precious, too important and hell, even if he broke down and cried, he had to get the words out.

"What's . . . sad . . . for me is that I miss having that person . . . who she was. . . . I guess I think she's the fifth person in this good old bunch. Hell, she would have been so proud. She would have had a hell of a good time being right here with us. I guess that's what's missing . . . for me . . . having Lexie's mom . . . see how . . . her baby turned out." The tears were flowing openly from his eyes as Lexie pressed her face against his.

Nick sniffled a little in the back seat, and Beulah pressed his hand silently. She'd been awake for most of what Marcus said, but she was too moved to speak.

Lexie thought, I love all of them so much. It almost doesn't matter whether I make a good showing, or even win. Real happiness is what's in this car, not what's out there.

*   *   *

"It feels huge," said Lexie. They stood at the entrance to the St. Louis Arena, and Lexie felt the warmth of the house lights on her face. Before them, the rink stretched empty, a vast, open expanse of scintillating white.

"Wait'll it's full," said Nick, looking at the rows and rows of empty seats.

"Wow," breathed Beulah.

Lexie forced a terrified smile. "Thanks a lot. Is that supposed to make me feel better?"

Marcus came striding down the aisle toward them, beaming. The payoff had been successful.

"Twenty bucks a night, three nights, before the preliminaries," he informed them. "Man said any time we want the ice we got it. Just so it's between the hours of one and four in the morning."

"That should be plenty of time," said Beulah, pleased.

Nine hours of practice time on a totally unfamiliar and huge competition rink. Would it be enough time for a blind skater?

Nick took Lexie by the hand and led her to the edge of the ice. Marcus and Beulah followed.

"The tunnel is about fifteen feet wide," said Nick, while Lexie listened attentively, knowing that she'd have to memorize all of it with her body, not only her brain. "Standard. It's about thirty feet after that in the open to the ice."

They had reached the ice now. Lexie, nodding to show she was paying attention, put one foot up on the step and touched the surface, adjusting her foot to the right height.

"I'll get some adhesive tape, run it along the leading edge of the tread," said Marcus. Nobody will notice."

Lexie nodded again, imagining the feel of the thin adhesive under her skate.

"Ready?" asked Nick in her ear.

Lexie took a deep breath. "I guess so," she said. She took her first steps out on the ice for her practice session.

"Without your skates?" asked Beulah dryly.

Lexie laughed. "You all think of everything, don't you?"

"We try," said Nick modestly.

* * *

For the first hour of practice, they skated together, Nick and Lexie, just as they'd done on the pond so many months ago. Then, Nick let her go, and Lexie skated hesitantly around the perimeter of the rink.

"It's so large. There's so much ice. I'm not used to it," she called to Nick, who skated beside her, but not near enough to touch her or get in her way.

It's an even barrier," he told her. "Easy to see."

"For you," scoffed Lexie.

"Nice easy corners. How does it feel?"

Lexie skated on for a few more feet. "Okay . . . it feels okay," she said at last.

Then the hard work began. Over and over, Lexie practiced the distances from the walls for the different parts of her routine. Working with a stopwatch, Nick gave the warning indications of distance and times over and over, until Lexie's mind and body and skating feet began to learn the dimensions of the rink by heart, and memorize the times.

When she'd worked over the rink three or four times all by herself, with no coaching from Nick, they decided to call it a night. Besides, their three hours of ice time were up.

The next night, Lexie worked on her jumps and her spins, going over her long program until it was coming out of her ears. But she intended to be judged not as a blind skater, but a sighted one, and she would gain or lose points according to how well her program fit the rink. Action in all the corners—that was one thing the judges were always looking for.

On the last night before the Sectionals, Beulah drilled Lexie in the figures, while Lexie's heart filled with despair. She could never get them exactly right, even when her vision had been perfect. How on earth was she expected to stay on her tracings now? Her brow furrowed in discouragement.

"Okay, four o'clock," announced Marcus.

Lexie and Nick skated off the ice and over to the tunnel where Marcus waited. Beulah picked up a towel and rubbed at her sweaty head. Figures were hard work for *both* of them.

"How do you feel?" asked Marcus, looking closely at Lexie.

"She knows it cold," stated Nick.

"We're not going to have any warm-ups," said Beulah. "You'll have to do it in the dressing room. All right?"

Lexie nodded. Did she have a choice?

"Don't worry about getting into place through the crowds and stuff like that," Nick advised her. "We'll handle the ice."

Lexie nodded again. This was it. Practice time was over; it was time to get serious. Tomorrow was the big day—today, rather, because it was already four o'clock in the morning, and she was one of the first skaters scheduled to be judged on the compulsory figures. In only a few hours she'd be back here on the ice, competing. She drew a deep breath.

"Well, all I can say is—whatever happens, I love you. I love you all," she cried, throwing her arms wide. And then they were hugging and kissing, all of them.

* * *

14

Lexie touched her collar nervously. Although she still owned every glamorous skating dress that Deborah Mackland had bought her, Lexie had chosen to wear the simple blue dress that Beulah had given her, the one with "Lexie" embroidered on the collar. After all, it had brought her a kind of luck in last year's Regionals, hadn't it? Besides, it was precious to her, and she never even gave a thought to its shabbiness, although it was the same shabbiness that had cost her so much embarrassment in Cedar Rapids.

The seats of the arena were far from filled. In fact, they were very close to empty. Who cared about the compulsory figures except a handful of friends and relations, and the coaches? Later, when the freestyle competitions were held, the stands would be overflowing with fans, all of them yelling and cheering for their favorites. But at this hour everybody, including the friends and relations, was sleepy.

Across the arena, over the stands on the judging side, a large banner was draped. It proclaimed the Midwest Sectional Figure Skating Competitions, and down on the ice, four girls were skating their figure eights in the four corners of the rink while judges took long, critical looks at the tracings in the ice.

"If you line up on the middle judge," whispered Beulah to Lexie as they stood on the sidelines waiting to be called, "your three turns will line up exactly on the cones."

The loudspeaker boomed through a squawking feedback.

"Betsy Meyer, Denny Peterson, Alexis Winston."

This was it. They musn't . . . above all they mustn't find out she was blind. She didn't want their pity, only to show them what she could do, what she was made of.

She took a deep breath and headed for the ice, walking up to the step. On the step, hidden from sight, was the adhesive tape that Marcus had placed there. Lexie found it with her skate; she could feel it and unhesitatingly she made it up the step and out onto the ice, heading for the dim shapes of the orange cones that marked out her figures.

"Miss Winston?" A referee was skating toward her. She turned at the sound of his voice and made out a dark blur.

"Hi," she smiled brightly at the blur as if it were a person.

"Your figures are eight forward paragraph double threes," the blur informed her.

Lexie nodded and lined herself up to the cone. Paragraph double three. She'd practiced that one a lot. She began.

From the sidelines, Beulah gave a little squeak of happiness.

"She's good. She got a good first tracing," she told them.

"It's lucky she got one of the first slots this morning. Nobody's here," whispered Marcus.

"Not lucky," said Nick with a mischievous smile. "Luck had nothing to do with it. A twenty-dollar bill had."

210

Marcus saw the light. "You are one enterprising young man," he granted Nick admiringly.

But Beulah's breath was hissing out in an explosive "Damn!"

"What?" demanded Marcus, looking at Lexie on the ice.

"She skated way off her tracings. Hang in there, honey, don't panic," prayed Beulah.

Lexie, aware suddenly of the difference in her tracings, *did* have a moment of panic. But only a moment. Because even sighted skaters sometimes went wide of their tracings. The thing was to get back on them as quickly as possible, and to look good while doing it. Deliberately, she arched her back and stretched her neck to achieve the best possible form, as she gave the judges a dazzling smile. And she was back on her tracings.

So intent were Beulah, Marcus and Nick on watching Lexie that they didn't see the woman standing on the other side of the rink. But she, too, was watching Lexie, and her mouth hung open in astonishment. And when the scores were posted, Deborah Mackland returned to her hotel room to telephone Brian Dockett.

"I just got in. It's incredible. Yes, Lexie Winston. No, I'm not seeing things. Yes, I'm certain. She did the compulsory figures. Her posted score was pretty bad, but the judges want it to be a freestyle competition, so they scored things pretty close. Everybody's score was bad." She fumbled with her cigarette pack, keeping the phone tucked under her chin and pressed to her ear.

"Yes, she'll do the short program tomorrow. Is she okay? I guess so. I haven't seen her . . . not to talk to, that is. She has a crowd around. Her father and a couple of other people. I haven't been near her. No, I don't think she saw me."

Deborah managed to get the cigarette into her mouth and lit just as Brian said, "I'm looking at a schedule here. I'll be in about eleven, your time."

"Why?" demanded Deborah.

"Why what?" asked Brian, surprised.

"Why are you coming?"

"What do you mean, why am I coming? Why are you calling? If she's there—and skating—Jesus! Of course I'm coming."

"All right," said Deborah grudgingly. He might come in useful; one never knew.

"I'll see you when I get in," said Brian. He was about to hang up the phone when he heard Deborah's voice, still coming out of it.

"Brian," she was saying.

"Yeah?"

"Did you see her . . . ever . . . I mean, since the accident?"

"She wouldn't return my calls."

Brian sounded defensive, thought Deborah. But who could blame him? Not me, certainly.

"I talked to her a couple of times," said Deborah sadly. "Toward the beginning . . ." her voice trailed off into silence. There seemed nothing more to say.

"I'll see you when I get in, Deb. Goodbye." And Brian hung up abruptly.

Deborah sat holding the buzzing phone for a minute, then she took a deep drag on her cigarette and hung up. She looked thoughtful.

The short program went went. It wasn't perfect, but it went well. As Lexie came off the ice, Beulah, Marcus and Nick surrounded her, flanking her sides and rear, walking her straight toward the tunnel. A couple of people in the crowd called out to Lexie, recognizing her as last year's celebrity, but all Lexie had to do was smile and wave in their direction. No problem.

"Finally got decent scores out of those judges." Nick was gleeful.

"It felt a little sloppy," said Lexie.

"You're on the board," Beulah pointed out. Lexie was in the running, one of the top ten skaters.

"Hey," said Nick softly. "Here comes Annette. Keep

going. Let's do our trick." "Our trick" was guaranteed—almost—to convince the onlooker that Lexie could see.

Annette Brashlout, complete with entourage of mother, coach, press, autograph seekers and skater groupies, was coming down the tunnel on her way to perform her long program. Her group and Lexie's were bound to pass each other. Nick stationed himself at Lexie's ear.

"Thirty feet. There's a lot of people crowding her." Nick nudged Lexie in the ribs. "She's looking. Look left. There are two or three layers of people between you. Now!"

Lexie flashed a warm grin to a spot she couldn't see.

"Hi, Alexis," said the spot coolly.

"Congratulations, Annette," called Lexie.

Annette smiled more warmly this time. "Not yet. Good luck."

"Thanks." And they passed each other, with Annette none the wiser.

"Made it," chortled Nick triumphantly.

There was a burst of distant applause from the arena as Annette skated out onto the ice to do her long program.

"Well, if it's any comfort, the crowd's faithful. They still like Annette Brashlout."

Everybody gave Nick a dirty look for that, including Lexie. By now, they had reached the small private dressing room they'd bribed for, a place where Lexie could be alone, away from prying eyes. Noisily they all burst in, closing the door behind them.

"Hi, Lexie," said Brian softly.

It was totally unexpected and caught everybody by surprise. How the hell did he get in here? Nick found his fists clenching. And Lexie, stunned by Brian's voice, looked for him in the wrong direction.

It took a split second for Brian to realize that Lexie was still blind. "Jesus," he breathed, staring at her. He had just seen her on the ice; nobody would believe that she couldn't see.

"What the hell are you doing here?" Marcus growled.

But Brian didn't answer; his eyes were fixed on Lexie, who stood, deeply troubled, realizing that her secret was out. Brian moved forward, past the others, to Lexie's side. He lifted her face and peered into her eyes. They were beautiful, but empty.

Turning to the others, Brian asked softly, "Could we have a minute, please?"

"No!" shouted Marcus. "This is—"

"Yeah. Sure." Nick interrupted. He turned and strode from the room. Reluctantly, Beulah and Marcus followed Nick, suspicious of Brian, unwilling to leave him alone with Lexie.

When the door closed behind them, Brian turned back to Lexie. She was even more beautiful than he had remembered; her coltish charm had been replaced by a mature kind of dignity that made her shine like a clear star.

"You can't tell," he told her gently. "I mean, I saw your program. I can't believe it."

Lexie had no answer to give him; she bent to unlace her boots. Instantly, Brian knelt to help her.

"No. I can do it." Her voice was lower pitched than it had been. She was more woman than child now.

"You look lovely, Lex," breathed Brian. "I saw you out there and fell in love with you all over again." He meant it only as a compliment, but as he spoke the words he realized they were true, and it shook him.

"That's a funny relationship," said Lexie lightly. "Only while skating."

"You didn't take my calls," Brian reproached her.

"No."

Lightly, he reached one finger out and touched her cheek with it, then cupped her small face in both his hands and looked at her hungrily.

"Do you remember me?" he demanded.

"Yes." She remembered every expression on his handsome face, and she could picture him now as he gazed at her.

"I missed you," said Brian.

"I missed you," said Lexie.

214

"Want to try again?" Funny, he hadn't meant to ask her that, but now he was glad he had.

Lexie hesitated, then she touched Brian's face in her turn. "I don't miss you anymore, Brian," she told him gently.

He stood up. There was nothing more to say. Something in her voice told him that she was telling the truth; there was no room in her life for Brian Dockett. "Does anybody know you're blind?" he asked her.

"No. Could you ask my friends to come back in, please?"

Brian nodded, then remembered that Lexie couldn't see a nod.

"Yes," he said. At the door, he turned. "Good luck."

"Thank you," said Lexie calmly, a stranger talking to a stranger.

In the hallway, Brian found Nick sitting on the stairs, his arms folded on his knees.

"Hold on a minute," Nick called to him as Brian headed up the stairs to the arena seats. Brian turned and waited.

"You going to tell anyone?" asked Nick, his face set.

"You know," said Brian, "I really loved her."

"Is that for her or me or you?" asked Nick hotly.

"Maybe for everyone." He started up the stairs again.

"You going to tell anyone?" Nick demanded again.

Brian smiled. "Not everyone who doesn't happen to be from Waverly is a complete phony," he said patronizingly.

"Yeah, maybe not." But Nick didn't sound convinced.

Brian moved away quickly. He had to find Deborah. She had to know as soon as possible, before she, too, made a fool of herself.

Nick sauntered back into the dressing room, just as Annette Brashlout completed her long program. The audience was cheering with passion; Annette had skated brilliantly.

Lexie stood smoothing out the skirt of Beulah's old skating dress.

"It's nice to see it again," Beulah said.

"How does it look?" asked Lexie shyly.

"Beautiful," approved Marcus proudly.

The cheering increased and came pouring through the door as Nick entered.

"Annette," he said briefly.

"How do you like it?" Lexie asked him, smoothing the skirt down.

Nick took a long look at her. "You're about the sexiest bozo ever to ride in a snowmobile," he told her from the heart.

Lexie smiled; to her, it was poetry, better than anything Shakespeare ever wrote.

From the arena came an accelerated, almost animal noise as the near-hysterical crowd gave Annette Brashlout a standing ovation. Flowers poured like hail down on the ice, and Annette skated to them happily and gathered up an armful to more cheers and applause.

The loudspeaker sounded throughout the arena, giving Annette's scores. In Lexie's dressing room, the four of them fell quiet and listened.

"5.8, 5.9, 5.7, 5.9, 5.8" came over the public address system, and the crowd went even wilder, although a moment ago that had seemed impossible. With scores like that, no other winner was possible. It would take a miracle to defeat Annette Brashlout now.

Quietly, they moved out of Lexie's dressing room and down the tunnel to the ice, Lexie walking on her blade guards. There was a delay when they reached rinkside; the flowers had to be cleaned off the ice.

"You okay?" whispered Nick to Lexie.

She nodded her head and kissed him lovingly.

"I'm fine. I'm really fine. Daddy?" She reached her hand out and Marcus caught it. "Daddy, I love you. Thanks for being my daddy." Happily, she returned Marcus' embrace.

"The next skater to perform a long program will be Alexis Winston," announced the loudspeakers.

Tossing her ponytail over her shoulder, Lexie skated out to the center of the ice and took her stance, waiting.

216

The audience recognized her, a skater making a comeback after an accident. A skater who had performed the short program well. There was a healthy round of applause for her, and then the music started.

It was her old tape, that haunting, spellbinding music that was hers and hers alone. But still Lexie stood silent, as though waiting for something else. A murmur went through the audience as the precious seconds ticked by. Why was she standing there?

Lexie took a deep breath, her eyes very wide. "Here's for my mom," she whispered, then she closed her eyes and began to move.

Years from now, people who were in St. Louis that night will be telling stories of how Lexie Winston skated. And people who weren't there will say they were, because the legend is so strong and still so beautiful that they want to be a part of it, to believe they had been a part of it. But even the most exaggerated stories cannot do justice to the symphony of motion that was Alexis Winston that night. It is possible that her artistry may never be duplicated, even by champions yet unborn.

There would be disagreement, too, in later years, among the people who had been there, as to Alexis Winston's exact program. The disagreement would be less the fault of dimming memory than the fact that describing a series of jumps and spins in a sequence is so flat that it cannot give the listener the feeling of what was actually seen that night. All accounts ended with the words: You had to be there.

What everyone did agree to was this. The best skaters, in preparing a program, take care not to telegraph their next moves. Every gesture carries a load of disguise, so that every daring jump or sparkling spin surprises the viewer and evokes gasps. But with Lexie, her every movement was so non-theatrical, so natural, so *organic,* that each move led inevitably to the next, and it was the *rightness,* the expectation fulfilled, that provoked the gasps. She skated totally without effort. It seemed as if there were no arena, no competition, no judges and no spectators. She was alone on the ice, just a girl and her music, and a pair of ice skates. And there was more—it seemed as though this girl had been born there, and had spent all of her life there, and that ice was her natural environment.

When the music lifted Lexie up and carried her, she glided backward in an arabesque that led naturally to a spread eagle, then a backward spread-eagle performed with such limber artistry that her entire body nearly touched the ice. Then, with perfect clarity, she skated forward in an incredible burst of speed and left the ice in a series of jumps that brought gasps of delight from the entranced spectators. In quick succession, she jumped a double axel, a triple lutz, a double salchow, gaining astonishing heights as she leaped in the four corners of the rink. And then, oh, then, the slender girl's body flew into the air once more . . . turning, turning, turning, and yet again. Free, free. She had taken the skills Deborah had taught her and added to them the joyous naturalness she'd regained.

It wasn't possible! She'd never make it! The spectators stopped breathing. A triple axel? No! But she did; she flew like a swallow, winging high and straight, and while the audience sat terrified at the prospect of her failure, Lexie Winston completed a perfect triple axel, landed gracefully on her toe picks and set off again into a series of spins that ended only with a deep sit-spin, only inches above the ice, a spin so fast that she was a blue and gold blur until she stood again and spun to a crossover and a stop.

And then it was over. Unbelievable! Had four minutes gone by already? An eternity. An unspecific time in which they had witnessed . . . been a part of . . . the perfect connection between body and spirit, the rare moment when excellence out-excels itself.

The music came to a stop, and Lexie stood silent and still in the center of the arena. She opened her eyes. For the first time, she was conscious of the stands filled with people, of the judges. She had been alone out there, performing to her music, aware only of the ice and her own body. Wanting nothing but to skate, to skate as she'd always pictured herself skating—not like a champion but with joy. She could see the crowd, as a large dark entity, and it was getting to its feet and roaring, long, heavy, noisy shouts. The crowd called her name again and again.

On the sidelines, Nick, Beulah and Marcus, weeping openly, cheered and yelled with hearts ready to burst. Even they had not expected anything like this.

In the stands, Deborah Mackland was weeping, too. She felt a sense of loss so overwhelming that it was matched only by a burning disappointment. Because what she had seen out there was not what she had given Lexie, but what Lexie had given herself. Lexie hadn't needed her after all.

The din of the applause had now become rhythmic; the crowd was demanding that Alexis Winston circle the ice. Smiling, Lexie obliged, skating easily around the perimeter.

The flowers began to fall, red roses on the chilly clarity of the ice. Flowers for Lexie.

Of course, she could not see them. What's more, she didn't expect them. And she was heading straight for them. On the ice, anything, even a hairpin, is a hazard to the blades of even the most experienced skater.

Nick realized this too late. "*Lex!* The flowers!" he shouted, desperately trying to shout against and above the applause. But Lexie didn't hear him and couldn't have stopped herself even if she had.

The first flower that caught in her blade made her stumble; the second, an instant later, made her fall. Terror filled her lovely face, and the crowd became suddenly very quiet, watching without understanding as this girl in the old blue skating dress groped around on the ice, on her knees, touching, touching the flowers. They didn't know. They still didn't know.

But Deborah knew. Even though Brian hadn't succeeded in reaching her, Deborah knew, and watched in pity and terror as Lexie's small white hands fumbled through the flowers.

In pain for her, Nick steeled himself and walked out onto the ice.

Now, a ripple began through the crowd, a whisper that

219

became a murmur, a murmur that became a roar. In an instant, with the speed of a ash fire, everyone knew. Alexis Winston couldn't see. Alexis Winston was blind!

Nick reached Lexie and gave her his hand. "We forgot about the flowers," he said simply.

Lexie nodded and squeezed his hand. She wasn't hurt; she was a little disoriented maybe, but she was happy to have him near. He helped her to her feet and led her gently through the mine field of red roses and into the center of the rink.

All at once, the crowd broke into a roar of applause and cheering, louder and louder, hoarse and emotional. Lexie knew that they knew and that it was her courage they were cheering. But it was all right; it wasn't pity. They had already cheered her skill, and she had earned that without their pity.

Lexie and Nick stood before the judges' table. Lexie smiled brightly, although she couldn't make out the judges' faces, couldn't see them clapping and weeping in tribute to her genius.

The thought came to Lexie suddenly that maybe she'd won after all, even against those odds of Annette's high scores in everything. But, at the same time she knew that it didn't matter.

Always before she had sought the privacy of her own world on the ice, looking there for the love and the peace that had eluded her in the real world. But I don't have to escape any more, she thought. I have it now, all of it. I have Beulah and Marcus and Nick, and they love me. They truly do, and now they know it and I know it.

Nick let go of her hand, so that she could take her bow alone. As he took a step away, Lexie called to him gently, "Stay with me."

"You bet," he answered, and she could hear the love in his voice.

* * *

THE END

220

NORAH LOFTS

Norah Lofts weaves a rich tapestry of love, war and passion. Here are her most entertaining novels of romance and intrigue. You may order any or all direct by mail.

Historical Romance

Sparkling novels of love and conquest against the colorful background of historical England. Here are books you will savor word by word, page by spellbinding page.

☐ AFTER THE STORM—Williams	23081-3	$1.50
☐ ALTHEA—Robins	23268-9	$1.50
☐ AMETHYST LOVE—Danton	23400-2	$1.50
☐ AN AFFAIR OF THE HEART· Smith	23092-9	$1.50
☐ AUNT SOPHIE'S DIAMONDS Smith	23378-2	$1.50
☐ A BANBURY TALE—MacKeever	23174-7	$1.50
☐ CLARISSA—Arnett	22893-2	$1.50
☐ DEVIL'S BRIDE—Edwards	23176-3	$1.50
☐ ESCAPADE—Smith	23232-8	$1.50
☐ A FAMILY AFFAIR—Mellow·	22967-X	$1.50
☐ THE FORTUNE SEEKER Greenlea	23301-4	$1.50
☐ THE FINE AND HANDSOME CAPTAIN—Lynch	23269-7	$1.50
☐ FIRE OPALS—Danton	23112-7	$1.50
☐ THE FORTUNATE MARRIAGE Trevor	23137-2	$1.50
☐ THE GLASS PALACE—Gibbs	23063-5	$1.50
☐ GRANBOROUGH'S FILLY Blanshard	23210-7	$1.50
☐ HARRIET—Mellows	23209-3	$1.50
☐ HORATIA—Gibbs	23175-5	$1.50

Buy them at your local bookstores or use this handy coupon for ordering:

FREE
Fawcett Books Listing

There is Romance, Mystery, Suspense, and Adventure waiting for you inside the Fawcett Books Order Form. And it's yours to browse through and use to get all the books you've been wanting... but possibly couldn't find in your bookstore.

This easy-to-use order form is divided into categories and contains over 1500 titles by your favorite authors.

So don't delay—take advantage of this special opportunity to increase your reading pleasure.

Just send us your name and address and 25¢ (to help defray postage and handling costs).